PALM BEACH SCAVENGERS

CHARLIE CRAWFORD PALM BEACH MYSTERIES
BOOK 15

TOM TURNER

Ten Hut Media

Ten Hut Media
www.tenhutmedia.com

This is a work of fiction. Names, characters, businesses, places, events and incidents are either the products of the author's imagination or used in a fictitious manner. Any resemblance to actual persons, living or dead, or actual events is purely coincidental.

ISBN: 978-1-964007-00-7

ALSO BY TOM TURNER

CHARLIE CRAWFORD PALM BEACH MYSTERIES

Palm Beach Nasty

Palm Beach Poison

Palm Beach Deadly

Palm Beach Bones

Palm Beach Pretenders

Palm Beach Predator

Palm Beach Broke

Palm Beach Bedlam

Palm Beach Blues

Palm Beach Taboo

Palm Beach Piranha

Palm Beach Perfidious

Palm Beach Betrayers

Palm Beach Schemers

Palm Beach Scavengers

Palm Beach Psycho

Palm Beach Rogues

SAVANNAH SLEUTH SISTERS MURDER MYSTERY SERIES
NICK JANZEK CHARLESTON MYSTERIES

**To find out more about Tom Turner and his books, visit
www.amazon.com/stores/Tom-Turner**

ONE

In Palm Beach, most people have a lot of spare time on their hands. For one thing it's a chic and fashionable vacation destination and for another, it's an exclusive place people—usually very rich people—live at least part of the year. These people, besides sleeping late and having long, alcohol-fueled meals, even breakfast—think Bloody Mary's and Screwdrivers—still need activities to fill their days. The list of those they partake in is long: golf, tennis, riding, polo, croquet, backgammon, bridge, cards, chess, art classes, book clubs, Pilates, yoga, fitness workouts, charity events, AA meetings, and afternoon trysts. To name just a few.

But nothing in Palm Beach is bigger than an annual event called, The Scavenger Hunt. Yes, *The* Scavenger Hunt because there is no other scavenger hunt that is more brain-challenging, complex and, without a doubt, extravagant. Hey, it's Palm Beach, what do you expect?

The Scavenger Hunt is actually a charity event, and it raises at least a million dollars for several good causes. How? There are two teams that go head-to-head against each other, and they are as competitive as any Super Bowl or World Series you'll ever see. Each team has ten members and each member kicks in fifty thousand dollars to play, creating an instant one-million-dollar prize pool for charity. No muss, no fuss.

DAVID BALFOUR, SILLA VANDER POEL, AND JACK REMBERT WERE ON the eighteenth green of the Poinciana Club in Palm Beach standing over the hole. They had just found a clue written on a piece of raspberry bordered Crane stationery that had been stuffed into the hole. Balfour read it, *Your next clue has a hole in it too. Specifically, the location where the holy (or holey) shop in Palm Beach.*

Silla raised a long, aristocratic finger. "I got it," she said.

"What is it?" Balfour asked.

"What else? The Church Mouse," she said referring to the rich man's Salvation Army a block away from the Palm Beach Police station.

The Church Mouse was owned by the Church of Bethesda-by-the-Sea, located further north on South County Road. According to its website, the Church Mouse is, "recognized as one of the top donation based resale shops in the country..." and goes on to say, "we sell everything from top shelf designer clothing, handbags, and accessories to furniture, crystal, china, and books."

Top shelf or not, you still might find that the occasional Pucci dress or Turnbull & Asser shirt has a tiny hole or tear in it. Moths don't know the difference between fancy designer labels and the Gap.

"Brilliant," Balfour said. "Holy as in church, and holey as in...something with a hole in it."

"Exactly," Silla said. "What would you boys do without me?"

The two different ten-person teams—the Pinks and the Greens—were divided up into smaller groups. This was the third straight year that Balfour, VanderPoel, and Rembert had teamed up, and they considered themselves the brain trust of the Green team. Each one had their areas of expertise: Silla's were music, history, and geography; Rembert's were sports, art, and theater; Balfour's were movies, literature, and current events. Between them, they ham-and-egged it pretty well and had no problem nailing the final question on *Jeopardy*.

The three hopped onto their high-powered, royal blue golf cart, Balfour at the wheel, and headed down Golfview Road, unaware of the black Audi SUV and its three occupants following them at a discreet distance.

Once a year, the Mayor allowed golf carts on the streets of Palm Beach and today was the day. Maybe it had something to do with the fact that the twenty Pink and Green team members collectively accounted for over twenty percent of the contributions to his mayoral campaign two years back.

Balfour had the golf cart up to thirty-five miles an hour on Golfview and hung a hard left onto South County.

"Good God, David, be careful. We're not in that race in Monte Carlo or something?" Silla swooned, tightening her grip on a safety bar.

Balfour laughed. "Let me remind you, Silla, we lost this thing last year. We can't let that happen again."

"Yeah, but I think they cheated somehow," Rembert said as they blew past Worth Avenue.

———

They split up after entering the Church Mouse, going to different parts of the store. Fifteen minutes later, Silla stumbled onto what they were looking for. It took some Sherlockian sleuthing but there in the breast pocket of a blue Charles Tyrwhitt shirt, she spotted a BB-size hole and a folded piece of paper. It said, *Go hang out with total strangers, 4, 5, or 6, on Dixie Highway, and take a photo with them.*

"What the hell?" a bewildered Balfour said, as they walked out of the Church Mouse.

"Do you suppose it means like homeless people?" Silla said. The idea was clearly distasteful to her. "And what about the 4, 5, and 6?"

Balfour frowned. "I'm not really sure I want to *hang out* on Dixie Highway period," he said of the commercial street in West Palm Beach, an area considered many notches below Worth Avenue in Palm Beach.

"Wait a minute," said Rembert, grabbing Balfour's arm. "At the Norton," he said, referring to the Norton Gallery in West Palm, "there are these sculptures in their sculpture garden of these three guys. I'm pretty sure it's called *Total Strangers*. Sculptor by the name of Wormley or Gormley or something."

"Well, come on, let's go," Balfour said, as they approached the golf cart.

"We can't take it," Silla said, pointing at the cart. "It's too far."

Rembert had his iPhone out and was dialing. "I can get my Uber guy here in five minutes."

"Can you drop me at my car?" Silla asked. "I'm going to want to go home and help Maya get that marvelous lobster risotto ready for you hungry men after we win this thing."

"Sounds delicious," Balfour said. "I'll go with you."

THE THREE PEOPLE IN THE BLACK AUDI SUV WERE DOUBLE-PARKED across from the Church Mouse watching the trio stand next to their golf cart.

"Guy's had quite a few pops," Greg commented from the driver's seat when Jack Rembert took a healthy pull from his Big Gulp cup.

"Yeah, I wouldn't let him behind the wheel of my golf cart," said the man in the back.

Greg nodded his head. "And the woman's got a bottle of wine in that cooler."

"And the other guy just killed the rest of whatever's in that flask of his," Gretchen, in the passenger seat, said.

"I noticed," said the man in back.

Gretchen patted her shoulder holster. "You know, I could always just take him out anytime. Be done with the whole thing in one quick shot."

"Have you listened to one damn thing I've said?" snarled the man in the back seat.

Gretchen held up her hand. "Sorry. I know, I know, make it look like an accident."

FIFTEEN MINUTES LATER, BALFOUR, VANDERPOEL, AND REMBERT walked through the Norton Museum on their way to the sculpture garden in back. Balfour had been Silla's passenger in her bright red Jaguar, while Rembert had been dropped off by his Uber driver, who was going to wait for him.

"I always liked that one," Silla said as they walked past an orange metal, abstract sculpture.

"That's Keith Haring," Rembert said, then pointed, "the sculptures I'm thinking about are over there."

They walked a little further and there they were: larger-than-life-size dark metal sculptures of three naked men, all looking away from each other. There was a small envelope stuck under an arm of one of the oversized metal men.

"There we go," Silla said, as Rembert extracted it and tore open the envelope.

"Says, *Take a selfie in front of the home of the messenger of the Gods.*"

Balfour chuckled. "That's easy," he said with a confident nod.

But Silla hadn't figured it out yet. "What are you thinking?"

"Hermes is the Greek name for the messenger of the Gods...and, little known fact, of thievery too," Balfour said, showing off a little.

Silla patted him on the shoulder. "Very good, David. So the Hermes shop in Royal Poinciana Plaza?"

"Exactly."

Balfour started walking.

"Hold on," Rembert said. "I've got another possible answer to that."

Balfour turned. "What is it?"

But Rembert had already started to walk away. "I'm gonna hop in my Uber and check it out. This way we got both covered. Meet you at your place, Silla."

"Okay," Silla said, "the lobster risotto will be waiting for us. By the way, I think we're killing the Pinks."

Balfour nodded. "Well, of course, we are. Vastly superior intellect. Last year was a complete fluke," he said, bumping Silla's raised fist lightly.

IN THE PARKING LOT OF THE NORTON THE BLACK AUDI SUV NOSED up next to Jack Rembert's Uber driver. The man in the back seat slipped down so he wouldn't be spotted He'd already told the husky blonde woman and Greg, the driver, how he wanted to play this. He'd handed Greg three one-hundred-dollar bills and the blonde a small plastic envelope containing three small pills, saying to her, "Take these with you, they may come in handy. Remember," he said, his eyes drilling into hers, "make it look like an accident."

She'd nodded and they waited as Greg hopped out, went over to the Uber driver, and tapped on his window.

The Uber driver hit the button that rolled down his window.

"Yo bro," Greg said, flashing the cash . "I gotta get to the airport in a hurry. I'll give you three hundred dollars if you can take me."

The Uber driver's eyes lit up. "Sure, but," he pointed at the Audi, "why can't you go in that car?"

"'Cause my boss is in the museum and would get real pissed if he came out and his car wasn't here."

The driver looked like he had a few more questions, and maybe something didn't quite add up, but the last thing he wanted to do was blow his chance of making three hundred dollars for a quick ten-minute ride. He figured since his fare, Jack Rembert, had entered the museum less than fifteen minutes ago, he could get back from the airport before Rembert came back to his car. Kill two birds with one stone and come out with some extra cash.

"Okay, hop in," said the Uber driver.

As they drove away, the blonde, dressed in a low-slung halter top and Daisy Mae short shorts with revealing rips, opened the passenger side door and walked around to the driver's side of the Audi waiting for Rembert to appear. She figured it was a good idea to let him scope out his new driver, particularly since the man in the rear seat of the Audi told her that Rembert had a thing for young women, especially blondes. Her guess was that he probably liked scantily clad ones even more.

Meanwhile, the man in back had put on his big-brimmed bucket hat and sunglasses, got out of the Audi, and quickly walked down the sidewalk away from the Norton. Then, he called another Uber to pick him up.

———

THE BLONDE DIDN'T HAVE LONG TO WAIT. TWO MINUTES LATER, Rembert, weaving slightly, walked toward her. When he got closer, a sloppy grin appeared on his face. The blonde, leaning against the car, shot him her most *come hither* smile.

"You Mr. Rembert?"

"That's me. What happened to Bill or Bob, whatever his name was?" Rembert said, sizing up the blonde. "Not that I mind his replacement."

The blonde put her hand up to shade the sun. "He had a family emergency. Don't worry, you won't be disappointed."

"I'm already not. You're a nice upgrade."

"Well, thank you. Where to?"

Rembert took a sip from his Big Gulp cup, but it only made a slurping sound. Rembert gave it a quick shake, trying to get one final slug out of it, but there was nothing left.

"I was going to the marina in Palm Beach, but I'm in no rush...and I'm thirsty. Maybe we swing by a bar before the marina?"

"Sure, whatever you want, Mr. Rembert."

"Jack," he said.

"Jack," she repeated.

"What's your name?"

"Gretchen."

"Pleased to meet you, Gretchen...very pleased."

"Me, too."

"Okay, let's go," Rembert said, walking around the SUV and sliding into the passenger side as Gretchen got in the driver's side. She started the car and pulled out onto Dixie Highway. "There's a place up on the right, next block, I forget the name."

Gretchen nodded. "You just tell me where."

They drove north one block. "There it is," Rembert said, pointing.

Gretchen nodded and hit the blinker. She parked and they walked toward the bar's front door.

"Nothing fancy, but the bartender goes heavy on the pour, light on the chit-chat," Rembert said, holding the door for her.

"Sounds good," Gretchen said. "I'm a nothin' fancy kind of gal."

"I don't know, you look pretty fancy to me," he said, following her into the dimly lit bar.

They sat down at a booth and after a few moments a waitress came over.

"Double Meyer's dark rum, please," Rembert said, holding out his hand, "and she'll have a..."

"Bud Light, please."

"That's all?" Rembert asked.

"I'm driving."

"Oh, yeah, right," he said, putting his hand on hers. "So what do you do for fun, Gretchen?"

"Um, well, I like to surf and...shop."

"That sounds like fun. You got a boyfriend?"

"Um, occasionally."

Rembert laughed.

Their drinks came and Rembert took a long pull and glanced down. "By the way, I'm crazy about your shorts, they're..."

She smiled. "Short?"

He laughed and took another pull on his rum. "Well, I'm gonna hit the head. Could you order me another Meyer's?"

"Sure," she said, as he stood and walked away.

She caught the waitress's eye and held up Rembert's glass.

She slipped the plastic envelope out of her purse and took out the three little pills, concealing them in her hand while the waitress brought over the Meyer's rum refill. As the waitress turned away, Gretchen popped the pills into Rembert's drink and placed it in front of where he had been sitting.

A few minutes later, he walked out of the men's room and headed over to her, still weaving ever so slightly.

He grabbed the back of a chair for support, sat down, and took another long pull of his rum. She watched him closely as he smiled at her. "Your boyfriend...you two live together or what?"

"Nah, he's out of town on business for a couple days."

"Oh," Rembert said, perking up, "is that so?" It came out, *zat so?*

She nodded, guessing he was going from a little drunk to a few minutes away from falling on his face drunk and quite incapacitated.

"Tell you what," Rembert said, putting a hand on her shoulder. "I gotta make a quick stop at the docks in Palm Beach, then maybe we pick up a bottle of champagne, head over to your place or something."

"Sounds like fun," she said. "I'd like that."

Rembert slowly got to his feet, but then his knees seemed to buckle, and he lurched to one side. Gretchen caught him before he toppled over. He put his arm around her shoulders, not as a form of coming onto her, but to keep from nosediving into the threadbare burgundy carpet.

TWO

CHARLIE CRAWFORD'S CELL RANG AS HE WALKED INTO HIS OFFICE AT the Palm Beach Police station at 8:15 in the morning. It was his friend, David Balfour.

"Hey, David, how's it going?"

"Hey, Charlie," Balfour said. "In a word, shitty. A good friend of mine drowned last night down at the docks."

"Oh, Jesus, I'm sorry to hear that. How'd it happen?"

"Depends on who you listen to. Official verdict seems to be that he drank too much, fell in the water, and drowned. Let's just say, I've got my doubts," Balfour said. "Hey, if all you've had so far is those blueberry donuts and coffee you always have, why don't you come over and get a real breakfast? I'll fill you in."

Crawford eyed the half-eaten blueberry donut on his desk. "Best offer I've had so far today," he said. "I'll be right over."

———

DAVID BALFOUR LIVED IN A BIG SPANISH-STYLE STUCCO HOUSE UP ON Emerald Beach Way in Palm Beach. He grew up with the proverbial silver spoon in his mouth in Grosse Pointe, Michigan, where people named Ford, Chrysler, and Dodge were neighbors. He had gone to a boarding school in the East, then to the University of Virginia where he partied prodigiously and played number one on the tennis team. After four years there, when his friends were headed off to corporate America, mainly Wall Street, Balfour didn't have a clue what he wanted to do. He decided halfway through the summer to give professional tennis a shot. The only problem was that it was the Andre Agassi / Jim Courier era and he'd have been lucky to take even a few games off either one of them.

Nevertheless, he stuck it out for five long years, playing satellite and Challenger tournaments in places like Gdansk and Little Rock. He rose as high as 126 in the world rankings, which was nothing to sneeze at but nothing that could support him either. Finally, with both a torn meniscus and a rotator cuff injury, Balfour decided it was time to hang up his racket. He ended up back at the University of Virginia as tennis coach and taught creative writing in the English Department. Eighteen years later at age forty-five, Balfour received a generous trust fund and retired to Palm Beach, where he had been for the last ten years.

The front door to Balfour's house had been left slightly ajar so Crawford walked in. The smell of bacon and coffee greeted him along with a sweet-smelling scent Crawford couldn't identify. Crawford went into Balfour's capacious kitchen and found his friend pouring two glasses of orange juice.

Balfour, wearing khakis and a long-sleeved canary yellow shirt, looked up and smiled. "Welcome, Charlie."

Crawford walked over and shook Balfour's hand. "Is that Nueske's bacon I smell?"

"Yup. Nothing but the finest for you. Plus, Celestine's award-winning French toast and, of course, tater tots, extra crispy, just the way you like 'em."

"Oh, man, it doesn't get any better than this," Crawford said, sniffing, "and what is *that* smell?"

Balfour pointed to a large bouquet of flowers. "I did a little snipping and clipping in my back yard. Gardenia's, night-blooming jasmine," Celestine, his cook, walked into the kitchen, "and what's that other kind of jasmine, Cel?"

"Confederate jasmine," Celestine said. "Hello, Detective Charlie."

"Hi, Celestine, the house smells amazing," Crawford said. "I'm giving you ninety percent of the credit."

"Make it ninety-nine," Balfour said. "Come on, let's eat. I've gotta tell you about my friend."

They sat down at Balfour's dining room table and a few minutes later Celestine served them French toast, Nueske's bacon—four thick slices each —tater tots, and as far as Crawford was concerned anyway, the best coffee in Palm Beach including what they served at his beloved Dunkin' Donuts.

Balfour took a bite of bacon and put the half-eaten piece down on his plate. "So my friend who drowned is named Jack Rembert. Ever hear of him?"

Crawford shook his head.

"Well, he's a sports agent. A very big sports agent. Couple months ago, he signed a baseball player to a 10-year seven hundred-million-dollar deal."

"Oh yeah, I read about that. Not a bad little commission on that."

"Yeah, you do the math. Ten per cent of that—"

"Is more than I make in twenty lifetimes," Crawford said. "So tell me what you know about what happened to him. How'd he drown? What had he been doing yesterday?"

"Well, I know a lot because I was with him before it happened. You know that scavenger hunt that happens every year?"

"Sure, raises a bunch of money for charity. Everyone buzzing around in golf carts."

"That's the one," Balfour said, spiking a few tater tots with his fork. "So Jack and me and a woman named Silla Vander Poel were at the Norton where we had just found a clue. Silla and I drove over to the Hermes shop on Royal Poinciana 'cause we figured out the clue—"

"What was the clue?"

"Something like, *take a selfie in front of the home of the messenger of the Gods*," Balfour said. "Hermes, of course, being the Greek messenger of the Gods."

Crawford thought for a second. "See, I would have gone with Mercury, the Latin name."

Balfour put his fork down. "Damn, you're right. They're both right answers, aren't they? I'm thinking now that was the answer Jack came up with too."

"Why do you think that?"

"Well, he just said to me and Silla that he had another answer, and he was going to check it out while we went to the Hermes shop. You know, cover both bases."

Crawford took a sip of his coffee. "So your friend drowned down at the docks...and I'm thinking...I'm thinking that there are probably more than a few Mercury boat engines down there. Maybe even a boat named *Mercury*. But Rembert didn't say that's where he was headed?"

Balfour shook his head. "No, he didn't. Just that we agreed to meet at Silla's for dinner. See, we just needed one more clue and we were done. We figured we were way ahead of the competition."

Crawford speared the last tater tot on his plate. "Do you know, by any chance, if an autopsy is being done?"

"Yeah, Bob Hawes." Balfour chuckled. "Your buddy."

Balfour knew Crawford wasn't a big fan of the Palm Beach County Medical Examiner.

"And do you know whether there were any techs at the scene?"

"Not sure. You mean, like Dominica?"

Palm Beach crime-scene tech Dominica McCarthy would have been Crawford's first choice. "Yeah, or any of them. You mentioned something about the theory being that Rembert drank too much, fell in, and drowned. I take it you guys had had a few."

Balfour nodded. "Yeah, Jack took a half-bottle of rum along for the ride."

"That's it?"

"Ah, no, Silla brought along a pitcher of bloodies."

"I hope the driver was abstaining."

"That would be me." Then like a kid caught smoking behind a barn by his parents, he added, "I actually had a small flask...of Maker's Mark."

"Jesus, David, not on my streets, please."

Balfour thrust his hands up in the air. "Sorry, I know, I know. But please don't give me a hard time."

Crawford let it drop. "So the theory about him being drunk and falling in...could that actually have happened?"

Balfour finished off his coffee and put the cup down. "He really wasn't drunk as far as I could tell. Well, maybe just a little. I mean the man could hold his booze pretty well. Let's just say, if you gave him a breathalyzer, he'd be close to the limit, but not over it. We didn't finish off all we had anyway. I'd guess the bloodies and my flask were more than half full."

"But maybe Rembert could have slipped, hit his head on something, then fell into the water?"

"Well, yeah, he could have, but I don't know, I just don't see it. I've been to a lot of docks in my day, sometimes after having a few, but I've never come close to falling in the water. Have you?"

"Can't say as I have, but it could happen...I guess. I mean sometimes they're wet, and you know, slippery," Crawford said. "Did he have any health issues?"

Balfour shook his head. "Guy was in fantastic shape. Ran five miles a day, went to the gym—I don't know—three, four times a week. Never smoked."

Crawford nodded. "And do you remember what he was wearing at the time?"

"Um, let's see," Balfour said, glancing away. "Yes, now I remember. This yellow long-sleeved shirt and blue-striped shorts."

Crawford nodded again and didn't say anything for a few moments. "Tell you what, I'll look into it. Things are pretty slow at the moment."

Slow wasn't the word for it. He and his partner, Mort Ott, hadn't had a murder in over five months. They weren't exactly eager for someone to get killed but wouldn't be heart-broken if someone did.

"I really don't see it, Charlie," Balfour repeated. "There're some guys, friends of mine, who I could see something like this happening to. Getting really drunk and falling in. But not Jack. He was just one of those guys who was always in control. Sure, he could have a few *pops*, more than a few, but not to the point where something like this could ever happen."

"I hear you," Crawford said. "So fill me in a little more. Married? Kids? Girlfriends? What?"

Balfour leaned his chair back on two legs. "Well, now that you ask, that's kind of a long story. First of all, there's his wife of like, I'm guessing, fifteen years. His second wife, actually. They almost got divorced a couple years ago, but the marriage kept limping along. I never got what Jack saw in her, except she was a piece of ass."

"That's enough for some men."

"Yeah, except she's so damn clueless and...well, kind of narrow-minded," Balfour added. "Anyway he had a long-time girlfriend or mistress, who's been chomping at the bit for him to divorce wife number two and so she can be wife number three."

"What's her name?"

"Weezie Gifford."

"Weezie?"

"Yeah, I think it's short for Louise."

"Okay, keep going."

"He's got two daughters. I always thought Jack was a good father but a...well, let's just say, maybe not such a great husband."

"All right, man, I'll look into it," Crawford said. "I'll get back to you with anything I find out."

"I appreciate it, Charlie."

"No problem. And hey, thanks for breakfast. I could make this a regular thing."

"But they'd miss you at Green's," Balfour said, referring to the workingman's luncheonette in Palm Beach where Crawford and his partner had their own table.

"Hey, speaking of Green's," Crawford asked, "did you guys beat the Pink's?"

"Oh yeah," Balfour said proudly, "crushed 'em."

THREE

Crawford left Balfour's house at a little past 9:30 and dialed Dominica McCarthy from his car.

"Hi, Charlie."

"Hey. By any chance, did you catch that drowning down at the docks last night?"

"No, Goldie got that one. Why are you asking? It wasn't a homicide, as far as I know anyway."

"David Balfour asked me to look into it. The guy who drowned was a friend of his."

"Gotcha."

"Have you heard...around the water cooler about it being anything other than an accident?"

"No. Not a thing. Why? Is that what David thinks?"

"He just doesn't think something like that could ever happen to his friend."

"But I heard there was alcohol involved."

"Yeah, but David downplayed that."

"You want me to talk to Goldie? Poke around a little."

"Yeah, would you mind?"

"Nah. I know you're dying of boredom. Looking for something to do."

Crawford chuckled. "You know me too well."

When Crawford arrived back at the station house, he went straight to his partner, Mort Ott, and filled him in on his conversation with both David Balfour and Dominica McCarthy.

Ott, shorter than Crawford by seven inches, rounder by four belt sizes, older by thirteen years, and balding, was an easy man to underestimate. That worked to his advantage because at fifty-three, Ott could bench-press his weight, outrun Crawford and outthink any Florida mutt, miscreant, or hardened outlaw.

Crawford, a highly-decorated New York homicide cop who burned out and moved down to the Sunshine State, was six three with piercing blue eyes and dirty-blond hair he wore a little longer than his crew-cut boss liked. Handsome without much fuss, he could have been a model if models wore clothes they bought on sale at Men's Wearhouse.

"So what do you want to do?" Ott asked Crawford.

"We've got to at least look into it," Crawford said. "Hear what Hawes comes up with. Maybe I speak to Rembert's wife and you talk to the girlfriend."

"Weezie, you said?" Ott asked, his eyebrows arching.

"That's her."

"Never had the pleasure of Q and A-ing a Weezie before."

"Well, now's your chance."

Later that afternoon, Crawford was seated in Christina Rembert's living room. She was a tall, skinny, cheerless woman, but maybe that had something to do with the fact that her husband had just died. But, then again, maybe not, since David Balfour had described her marriage as having devolved into a loveless relationship with Rembert spending more time with his girlfriend than her. Maybe she was happy to see him go. The living room was a lot cheerier than Mrs. Rembert with spectacular profusions of expensive-looking chintz and vibrant colors everywhere Crawford's observant eyes traveled. The artwork was big, bold, and abstract. Reds and yellows predominated.

Crawford had just done his usual 'sorry about your loss' spiel and was ready to cut to the chase.

"Mrs. Rembert, in your opinion, was your husband's death just an unfortunate accident?"

She scratched her cheek. "Well, what else could it have been?"

Crawford didn't plan on voicing David Balfour's suspicions. "I'm not suggesting it wasn't. I just wanted to hear your opinion since your husband was relatively young and seemed to be in good health and good shape."

She yanked her head hard to her right. "Who said he was in good shape?" she snapped. "Did you hear that from *that woman?*"

Crawford held up a hand. "No, it was just the impression I got," he said. "What woman are you referring to, ma'am?"

"Never mind."

"Well, let me ask you this, did your husband have any enemies that you're aware of?" Crawford asked. "Anyone who might have wanted to do harm to him?"

She laughed sarcastically. "*Do harm to him?* You mean like conk him on the head and push him into the water?"

He was getting a little sick of her answering a question with a question.

"Well, it's unusual for a man to drown even if he falls, trips, or is pushed into the water. It can happen, and has happened I'm sure, but it's just...unusual."

She shrugged dismissively. "Well, I don't know what to tell you. It's your job to get to the bottom of it."

"Which is why *I* asked the question."

"Next," she demanded.

"You still haven't answered," Crawford said. "Was there anyone you can think of who might have wanted to do harm to your husband?"

"No, not that I know of," she said, then had an afterthought. "Though he did have to deal with some pretty unsavory characters."

Crawford leaned in closer. "Can you tell me who?"

"Oh, my God, I have no idea what their names were, but those ghastly baseball, football, and basketball players."

"What do you mean? How were they *ghastly*?"

"Well, just look at them. How they dress and their haircuts and, and... how they talk. They speak in a language that seems indecipherable to me."

Crawford was getting a strong sense that Christina Rembert might just be a raging bigot, so he figured he'd push it a little.

"I'm not sure what you mean. How they dress and their haircuts and—"

"Just so flashy and uncouth and all those braids and tattoos and everything."

"Are you referring to black players, Mrs. Rembert?"

"Well, yes...and Hispanics too."

Crawford was close to pointing out that Black and Hispanic athletes had made her cushy lifestyle possible, but he figured what was the point. It wasn't as if Balfour hadn't warned him about her.

"So did Mr. Rembert ever say to you that any of his clients might have a reason to, I'll say it again, do harm to him?"

"No, except there was one very unpleasant man. I think he was a coach. Actually a white man."

"What is his name?"

"Um, Daryl something. He's the coach of the Jacksonville...whatever-their-name is. The football team."

Crawford knew she must be referring to Daryl Boone of the Jacksonville Jaguars, who had a reputation for being feisty and outspoken.

"Daryl Boone?"

"Yes, that's his name. He and Jack butted heads a lot."

Crawford typed Boone's name into his iPad. "Thank you. Anyone else?"

She shrugged. "Not that I can think of...but, of course, Jack and I didn't talk about his business much. I mean, what interest did I have in big black men who run fast and jump high? I had better things to talk about."

Crawford didn't ask the question that immediately came to mind: *Oh yeah, like what?*

FOUR

Weezie Gifford, Jack Rembert's not so secret mistress, lived on the top floor of 1801 South Flagler Drive, also known as Rapallo North, in West Palm Beach. It had a commanding view of the Intracoastal directly below, then the long thin sliver of Palm Beach, and finally the ocean beyond and forever. The equivalent condominium in Palm Beach would have probably sold for fifteen to twenty times what Gifford's Rapallo condominium was worth, simply because it was Palm Beach. But there was no equivalent building in Palm Beach since Palm Beach had a height restriction and the tallest buildings there were only seven stories high versus West Palm Beach's "the sky's the limit" zoning.

Weezie had a rock on her finger that looked like it could give the 45-carat Hope Diamond a run for its money. Mort Ott was having a tough time keeping his eyes off it. He had called Weezie and introduced himself as a Palm Beach detective looking into the death of Jack Rembert and told her he would like to ask her some questions. He had no idea how she'd respond. He'd imagined a wide range of reactions she might have: *I barely knew the man* or *I have nothing to say on the subject.* She might just hang up on him. That was a not uncommon reaction in his line of work.

Instead, she'd agreed to meet with him, claiming that she had heard the news about Jack Rembert's drowning from a friend and was "terribly chagrined."

They were seated in her living room which faced southeast so Ott could clearly see the tower at Mar-a-Lago a mile away. Weezie Gifford was, like so many young, stylish women, a blonde. Natural or otherwise, Mort couldn't be sure. She was on the short side but had what Ott would have called a "killer" body if he were talking to Crawford, and something much more anatomically restrained if he were writing up a report.

"Thanks for seeing me, Ms. Gifford, I appreciate it," he said.

"You're welcome."

"Well, as far as Mr. Rembert's unfortunate death goes, we're making the assumption that it was an accident at this point."

She blinked a few times. "Well, I haven't heard it was anything but that."

"We're really not sure, but we also need to at least look into it as a possible..." Homicide was too jolting of a word. "...intentional act."

She blinked a few more times. "You mean, like, someone killed him?"

"It's not uncommon for us to pursue all angles."

"I understand...but who?"

No, that's my question.

"Did Mr. Rembert ever mention to you anybody who he had...let's say, reason to fear. Who might have had a reason to...harm him?"

Weezie Gifford actually gasped at 'harm him' but didn't say anything for a few moments. Then, she inhaled deeply. "Look, Detective Ott, I'm going to level with you because, for all I know, you might be..." Her voice trailed off.

"Might be what, Ms. Gifford?"

"For all I know you might be thinking I had something to do with what happened to Jack."

"Actually, that had never crossed my mind."

"Well. Good. Because, you see, Jack was going to divorce his wife and marry me, but..."

"But?"

"His two daughters got involved...and said they'd never speak to him again if he married me..."

"Keep going, please."

"Jack adored his daughters...God knows why," she said, with an emphatic shrug. "So after a lot of hemming-and-hawing, he told me he wanted to call it off."

"Divorcing his wife and marrying you?"

"Yes, exactly," Weezie said. "So I guess you could come up with some scenario whereby the spurned woman, i.e. me, killed him out of spite because I wasn't going to have him...or something like that."

"Well, since you brought it up, yes, I guess I could," Ott said. "But you're saying that was not the case?"

"I was mad and I was upset, but the more I thought about it the more I realized Jack wasn't the man for me. I mean, if he could be talked out of something as serious as marriage by his daughters, then he really wasn't ready for it. If you talk to his daughters, though, they'll probably tell you I was in it for the money. But the reality is I could get by just fine without Jack Rembert and his millions."

"What do you do, if you don't mind me asking? I mean, do you work?"

"Yes, I work very hard. At the Hammer Gallery in Palm Beach. I do pretty well for myself, in fact."

"Mr. Rembert's daughters, do they live in Palm Beach?"

She nodded.

"Can you give me their names?"

"Sure. Sally Hemmes and Muffie Drexel."

Ott nodded and glanced again at Weezie's diamond ring.

She noticed. "Yes, Jack gave it to me."

"It's a beautiful ring."

"It's my engagement ring," she said. "After he broke the engagement, I told him I wasn't giving it back to him."

Ott made a mental note to check marital law and see if she had a right to keep it.

"When did you last see Mr. Rembert?"

"Oh, God, it had to be at least a week. He took me out to dinner at Cafe

Boulud to drop his little bomb. Had to have half a bottle of wine to get his courage up."

"That's when he told you he was not going to marry you?"

"Yes, he said it would 'shatter' his wife Christina and he couldn't have that on his conscience. Then he said, *'I know it won't shatter you because you're a lot tougher than Christina.'*"

"What did *you* say to that?"

"I just shrugged and said, *'No man's ever going to shatter me. And they're completely delusional if they think they can.'*"

FIVE

CRIME SCENE TECH DOMINICA MCCARTHY HAD GOTTEN BACK TO Crawford by cell phone on his way back from his interview with Christina Rembert.

"So whatcha got?" he asked her.

"Well, so far everyone's sold on it being an accident. I spoke to the guy who first spotted the body. He was fishing from the northern most dock and called 911. Shaw and Lorentzen responded and were first on scene. They figured he had been in the water since last night sometime—early evening probably—and there were no signs of foul play."

"No contusions, no visible injuries, or anything?"

"No, nothing. Guy clearly had drowned," Dominica said. "Anyway, it's in the hands of the medical investigator now and Bob Hawes. They've got his personal effects and his clothes. That's all I know."

"Thanks, I appreciate it, I'm gonna head down to the marina in a while and see what I find out," Crawford said. "There's a bottle of wine in it for your hard work."

"As long as I get to drink it with you."

"I'd never let you drink alone."

CRAWFORD AND OTT WERE BACK IN CRAWFORD'S OFFICE. CRAWFORD had filled in his partner on his interview with Christina Rembert, and it was Ott's turn to tell him about Weezie Gifford.

"I liked her," Ott said. "Down-to-earth kinda broad."

Crawford laughed. "Thought you said you were going to banish *broad* and *bimbo* from your vocabulary. As part of your sensitivity training."

"Yeah, I know, but in certain cases, *broad* is a compliment."

Crawford shrugged. "Okay, I'll take your word for it. What else?"

"Rembert gave her a rock half the size of Texas. An engagement ring. Then he called it off."

"So the long and the short is, you ruled her out?"

"Ruled her out? Ruled her out of what? Why do we think we've got a murder here? Just 'cause David Balfour doubts his buddy fell in the drink and drowned?"

"Yeah, I know," Crawford said nodding. "I'm not seeing anyone who jumps out as having a motive. But then again, we've barely scratched the surface of possible suspects, except the airhead wife and Weezie. Tell you what, why don't I go track down some of Rembert's players and you go talk to his daughters."

"You mean, those 'ghastly' players of his?"

"Yeah, with all the nasty tats, hairdos, and funky clothes," Crawford said. "And don't forget that badass white coach ol' Jack butted heads with."

Ott laughed. "Yeah, maybe head-butted him into the drink?"

CRAWFORD HAD ASKED OTT IF HE WOULD INTERVIEW JACK Rembert's two daughters for two reasons. One, no one was a better interrogator, and two, Crawford wanted to go down to the docks and nose around to see what he could dig up there. He was hoping for maybe an eyewitness or two, who might have either seen Rembert or else noticed something that looked suspicious. Then he'd try to line up and question a few of Rembert's players.

Ott had gotten the phone numbers of Jack Rembert's daughters by calling their mother, Christina, and had made an appointment at Sally Hemmes house in Palm Beach for 4:00 that afternoon. He was going to meet with Muffie Drexel the next morning.

Sally Hemmes lived in a modern boxy house constructed from concrete, which Ott remembered was from an architectural style called Brutalism. Palm Beach had strict guidelines about what was architecturally acceptable and what wasn't. Ott was surprised Sally Hemmes' house had passed the test. He wondered whether a friendly bribe might have been involved but then thought...in lily-white Palm Beach...*never*! Unless, of course, it was a really big bribe with lots of zeroes.

The interior of the Hemmes house on Reef Road could best be described as spartan or even barren as there were only five pieces of furniture in the entire living room, three of which were currently occupied. Sally sat in a love seat, Ott in a chrome and leather Breuer chair facing her, and Sally's lawyer on a white leather chair next to her.

Sally had explained that she wanted Arthur Meckler, her lawyer, to join them and further explained that he was a family friend. Ott guessed after a few minutes that Meckler was more than just a family friend because there seemed to be a certain unspoken familiarity between the two. Sally looked to be somewhere in her late twenties, a comely brunette with a large mole between her lower lip and chin. Arthur Meckler, thirty or so, was stocky, pink-faced, and had puffy jowls. Ott guessed jelly donuts and ice cream were mainstays in the man's diet.

"Ms. Hemmes, I spoke to Weezie Gifford earlier in the day—"

Sally mumbled something to Meckler that sounded a lot like 'bitch.'

"What was that?" Ott asked.

"Nothing," Sally said. "Proceed."

"Anyway, as I explained to you on the phone, my partner and I are looking into the death of your father as something that might not have been an accident. It's something we routinely do. Ms. Gifford told me that you and your sister were instrumental in breaking off the relationship between your father and her."

"What's that got to do with anything?" Arthur Meckler asked as spittle flew from his flaccid mouth.

"I'm just making sure that I have all the facts straight," Ott said. "Is that correct, Ms. Hemmes?"

"Yes, he broke it off when he figured out she was a gold digger and all she was after was his money."

"Weezie Gifford is a scheming, calculating woman," Meckler added, heavy on the scorn.

Ott nodded and thought for a second. "Can you tell me what Ms. Gifford looks like, Mr. Meckler?"

Ott had a hunch Meckler had never met Weezie Gifford and was just spouting the party line.

Meckler looked agitated. He ran his hand over his mushy chin. "I'm just telling you what's common knowledge. What else would you like to ask Ms. Hemmes, detective?"

Sally Hemmes raised her hand. "Before you ask me anything else, do you know that woman refused to return the very expensive diamond ring my father gave her?"

"No, I didn't know that." Ott bent the truth a little.

Sally nodded. "When my father ended the engagement, he asked her to return the ring, which, by the way, he paid over seven hundred thousand dollars for." Ott was not surprised by that. "And she refused to return it."

Ott had checked the law on this subject, as he'd made a note to do, so he decided to let it fly. "Mr. Meckler, my understanding of the Florida statute on this subject is that the donee gets to keep the ring, if the marriage is called off by the donor."

"Now *you're* a lawyer?"

"But isn't that correct, Mr. Meckler?"

"The law's somewhat ambiguous on this," Meckler said, clearly clueless. "Why don't you go ahead and ask Ms. Hemmes your questions."

"Did your father have any health issues, Ms. Hemmes?"

"No, he was as healthy as a horse," Sally said. "Had his hips replaced at HSS last year but that's all."

"So how did you react to the news that your father had fallen into the water at the marina and drowned?"

Sally rubbed her forehead. "Of course, I was devastated. But then, I thought it was strange. Extremely unusual. That was about the last way I'd ever expect him to die."

Ott wanted to probe this a little deeper. "Is that...is that something you gave thought to...how your father was going to die? I mean, he was only fifty-seven years old."

Arthur Meckler bridled. "What kind of a question is that? She was just saying that it struck her as somewhat, ah, surprising and unusual. Of course, she didn't sit around thinking about how her physically fit father was going to die."

Ott just nodded.

"So if you don't have any more—"

"I do," Ott said. "Ms. Hemmes, I asked your mother this same question: did your father have any enemies? She mentioned a football coach. Did your father ever happen to mention anyone to you who he...feared might do him harm?"

Sally shook her head. "Not really."

"What about his partner?" Meckler said to Sally.

"I don't really think—"

"Who is his partner?" Ott asked. "I've never heard him mentioned before."

"Well, really, his junior partner," Sally said. "Del Lewis."

"The very ambitious Del Lewis," Meckler added, and Sally nodded.

"When you think about it," Meckler said to Sally, "he would like nothing better than to take over your father's business. Go from second-in-command to head honcho."

"I'd like to hear more about this man," Ott said.

Sally looked away for a moment, then back to Ott. "Okay, Del started out in the mail room when my father worked out in Los Angeles, the way a lot of agents do, then I guess my father saw something in him he liked and made him his assistant."

"How long ago was that?"

"Oh, about fifteen years ago, I think. Then Dad started his own shop and moved it here. Close to where he grew up. Del came here with him."

"So would Mr. Lewis now become agent for all those athletes your father used to represent?" Ott asked.

"I don't know exactly," Sally said, "but probably a lot of them. As I said, Del worked with my father for about fifteen years and isn't that much older than some of the players. I think a lot of them trusted him 'cause they were close in age. So I'd guess most of them probably wouldn't jump ship to other agents."

"Would *not*?" Ott said.

"Correct," Sally said.

"Del had a way of being very skillful at worming his way into their good graces," Meckler said and then added to Sally. "*Unctuous* is a word I heard your dad use."

Sally threw up her hands. "I don't really know. It's not as though my father talked to me a lot about it."

Ott made a mental note to interview Del Lewis as soon as possible.

"Anyone else, Ms. Hemmes?"

"Anyone else *what*?" she asked.

"I think he's asking whether there's anyone else you think might have had a reason to kill your dad," Meckler assisted.

"Good God, no, and I wasn't suggesting that Del might have," Sally said. "Can we be done with this now, please?"

Meckler nodded vigorously. "Yes, we absolutely can," he said, turning to Ott. "What she's saying is, she'd like you to leave now."

Ott could take a hint. He got up smiled at both, said good-bye, and showed himself out the door, thinking to himself, *this thing is starting to get interesting.*

SIX

CRAWFORD DECIDED TO WALK TO THE DOCKS SINCE IT WAS ONLY FIVE blocks from the station house. In retrospect, he wished he had driven there because on his way he spotted an older woman coming toward him wearing shorts, a sleeveless T-shirt, and black Chuck Taylor hi-tops. He recognized her immediately and hoped she didn't recognize him.

His wish was not granted. "Hello, detective," she said warmly. "How've you been?"

He nodded. "Great, Mrs. Halsey, nice to see you again," he said and kept on walking.

But the first time he had *seen* her had not been particularly nice at all. In fact, it had been downright...well, astonishing was one word for it. Eye-opening was another. Even for Palm Beach. That was because the woman was skateboarding naked, well, except for the same Chuck Taylor's she was now wearing, down Australian Avenue. A call had come in from a concerned citizen, a man, who ended his call by saying, "it would have been one thing if she was fifty years younger." Crawford had been called by Bettina, the receptionist, who prefaced it by saying, "Sorry, Charlie, hate to bring you into this, but you're the only one around..."

So Crawford had driven to Australian and, sure enough, there was

Wendy Halsey...in all her splendor. He'd offered her his jacket to cover up as much as it could and drove her back to her house two door down from the Brazilian Court Hotel. He did not write her a citation but requested that she please refrain from naked skateboarding in the future. She might get a painful sunburn, he added. She promised she would and told him she appreciated his concern.

After the surprise digression, Crawford arrived at the marina and walked up to the northern most dock where Dominica had told him Rembert's body was discovered. The first thing he noticed were the cameras on many of the boats, something that had not occurred to him. Of course, there would be security cameras on boats, just like there were on houses.

As he was walking down the dock, he saw a man in a white uniform coming toward him. He looked like he was maybe the captain of a private yacht.

"Excuse me, sir," he said to the man, taking a photo out of his pocket. "My name's Detective Crawford, Palm Beach Police. This is a photo of the man who drowned here the other night, I'm sure you heard about it. Did you, by any chance, happen to see him then?"

The man took a look at the photo. "Oh, yes, I certainly did hear about it," the man said in a German accent. "But no, I'm sorry, I never saw him."

Crawford thanked him and kept walking until he saw a woman standing on the aft deck of a boat and waved at her.

"Hi," he said, as she came up to the edge of the boat. "I'm a detective with the Palm Beach Police Department. As I'm sure you know, a man drowned here the other night." He held up the photo. "I wondered if you had seen him?"

"You know what? I actually did." Crawford took a few steps closer to her. "He looked like he was really intoxicated. He was staggering, like he was about to face plant on the dock. I figured he was maybe on his way back to his boat. I mean, trust me, the guy was in really bad shape."

This was not jibing with what David Balfour had told him.

"If you could tell me *exactly* what you saw, please?" Crawford said.

"Of course," said the woman. "Well, for one thing I saw this woman behind him, almost like she was following him. She stopped when she saw me and kind of turned to one side. Like she didn't want me to see her face."

"Really? Did you get much of a look at her at all?"

"No, not really. Just that she was a blonde," she said.

He saw a camera facing out from the boat she was on. "I was wondering...would it be too much to ask for me to take a look at the film from your security camera?"

She shook her head. "You know what, that's actually a really good idea. Who knows what you might see, right?"

Crawford nodded.

"Well, come on board," the woman said, pointing to the gangplank near the bow of the boat.

———

CRAWFORD SPENT THE REST OF THE AFTERNOON—THREE SOLID HOURS —going from one boat to another looking at security footage which covered the window of time when he figured Jack Rembert arrived at the docks until the approximate time when he drowned. He had found only one camera so far that had recorded Rembert walking—very crookedly and unsurely—down one of the docks. Crawford decided that he was going to spend more time looking the next day and get Ott to join him.

On his way back to the station, he dialed David Balfour.

"Hi, Charlie."

"Hey, I just spent a lot of time down at the dock and I've got some questions for you."

"Fire away."

"Okay, I know what you said, but is it possible Jack Rembert was really drunk the last time you saw him? He just hid it well."

"No. Like I mentioned at my house, Jack was a guy who could handle his liquor really well—"

"Define that."

"He could have four or five drinks and you'd never know it. No slurring. No trouble walking a straight line. Like he hadn't had much. And two, he only had like two, two and a half drinks in the hours before we went to the Norton. We were pretty serious about the scavenger thing. We lost to the Pinks last year and weren't about to let it happen again."

"Gotcha. 'Cause to hear a few people who saw him tell it, he was falling-down, stumble-bum drunk. And that's how he looked on security footage."

"You sure it was Jack?"

"I'm sure. No question about it. He was wearing that same yellow long-sleeved shirt and blue-striped shorts you mentioned. It was definitely him," Crawford said. "Second question: do you know what time it was when you split up with him at the Norton?"

"I know exactly. 'Cause I checked on my way over to Silla Vander Poel's. It was 6:15 on the dot."

"Okay, so for him to get to his Uber and then to the docks, it couldn't have been any more than, what, ten minutes?"

"Yeah, exactly, up Dixie to Ocheechobee, over the bridge and the marina's right there," Balfour said. "Unless the bridge was up?"

"Good point. That could have happened. But that would only have added five to seven minutes."

Crawford made a mental note to see whether the draw bridge had been raised and lowered around that time.

"Why are you asking, Charlie?"

"Because there's a shot from a security camera of Rembert getting out of a car at 6:45 at the docks."

"So, you mean...a half-hour after when I figure he left the Norton?"

"Exactly. So my third question is, what kind of car was the Uber, and what can you tell me about the driver? See, problem is I can't get any info on an Uber account or any other phone info 'cause his phone was in his pocket and it's obviously ruined."

Balfour didn't say anything for a few moments. "I understand. So I think it was a white, um, Camry or maybe a Honda Accord. One of those. And the driver was a guy who Jack had used before. Tall, skinny guy I think his name is Ted."

Crawford felt a jolt of adrenaline.

"That's very interesting."

"What do you mean?"

"'Cause the car that dropped him off was a black Audi SUV. And the driver was a blonde woman. I couldn't really make her out except she clearly was a blonde."

Balfour scrunched up his eyes. "None of this jibes, Charlie."

"I know. Three things: the fact that Rembert was sloppy, falling-down drunk, how long it took him to get from the Norton to the docks, and the driver and the car."

"So what do you do now?" Balfour asked.

"Security cams. And me and Ott get to the bottom of it."

"What are you thinking at this point?"

Crawford thought for a moment. "That all of a sudden I've got a hell of a lot more questions than answers."

SEVEN

CRAWFORD HAD HATCHED A THEORY THE NIGHT BEFORE AND WENT TO
his office early to think it through and research it. At nine o'clock—an hour
and a half later—he called the medical examiner, Bob Hawes. As he could
have guessed, Hawes was not in yet. He and Ott had observed Hawes kept
"banker's hours," which were very different from detective hours. They
calculated that detective hours, at least when they were on a case, were
probably twenty hours a week more than those clocked by Hawes. He left a
message for Hawes and about forty-five minutes later, the M.E. called back.

"What's up, Crawford?" Hawes said. "You calling about Johnny
Weissmuller?"

Crawford had to think what he meant, then he got it. Hawes' very
dated reference was to an Olympic swimmer back in the 1920's who won
many gold medals and went on to play Tarzan in the movies. Mort Ott had
pointed out on more than one occasion that it was a toss-up who had the
worse sense-of-humor, Hawes or their chief, Norm Rutledge.

"That's very funny, Bob," Crawford said. "His name is Jack Rembert."

"Yeah, I know. I don't have a tox report yet, but it seems accidental,"
Hawes said. "His body's at Quattlebaum's Funeral Home now."

"I've got a question or two for you."

"Well, as you know, I'm the man with all the answers."

Aww, conversations with Hawes were so damn tiresome but Crawford plowed on.

"Okay, so those date-rape drugs like Rohypnol and GHB...how long do they stay in the system?"

"Has it gotten so bad you have to resort to those things?" Hawes said.

Crawford just ignored him.

"What's the answer, Bob?"

"Well, normally they don't stay in the system very long. Like, say, eight to twelve hours is all. Why do you ask? Are you thinking Rembert was a homicide?"

"I'm not saying that. I'm just looking into something."

"But do you think someone gave him one of those drugs?"

"I don't know, it's just something that's got me curious. I'm shooting in the dark at the moment," Crawford said. "So by now you're saying—36 hours later or so—there's unlikely to be any trace of anything?"

"Correct, but...hold on a second...hair is different. Stays there a lot longer. Like up to a month or so."

"So, you mean, if you took a hair follicle and put it under a microscope, traces of the stuff might show up?"

"Yeah, I've never done it myself but I've read and heard about it. Traces of those two you mentioned—Rohypnol and GHP—show up and also keta-mine and another one called scopolamine."

"That's good to know," Crawford said. "So how would you feel about getting a hair sample of his?"

"Yeah, sure, but you better ask the family," Hawes said. "I don't think they'd like it much if they were at Quattlebaum's and I showed and plucked a hair out of Jack's head."

Crawford almost laughed at the mental image but didn't want to encourage Hawes. "Tell you what," he was getting amped up now, "I'll clear it with Rembert's widow. I'll get back to you as soon as I do, and you can go get a hair follicle and check it out."

"Anytime. Just let me know and I'll see what I can come up with,"

Hawes said. "Basically, you're just trying to find out whether your vic ingested any of that shit, right?"

"Yeah, basically."

"I'll get on it," Hawes said, with a chuckle that announced he was about to unleash what he considered a real knee-slapper. "In the meantime, I'll get my tweezers ready."

EIGHT

CRAWFORD WENT DOWN TO OTT'S CUBICLE AND FILLED HIM IN ON the latest development and the conversation with Hawes. After he finished Ott told him about his conversation with Jack Rembert's oldest daughter, Muffie Drexel.

"You know the word *kvetcher?*" Ott asked.

"I've heard it, but I'm not sure what it means."

"It means someone who complains morning, noon, and night," Ott said. "In this case about her dearly departed dad."

"Okay, talk to me. What did she say?"

"So right after I get to her house, she starts bitching about how her father refused to co-sign on the mortgage for her house. Then she says how he refused to pay for her son's first grade tuition at Palm Beach Country Day and goes, 'this is after I honored him by naming my son after him.'"

Crawford chuckled. "So is it written somewhere that if you name your kid after your father that he has to pay the kid's tuition?"

"Right? I mean, Jesus, come on lady, you're s'posed to be in mourning," Ott said. "And this is after she tells me what a cheap bastard the guy is. How her husband works for her father as an agent and pulls down a measly two hundred grand a year and her father clears like eight to ten mill."

"Maybe two hundred K is all the guy's worth," Crawford said. "And last time I checked, that's not a bad paycheck."

"Exactly."

"So what else?" Crawford asked. "What'd she have to say when you asked her the, 'did-your-father-have-any-enemies-who-might-have-wanted-to-kill-him' question?"

"A ton."

"Really? Let's hear."

"Well, first of all is our friend, Weezie Gifford."

"Because of the ring?"

"Yeah, but according to Muffie..." Ott shook his head and laughed. "Jesus, what's with these names—Muffie and Weezie—next we're gonna have a Binky or a Bunny...anyway she says that the ring cost Rembert seven hundred fifty grand and he didn't give a damn what Florida law says, he was gonna claw it back."

"So Muffie's saying that Weezie killed him so he wouldn't come after her to get the ring back?"

"That's the gist. And then she says how Weezie's as poor as the proverbial church mouse and is desperate for the money she's gonna get hawking the ring."

"Despite what Weezie told you about having a good job at Hammer Gallery?"

"Yeah, I brought that up and she goes, 'oh, that's a commission job and, trust me, she's starving.'"

"Okay, so Weezie's still on the list. Who else?"

"Oh, man, you'll love this. Remember the football player, Robert Smallwood?"

"Sure, all-pro linebacker for the Chiefs and the Bills. What about him?"

"Well, turns out he ended up being an agent at some other place after he retired, and according to Weezie, he and Jack Rembert were bitter enemies."

"Muffie, you mean?"

"Yeah, sorry, Muffie. I get confused."

"I hear you," Crawford said. "Smallwood also had that manslaughter charge. Remember? Killed his girlfriend in a bar or something, right?"

"Yeah, exactly. His lawyer claimed it was a freak accident. He got off on some technicality with a wrist slap. A couple years later he became an agent."

"So what was the thing between him and Rembert?"

"Muffie didn't really know any specifics, just that she heard him go off on Smallwood, called him 'the bar room killer.'"

"Where's he live? Smallwood?"

"Just down the road in Boca. I checked him out. Works at a sports agency called, Just the Best Sports Management."

"I've actually heard of it. I think they just did a contract for that pitcher for the Astro's, Luis Santana. Well, guess Smallwood jumps up high on our list."

"That is, if we got a murder here," Ott said. "We're still not absolutely sure."

"I'm beginning to feel pretty certain we do," Crawford said.

Then he told Ott his theory about Rembert being drugged and how it would make him more susceptible to falling in the water and drowning. Or being pushed in.

"All right," Crawford said. "So two suspects doesn't add up to a 'ton.' Who else?"

"Oh yeah," Ott said. "How about Muffie's mother? Well, stepmother actually. Apparently, Christina Rembert and she aren't on real good terms. She said dear old stepmom threatened dear old dad a time or two. I guess 'cause he messed around with other women."

"Jesus, Mort, talk about a dysfunctional family?"

"With a capital D."

"Did she give any specifics about these threats?"

"Not really. Except they'd both get a couple cocktails in 'em and start yelling and screaming and hangin' out the dirty laundry."

"And Muffie was around to hear it?"

"Yeah, except she remembers it from back when she was living under the same roof with them ten or twelve years ago."

"All right, speaking of Christina Rembert, I've got to get her permission for one of the oddest requests, I guarantee you, she's ever heard."

"And that would be?"

"For Bob Hawes to pluck a couple of hairs out of her dead husband's head."

NINE

It was a little past ten when Crawford and Ott got in their Crown Vic and headed down to the Palm Beach docks. The first person they spoke to was a young man in a white uniform pushing a large cart of what appeared to be bags of groceries and two equally large brown cartons, which Crawford guessed, contained bottles of liquor. As the man got closer, Crawford noticed the words *Day Trader* in script on the man's breast pocket.

"Excuse me," Crawford said, "we're Palm Beach detectives investigating the drowning of a man here the other night, can we ask you a few questions?"

"Of course," said the man in a British accent. "That was terrible...what exactly happened?"

"Did you, by any chance, happen to see him?"

"No, I did not, but the scuttlebutt seems to be that he was very drunk."

Crawford had noticed that a camera on board the boat they were standing next to was aimed in the direction of the parking lot.

"Is this your boat?" Crawford asked.

"No, the *Day Trader* is two down from this one," the man said pointing at a massive yacht that had to be at least a two hundred fifty feet long.

"The man who owns it must have done pretty well in the market," Ott said, referencing the boat's name.

"It's a she," the man said. "One of the best traders ever, I read. Made a fortune on bitcoins too."

"Did you hear any other scuttlebutt about the man who drowned?" Crawford asked.

"Just that he was a big sports agent. That's about all I heard. As I said, I never saw him."

"Well, thank you," Crawford said, pointing at the boxes of liquor. "Having a party or something?"

The man chuckled. "No, the madame and her friends just love their cocktails."

"Okay, thanks," Crawford said, and they walked further down the dock.

"You ever heard that expression, *the haves and the have yachts?*" Ott asked, taking in the staggering array of colossal yachts moored at the docks. "I read somewhere that at any given time the boats at all the docks here are worth between five and ten billion dollars."

"I believe it," Crawford said.

"Oh wow, see that one," Ott said, pointing to a ship's name on its bow further down the dock. *Privacy,* it said. "Tiger Woods owns that one. He lives up on Jupiter Island."

Ott was referring to an exclusive island forty-five minutes to the north of Palm Beach.

"Sleek as hell," Crawford said about the boat. "Wonder why he keeps it here instead of up there."

"Who knows?" Ott said, with a shrug. "Maybe just came down here to go shopping or something."

Crawford chuckled. "You mean, a couple thousand dollars in gas to get a few shirts."

"Hey, he's Tiger, what's a couple thou in gas?"

Crawford chuckled. "So you want to wait around here and get his autograph?"

"Nah, I'd do a selfie anyway," Ott said. "Come on, we got work to do, security cams to check out."

An hour later, Crawford left to meet with David Balfour. He took the Crown Vic and Ott was either going to walk back to the station or still be at the docks when Crawford came back later, depending on how much ground he covered. Crawford had decided at the station earlier that he needed to pick Balfour's brain a little more. He called him, but Balfour didn't answer and, looking at his watch, Crawford realized this was when Balfour had his usual late morning golf game at the Poinciana Club.

"Hi, it's Charlie, I want to ask you a few more things about Jack Rembert. So if you have any time early this afternoon, after lunch say, I'd like to stop by and ask you some more questions about him."

A little later he got a call back and Balfour said he could meet him at 1:30. Crawford thanked him and said he'd be there then.

Meanwhile, Crawford figured that his strange request for a sample of Jack Rembert's hair required an in-person visit. So he called Christina Rembert next and she agreed to meet with him after he met with Balfour. After setting up the appointment with her, he spent some time plotting out how to proceed with his different suspects...except, of course, they weren't full-fledged suspects yet and wouldn't be until he was absolutely convinced he had a murder on his hands. He was, however, about ninety-per-cent there.

He got to Balfour's house at a little after 1:30 and the two of them were seated at a glass-topped table out by Balfour's pool, drinks in hand. Crawford nursed a ginger gle, and Balfour a concoction called a Blood Bull.

"Gotta boast a little. I shot six-over," Balfour said, meaning he shot six over par on the golf course.

"Nice going," Crawford said. "You're an eleven handicap, right?"

"Yeah," Balfour said. "Won a few bucks."

Crawford knew that Balfour and his golf buddies played for big money and guessed that "a few bucks" was probably high three figures, possibly four figures.

"I gotta get you out there again, Charlie," Balfour said, referring to the golf course. "So what do you want to know about Jack Rembert?"

"Everything," Crawford said. "From what I've heard so far, the man, let's just say...got around. With women, I mean."

Balfour laughed. "That's the understatement of the week...maybe the year," he said. "No question about it, 'ol Jack liked the ladies...and the ladies liked him. His money didn't hurt either."

"Okay, so give me some names."

"Well, let's see...I already told you about Weezie Gifford who was all set to marry him—"

"Until he called it off and wanted the ring back."

"Yup, then there was Sally Shuman, married to a guy named Mark Shuman. She and Jack were having a nice, quiet affair until it went public."

"What do you mean? How?" Crawford said putting his ginger ale down on a table.

"He took her to a charity ball, the Red Cross ball, I think it was. I wasn't there but I heard all about it. Mark was out of town on business and Jack showed up with her and the two danced the night away. It was like he didn't give a damn if anyone knew."

"That was pretty stupid. Why be so obvious?"

"That I don't know. In the past, he was always a lot more discreet," Balfour said, putting his feet up on another chair.

"Who else?"

"Well, this is a really odd one," Balfour said. "How about a six-foot four black woman basketball player from Russia?"

"What? Since when are there black people in Russia?"

"Since almost never. I bet if you looked it up, they'd be less than one percent of the population."

"A *lot* less is my guess."

"So you ever heard of Anoushka Novokov?"

"Can't say I have?"

"She plays for the Dallas Wings and is one of the highest paid women's basketball players."

"But they don't make anywhere close to what the men make, do they?"

"I'm sure they don't, but anyway Jack repped her," Balfour laughed, "and did a lot more than that."

"How do you know this?"

"He told me, sometimes he'd boast about his conquests," Balfour said. "One time we were in the locker room at the Poinciana and a women's hoops game was on TV in the background. He looked up and pointed at this good-looking black woman dunking a ball and said, 'I just signed her to a five-year contract with the Dallas Wings. Anoushka Novikov's her name.' Then he gave me this big wink and lowered his voice. 'Plus a personal contract with me...amazing in the sack.'"

"Did he have any other women clients?"

"I think maybe a couple of tennis players. One from Argentina and an Italian one, as I remember," Balfour said. "I remember he told me that Anoushka used to be, or maybe still was, the mistress of this Russian oligarch, so he had to be careful about his dalliances with her."

Crawford laughed. *Dalliances* was such a Balfour word. "Wow, so if, in fact, he was murdered, you just gave me two new suspects."

Balfour nodded. "Mark Shuman and the Russian oligarch."

"Exactly. What's the Russian's name?"

"Um, let's see." He stared at the pool before snapping his fingers. "Now I remember, Stanislav Dalyagin."

"Thanks. Who else you got?"

"Let me think a second..." Balfour leaned back in his chair, so the two front legs were off the ground. Suddenly, his face lit up with a big wide grin. "Oh, Christ, this one's a real doozie...remember the name Sumner Redstone?"

"Sort of. Didn't he have something to do with CBS?"

"Yeah, something to do with CBS, Paramount Pictures, Viacom...guy was a multi- billionaire. Anyway, Jack knew him from LA, where he used to have an office. They played cards together, I think it was, got to be pretty good friends. Anyway, pay attention here, 'cause this gets complicated."

"I'm listening."

"So Redstone apparently had like a flock of mistresses and hookers who he'd pay big money for their, ah, services. Apparently even put a couple of 'em in his will. So there was one who Redstone introduced Jack to who Jack really fell for, and I guess after a while they got something going. And so when Redstone died, Jack kind of...well, inherited her. Chloe's the name. She was like the creme de la creme of high-paid hookers. Jack told me Redstone had her on this yearly retainer for a couple of years. A million a year or something, which, when you think about it is chicken feed for a guy who's worth around three billion. Anyway, she was expecting to get the same deal from Jack, but Jack was nowhere near in Redstone's league and paid her like ten grand for every time he saw her."

Crawford shrugged. "Sounds pretty good to me."

"Well, for her it was nowhere near enough," Balfour said. "So to placate her, Jack said he'd put her in his will for a million."

Crawford nodded. "I get it. So you're thinking to get at the million she, or someone she hired, might have killed him."

Balfour nodded his head. "Well, yeah. I'd say she's a possibility," he said. "And, if not, I figured you'd at least appreciate the story."

Crawford shook his head and smiled. "Let me ask you, David, is that what you do when you get rich? I mean, round up as many mistresses as you can and spend the rest of your days screwing. And, by the way, what's the difference between a mistress and a hooker?"

Balfour laughed. "Not much. A couple hundred thou maybe."

Crawford wasn't sure that super-escort Chloe was shaping up as much of a suspect, but he was still curious.

"So rich guy's wives...what do they think about all these mistresses and hookers their husbands are doing? I mean, they find out about them, right?"

"Oh yeah, definitely," Balfour said. "It's like this pact. The wives get pretty sweet lives, everything they want, they just have to look the other way. In reality, they're probably pretty happy they don't have to have sex with their husbands. This one, Mimi somebody, told me at a dinner party after she had a few glasses of champagne, that when she and hubby did it, it was over and done in sixty seconds flat. Or else he'd be chugging away for hours with nothing happening. She told me she felt like picking up a maga-zine while he was banging away—"

"Okay, David, TMI," Crawford said shaking his head. "Gotta say, you have some pretty weird dinner party conversations."

"Yeah, people get a little booze in 'em and you never know what's next."

"I'll take your word for it," Crawford said, looking at his watch. "Well, thanks for all that. I've got to meet with Christina Rembert pretty soon," he said, getting to his feet.

"I'm going to see her day after tomorrow," Balfour said.

"Another dinner party?"

"Nah, Jack's funeral."

Crawford nodded, realizing that was an event he and Ott should defi-nitely attend.

TEN

CRAWFORD AND CHRISTINA REMBERT WERE SITTING IN HER brightly-colored living room again and she was telling him about a note she had received from one of her husband's mega-million-dollar-a-year football players.

"It was very nice of him to write, even though every third word was misspelled. I mean, do these men even get past kindergarten?"

The man was a wide receiver for the Buccaneers and had about the best hands in the NFL, so a few spelling mistakes weren't going to slow him done. Besides, it was a damn thoughtful thing to do, Crawford thought.

"Have you had any other players who your husband represented write to you?"

"A few. Frankly, I was amazed, but then again Jack made them a lot of money."

Crawford was amazed at how she couldn't see it the other way around: how much money they made Jack.

Crawford just nodded. "Mrs. Rembert, I have an unusual request to make. Actually two."

Her eyes fluttered like hummingbird wings. "What, what are they?"

"I have a theory that your husband may have been murdered and that it was disguised to look like an accident."

She leaned closer to him. "You're kidding."

"See, my theory is that he may have been drugged, which led to him becoming very unsteady and incapacitated. That might have led to him falling into the water at the docks and drowning. Or maybe someone actually pushed him."

She put her hand up to her mouth. "Oh, my heavens, do you really think so?"

"I have no definitive proof yet. That's why I keep referring to it as a theory, but I want to pursue it and see where it goes."

"Well, in that case, I urge you to do so," she said earnestly.

"Thank you, so the unusual request is this: if a drug was used, traces of it may be observed in the hair of your late husband."

She shook her head. "I still can't get used to that. The 'late' part," she said. "So you want to...pluck out one of his hairs, is that it?"

Crawford nodded. "A few, actually."

She didn't hesitate. "Sure. I mean, if it'll help, why not?"

"Thank you very much, Mrs. Rembert, I really appreciate it."

"His body is at Quattlebaum's Funeral Home in West Palm Beach."

Crawford nodded. "I know where it is. On Parker Avenue, I believe."

"That's right. I'll call the funeral director and tell him to expect you."

"Actually, it will be our Medical Examiner, a man named Robert Hawes, who will do it."

"Okay, I will tell the director."

"And my second unusual request is that you allow my partner and me to attend your husband's funeral tomorrow?" he asked.

A quick frown appeared, so he charged ahead.

"You see, it's something we do quite often. We just want to see who appears for the funeral. Maybe—very discreetly, of course—ask a question or two. It can be a very useful thing for us."

"Okay, well, if you think it might help." She shrugged. "I guess that's okay."

"I do think it might help," Crawford said. "In the meantime, we can find out if, in fact, your husband was drugged or not."

She just shook her head. "Who would do such a thing?"

"That's what I intend to find out."

ELEVEN

Since Crawford hadn't yet gotten around to speaking to any of the athletes Jack Rembert represented, he thought Rembert's funeral might be the place to do so. He figured some of them could possibly shed light on Rembert's death. Specifically, who, if anyone, Rembert had a falling-out with? These were giant men, after all, who had giant egos to match. Many of them played in physical, sometimes violent sports. There had to be more than a few stories there.

Right after leaving Christina Rembert's house, Crawford got a call from Ott.

"Where are you?" Crawford asked, when Ott picked up.

"Still here at the docks," Ott said. "I may have gotten us a case-buster."

"Talk to me. Whatcha got?"

"On one of the security cams, I saw Jack Rembert get out of this black Audi SUV, and I got the license plate clear as day."

"No kidding," Crawford said. "That's big all right."

"Leave it to Mortie," Ott said. "I'll take a ride over to Motor Vehicles later on and try to ID the owner."

"Okay, I'll be there in five minutes," Crawford said. "Where exactly are you?"

Ott gave him directions and they met up five minutes later.

Ott showed him the shot of the Audi SUV and Rembert getting out of it. Then another shot of the Florida license plate, then a third one of the blonde woman driver. It was much higher-resolution than the one Crawford had previously seen.

"She's a big woman," Crawford said.

"That was my first reaction, too," Ott said. "Big, good-looking, and scary dangerous."

Crawford looked at his watch. "You still have time to get to Motor Vehicles and ID the owner of the Audi."

"I'm on it," Ott said.

"Meantime, I'm gonna go talk to an Uber driver named Ted who was supposed to be driving Rembert the night he drowned."

"Sounds good. How'd you find out about him?"

"Balfour gave me his name and I tracked him down."

"Question is, why was mystery woman driving Rembert instead of him?"

Crawford nodded. "That's the question."

OTT WAS NO STRANGER AT MOTOR VEHICLES ON OLIVE STREET IN West Palm Beach and had cultivated a relationship with a long-time clerk by the name of Magda. The first time he met her there, he had slipped her two twenties to expedite a search and she was very appreciative. Of course, Chief Norm Rutledge squawked about it when Ott tried to get reimbursed for the forty bucks, claiming 'twenty would have been plenty.' He'd OK'ed it anyway. One other time when Ott wanted to find something else out at Motor Vehicles, he'd swung by Publix first and picked up a nice bouquet of flowers for Magda. She seemed to like that even better and thanked him profusely. He stilled remembered her words, 'you're such a gentleman, Mort, no one else ever gives me anything but grief.'

This time he got in line at the counter where Magda was working and tried to make himself conspicuous. She spotted him after a few minutes and waved him up to the front of the line, explaining to the woman who was there: "This is a police officer who is here on an urgent police matter." The woman stepped aside as Ott excused himself saying, "Thank you ma'am, this shouldn't take long."

"Hello, Magda," Ott said, taking out his wallet and slipping her a twenty-five dollar gift card for T.J. Maxx, "I remember last time you told me you like to shop there."

Her eyes went wide, and a big smile lit up her slightly lop-sided face. "Oh, Mort," she said, lowering her voice, "you are such a thoughtful man, how can I help you?"

Ott took out a scrap of paper, on which he had written, *X71119- Fl.* "I need you to ID a plate for me," he said, handing her the scrap of paper.

Magda smiled at him. "Child's play, my friend."

And two minutes later, she gave him the information he had asked for. The owner of the black Audi was named Gretchen Bull, and she had an address in downtown Miami.

"Thank you, Magda, I really appreciate it," Ott said, smiling up at the woman in horned-rim glasses. "Well, happy shopping."

"Anytime, Mort." She flipped him a thumbs-up. "And happy crime-busting."

TWELVE

"Gretchen Bull, huh?" Crawford said, when Ott came back to the car and told him who the owner of the Audi was and where she lived.

"Guess we're going down to Miami," Crawford said.

Ott nodded. "Not your favorite city."

"Before we go, I want to hear from Hawes. See what he finds out about Rembert's hair sample."

And right on cue, Crawford's cell phone rang. It was Hawes.

"Hey, what did you find out?" Crawford asked, hitting the speaker button.

"Good hunch," said Hawes. "Guy had roofies in his system."

"Rohypnol or what?"

"Can't tell yet but something in that family," Hawes said. "Enough to make him very unsteady on his feet and seem drunk, like your witnesses described him."

Crawford turned to Ott. "Looks like it's official—"

Ott finished, "—we got a murder."

"Thanks, man," Crawford said. "I appreciate you getting on it so fast."

"No problem," Hawes said. "Thought you'd want to know right away. I'll fill you in if I get more details."

"Later," Crawford said, and clicked off. "Magic City…here we come."

"Bring on the 305."

<hr />

THEY DECIDED TO GET AN EARLY START THE NEXT MORNING. Crawford's alarm went off at 6:00 a.m, he hit Dunkin' Donuts at 6:15, met Ott at the station at 6:30, and they were on the road at 6:35.

"We're kidding ourselves if we think we're gonna beat the traffic, you know," Ott said, in the driver's seat of the Crown Vic.

"Well, maybe some of it," Crawford said.

"Doubtful."

"You plug the address into the GPS?"

Ott nodded. "16185 SW 136th Terrace, Miami."

"If that was my address, I'd never be able to memorize it."

Ott nodded again. "No shit, eight numbers. No way in hell."

For the first half of the trip, they made decent time. The second half was a nightmare. Two fender benders and, if they were lucky, they averaged fifteen miles an hour. And Ott was a driver who was most comfortable going between eighty and ninety.

On the way, Crawford told Ott about meeting with the Uber driver, Ted, the day before and how Ted was reluctant to say much at first. Upon Crawford's aggressive questioning, Ted admitted that he had been offered three hundred dollars to drive a man to the airport. And that when he came back to the Norton Museum, Jack Rembert was gone. Crawford got a description of the man who had offered Ted the three hundred dollars, but he wasn't optimistic that would go anywhere.

At 8:42 a.m., they rolled up to the house at SW 136th Terrace. It was a beige, square building with lots of large windows and a three-car garage. It looked like a neighborhood where prosperous people lived.

"Looks like a pretty ritzy neighborhood," Ott said, observing the expensive houses in the area and pulling up to the address he had for Gretchen Bull.

Ott was the designated driver and doorbell pusher. He pushed the button.

A few moments later the door opened and a six-foot man who appeared to be in his mid-thirties opened the door. He was not what they expected because he was almost soap opera star handsome, marred only by a broad scowl on his face.

"Who are you?" he demanded.

"Mr. Bull?"

"Who wants to know?"

Crawford hated that passive-aggressive question.

"My name's Crawford and he's Ott. We're homicide detectives up in Palm Beach."

"Okay, and what do you want?"

"Are you Gretchen Bull's husband?" Ott persisted.

"Suppose I am."

His answers were getting tiring, and Crawford was losing patience. "Okay, we're going to assume you are," he said. "Do you own a black Audi SUV, Florida plate number X71119?"

"Yeah, I do. What of it?"

"And would you tell us where were you three nights ago, the 17th, at around six to seven-p.m.?" Crawford asked.

"Right here, why?"

"Because," Ott said, "we have your Audi on a security cam up in Palm Beach at that time."

Something resembling a smile cropped up on Bull's face. "Oh, so that's what happened to it," he said. "See, someone boosted it that afternoon. I found it on my run the next morning a couple blocks away."

Crawford looked at Ott, who was having a hard time disguising his incredulity. "Okay, and did you report this to the police, Mr. Bull?"

"Nah, figured some kid took it on a joyride or something."

"And was it in your garage when this...allegedly happened?" Crawford asked.

"Yeah, it was."

Crawford cocked his head. "What's your first name, Mr. Bull?"

"Greyson, why?"

"Just wanted to know who we're talking to."

Crawford noticed Ott was studying the man like he would a rare animal at the zoo. His unblinking gaze was as intense as Crawford had ever seen it.

"And how do you figure this...joyrider opened the garage door?" Ott asked.

"How the hell would I know?"

"Mr. Bull," Crawford asked, reaching into his jacket pocket and taking out a photo. "Do you have any idea who this is?"

It was the photo of the blonde woman at the wheel of the Audi at the Palm Beach dock.

Bull gave it a fast glance. "No idea."

"It's not your...wife, is it?"

"My wife? No way, she was right here when the car got stolen."

"Is she a tall blond?" Crawford asked.

"Yeah, so?"

Ott's eyes were boring into Bull's. "But does she look like this woman? Your wife?"

"She's a blonde," Bull shook his head in disgust. "Look, I've given you guys enough of my time on this wild goose chase or whatever the hell it is. It's time for you to get the hell out of here now."

Crawford and Ott didn't move. "Do you work, Mr. Bull?" Crawford asked.

"Okay, this is the last damn question I'm gonna answer and then I want you out of here. I'm an independent contractor. Why?"

"But what exactly do you do?" Ott asked.

"What did I just tell you? I'm an independent contractor. And now I'm going to shut the door and you're going to leave me in peace."

Bull did just as he said he would and shut the door. Actually, slammed the door. But Crawford and Ott, once again, didn't move.

"You thinking what I am," Crawford said.

"I bet I am," Ott said. "That the blonde in the photo might be Mr. Bull himself in a nice, expensive wig."

THIRTEEN

A FEW MINUTES LATER THEY DROVE OUT OF SW 136TH TERRACE.

Crawford turned to Ott. "Did you notice how smooth his face was?"

"Yeah, like he didn't need to shave. Maybe had some kind of plastic surgery or electrolysis or something?" Ott said, "And how about the two little holes in his ear lobes."

"For earrings, you mean?"

"Yup, and the eyebrows," Ott said.

Crawford nodded. "Faint trace of eyeliner, right?"

Ott nodded back.

"That was the biggest giveaway."

"So we got a transgender suspect here," Ott said. "Just where does that get us?"

"Damn good question," Crawford said. "I got another one. Do you know the difference between a transgender person and a transsexual one?"

Ott scratched his head as he pulled up to a light. "I'm not sure, you better Google it."

Crawford took his iPhone out and typed.

"Here we go," he said. "Says, 'the word 'transgender' is an umbrella term that describes those who have a gender that's different from the sex assigned at birth: male, female, or intersex. 'Transsexual' is a more specific term that fits under the transgender umbrella. This word can be contentious and shouldn't be used unless someone specifically asks to be referred to this way. Read on to learn more about the difference between being transgender and being transsexual.'"

"Wait, what's 'intersex' mean?"

"Hang on, I'm reading...here's some more, 'the terms transgender and transsexual can refer to a person who has a different gender identity to the sex that a doctor assigns them at birth. However, many people find the term transsexual outdated and offensive.'"

"Okay, so I guess we better go with transgender."

"I guess so."

They both were silent for a few minutes.

"How 'bout that bullshit about not calling the cops when the Audi was stolen because he knew it was just a joyrider out for a little fun," Ott said.

"And the joyrider being so thoughtful to bring it back and drop it just down the street."

"What a crock of shit."

"And that whole thing about being an independent contractor was pretty sketchy. I mean, an independent contractor can be a million things other than a contractor who works on your house. Doctor, dentist, lawyer, accountant—"

"Fisherman, fire man, post man—"

"Hitman?"

"Hitwoman?"

A few minutes later, Crawford started working his iPhone.

Ott glanced over. "What are you looking for?"

"I think we should swing by the nearest police station. Something tells me that Mr. Greyson Bull either has a sheet or someone in local law enforcement knows something about him."

"Good idea. Just tell me know where to go," Ott said.

"Okay," Crawford said. "Looks like the nearest station is either 799 NW 81st Street or 1000 NW 62nd Street." Crawford looked up at a street sign. "Let's try the one on NW 81st."

"Okay, what's the number again?"

"799."

"I'm on my way," Ott said, taking a sharp U-turn.

Crawford was still reading. "You know how they give stars for every-thing? Hotels, restaurants, everything."

"Yeah?"

"So the station on 62nd Street gets a whopping 2.6 stars and the one on 81st only a 2.1."

"I got news for you, my friend," Ott said.

"What's that?"

"Palm Beach only has a 3.5."

"That must be because of Rutledge."

FOURTEEN

They walked into the police station on NW 81st Street and the first thing that struck Crawford was how similar it was to the Palm Beach Station.

"I know what you're thinking," Ott said, as they approached the receptionist. "Same architect, right?"

"That's exactly what I was thinking," he said, smiling at the skinny, bespectacled woman receptionist. "Hi, we're detectives from Palm Beach and just wondered if there's someone we could speak to regarding a possible murder suspect of ours who lives here."

"Sure, were you thinking homicide guys?"

"Yeah, that would be good. Any of 'em here now?"

"I got at least one. Maybe two. Hang on."

She pressed a few numbers. "Hey, Santiago, I got a couple detectives from Palm Beach out here looking for a murder suspect who may live around here. You got a minute?"

She nodded. "How about Rick? Is he here?"

She nodded again "Okay, yeah, come on out, would you?" she said.

She clicked off and turned to Crawford and Ott. "He'll be right out. The other guy's not around."

"Thank you," Crawford said. "Appreciate it."

"Always so quiet here?" Ott asked the receptionist, making conversation.

"Nah, this is unusual. I like it like this."

"I hear you," Ott said.

A dark complected Latino man with a buzz cut came toward them from across the room.

"That's Santiago," the receptionist said.

Crawford and Ott nodded to the man as he approached.

Crawford put out his hand. "Hey Santiago, Charlie Crawford, Palm Beach homicide and my partner, Mort Ott,"

"Hey, fellas," Santiago said and the three shook hands. "Santiago Vasquez, welcome to our little slice of paradise. Wanna come back with me?"

"Sure," Crawford said, and they followed him back to a room full of cubicles.

"That's mine over there." Santiago pointed to a cubicle. "You know, better yet, there's more space in the interrogation room."

They went with him through the cubicles to a room with four chairs, no windows, and a funky smell to it. Crawford and Ott sat down, and Santiago pulled up a chair facing them.

"So what brings you boys down this way? Doreen mentioned something about a possible murder suspect?"

"Yeah, we had a drowning a few nights back which first looked like an accident, but now we have reason to believe the vic may have been drugged," Crawford said. "Maybe hit over the head, pushed into the water, we're not sure."

"Ever hear the name Greyson Bull, lives at SW 136th Terrace?" Ott asked.

Santiago scratched the back of his head.

"It's a little tricky," Crawford explained, "because we believe he may be transgender. May have been presenting as a woman when the drowning went down. A blonde, close to six-feet, goes by the name of Gretchen Bull."

Santiago shook his head. "Jesus, that *is* tricky. That name sounds kinda familiar. There's another guy here I want to ask," he said standing up. "Can you guys hang tight for a few?"

"Yeah sure," Crawford said, as Ott nodded.

Santiago walked out.

"Smell a little gamey to you?" Ott said, sniffing.

"Yeah, he'd probably say the same about ours."

A few minutes later Santiago came back with a black man with tinted glasses and a full beard.

"This is Nate Barber, Street Crimes and Vice," Santiago said introducing them. "Charlie and Mort, Palm Beach Homicide."

The three shook hands. "So you want to know about Greyson Bull, who sometimes changes his gender and goes by Gretchen?" Barber asked.

Crawford nodded. "So they are one and the same?"

"Yup, but Gretchen's the worst of the two," Barber scratched the side of his face. "See, the long and the short is, she hurts people for a living. Did an eight-year bit up in Raiford for manslaughter a while back."

"As Gretchen, you're saying?" Crawford asked.

"Yeah, like I said, Greyson's the nicer of the two."

"He wasn't all that nice with us," Ott said.

"Yeah, guess it's all relative," Barber said. "We been trying like hell to hang something on her that'll put her away for good. We suspect she's done a couple murders for hire."

"Well, we're thinking you can probably add our drowning vic to the list," Crawford said.

"Someone hired her, probably someone in Palm Beach," Ott said, "who didn't want or know a local hitter."

Barber and Santiago nodded.

Crawford tapped the metal table. "I think what would really help is a shot of her maybe from a security cam around here somewhere. So we can match 'em up. Or maybe you have one in your system?"

"I'll check, but I'm pretty sure we just have one of Greyson," Barber said.

Crawford nodded.

"That way she won't be able to deny it was her up in Palm Beach, if they match up," Ott added. "Wait a minute, what about if a camera was mounted across from her house on 136th Terrace aimed at her front door? Blend it in with what's around it. That way we could see her coming and going."

"Good idea," Barber said. "We just gotta put it up where she can't see it and isn't around when we do it. We'd have to hit you up for the expense."

"No problem," Crawford said.

"Like at night maybe," Santiago added. He volunteered that he had a man at a company that could probably install the camera right away—likely that night—and without Gretchen being the wiser, and Crawford told him to send the bill to Chief Norm Rutledge. He knew Rutledge would balk at it, but Crawford was sure he could sell him on it.

Ott turned to Crawford. "You think we should go back to her house now?"

Crawford thought for a moment. "Nah, 'cause now she knows we're looking for her. No way she's gonna open the door again."

Ott nodded. "Plus we should probably wait until we've got an unmistakable match. So she can't deny it's her."

"I agree," said Santiago. "I'll call my guy from the security company right now."

"All right," Crawford said, getting to his feet. "Well, thank you, boys. You've been real helpful."

Ott stood up. "Yeah, pleasure doing business with you." They all shook hands again.

Crawford and Ott left the station a few minutes later, headed back up to Palm Beach.

"Well, what did you think...what rating?" Crawford asked as they climbed into their Crown Vic.

"Umm, I'd say...interrogation room 1 point 7. Santiago and Nate, 5 point o's."

FIFTEEN

Henry Flagler, who made his mark all over the state of Florida a hundred years ago, created Woodlawn Cemetery on 17 acres of pineapple fields in 1904. Back when it was done, it had a wrought iron gate, which was later replaced with a massive concrete arch. On top of the archway were the words: *That which is so universal as death must be a blessing.*

"Not sure I buy that," Ott said, as he drove through the archway.

Crawford nodded. "Yeah, who came up with those words of wisdom?"

Woodlawn Cemetery is located just a hundred feet north of the Norton Museum on Dixie Highway. The irony of the Norton Museum being so close to where Jack Rembert had probably been driven to his death was not lost on Crawford, who pointed it out to Mort.

Ott nodded. "Yeah, I was just thinking the same thing," Ott said, as he followed a black BMW into the cemetery parking area.

"I'm hoping some of his players are gonna be here," Crawford said, looking back in the rearview mirror as a sleek red sports car followed them in. Ott saw it too.

"There's you answer," Ott said, seeing a large black man inside it. "At least one anyway."

"What is that?" Crawford answered.

"A McLaren 250 S," Ott, a car guy, said, "which is about what it costs. Two hundred fifty grand."

"You're kidding," Crawford said. "For that little thing?"

"Yup, if not more," Ott said. "But that's nothing, the McLaren 765SLT goes for close to four hundred K."

"So you get one little dent and—"

"— that's twenty grand."

"Which is about what my used Lexus cost me. The whole car."

"Just think, Charlie, you were a great athlete, but if you were just a little better, Jack Rembert coulda repped you and you'd be driving one of those little things. You'd be living in the lap of luxury in a place like the penthouse of the Bristol, instead of the fifth floor at the Trianon."

"I like my place."

"Well, good 'cause your playing days are over."

Crawford nodded as Ott slowed to a stop. "Not to mention, I don't think professional lacrosse pays a hell of a lot anyway."

"Yeah, but you played football too."

Crawford laughed. "Ivy League."

Ott chuckled. "Well yeah, there's that," he said. "I bet a few Ivy League guys made it to the NFL."

"Damn right. Sid Luckman, Chuck Bednarik, Calvin Hill, Pat McInally, the list goes on."

"Yeah, but they were from the dark ages."

"Okay, how 'bout Jay Fiedler and Ryan Fitzpatrick?"

"Um, not exactly All-Pro candidates."

"How many from Cuyahoga Community College?"

Ott laughed. "Okay, you got me there."

They parked and got out of the car as another sports car came through the archway.

"What's that one?" Crawford asked flicking his head at an approaching blue sports car.

"That, my friend, is a Pininfarina Battista. Runs you around two million."

"Come on! For a car?"

"Hey, believe it or not, you can spend twenty million on a car."

"I'd rather have a private plane."

"You could get a nice one for that."

Ott watched as a large black man squeezed out of the McLaren that had followed them in.

"Holy shit," he said under his breath. "That's Amari White."

Amari White was the six-foot four-inch, two-hundred-forty pound quarterback for the Atlanta Falcons.

Off in the distance, they saw Christina Rembert and her two daughters, Sally Hemmes and Muffie Drexel. With them was the attorney Arthur Meckler, the man who had been with Sally when Crawford interviewed her. There was another man, who looked to be in his thirties. Crawford assumed he was Muffie's husband. Off to the side, probably twenty yards away, he was surprised to see Weezie Gifford, who he would not have expected to put in an appearance.

Ott nudged his arm and flicked his head in the direction of a stout older white man. "Daryl Boone," he said.

Crawford turned to see Boone, the coach of the Jacksonville Jaguars, who Christina Rembert alleged had "butted heads" with her husband.

"What's he doin' here?" Crawford said in close to a whisper.

"Looks like we got a few surprise guest appearances."

Crawford nodded as he watched a man drive in at the wheel of a hunter green Cadillac convertible. It was Robert Smallwood, the former Buffalo Bills and Kansas City Chief linebacker who became an agent after retiring. Crawford remembered Ott telling him that Muffie Drexel mentioned that her father had referred to Smallwood as "the bar room killer." Then something about Rembert having "stolen" three major clients from Smallwood and how Smallwood, living high on the hog at the time, was fired from his company, had to sell his boat, went through a messy divorce, and experienced a major fall from grace. Smallwood was wearing a double-breasted white jacket and an open-collared purple shirt. Crawford could clearly see a big gold chain around his neck. If it was real, Smallwood was probably not as destitute as had been implied. Not to mention the

Cadillac convertible had to go for seventy-five, eighty-thousand...though, of course, it could have been a lease.

"All these guys showing up who are s'posed to be on Rembert's shit list," Ott said, under his breath, as they walked over to where about a hundred white chairs were lined up facing a coffin on a heavy dark table.

"Shhh," Crawford said, "no cursing at a funeral."

Ott put his hands up. "Oops, sorry."

Crawford and Ott sat in the last row, which was about ten rows back from where the Rembert family members were seated.

They watched as other guests filed in. It was a cavalcade of primarily very large black athletes and much smaller white men and woman who, Crawford guessed, by their fashionable clothes, were Rembert's Palm Beach social friends. Five minutes later, Crawford saw David Balfour walk in wearing a well-cut black flannel suit. Balfour saw him, gave him a quick nod

and sat in an aisle seat a row behind Rembert's family. As he sat, he gave Christina

Rembert a pat on the shoulder. She turned and smiled at him.

Soon after that, the funeral began, and a priest Crawford recalled having seen somewhere proceeded to conduct the funeral.

Crawford figured if Henry Flagler was still around, he would have been very impressed with the exotic cars and the staggering net worths of the men at his former pineapple grove. Having read about what many of these football, basketball, and baseball players made, Crawford estimated that there was over 500 million worth of annual salaries sitting in the little white chairs that looked so fragile beneath the mountainous physiques of the men.

The funeral ceremony was surprisingly short with only the priest making remarks, then Rembert's body was lowered into a nearby grave by the man who Crawford assumed was Muffie Drexel's husband and another man who Crawford guessed was also a family member.

Then it was over, and Crawford watched as the guests in front of him got up out of their chairs. Suddenly there was a loud cracking sound off to Crawford's right and he saw Robert Smallwood crash to the ground, splintering his chair into a hundred tiny pieces. Crawford took a few steps forward to help him up but the giant man, his face flushed with embarrassment, shoved Crawford's hands away.

Another large black man approached, looking down at Smallwood. "Guess you didn't see the sign, dude. 'Anyone over four hundred pounds gotta stand,'" the man said with a loud guffaw.

But the man made no effort to help Smallwood get up as he struggled to his feet.

It was clear Smallwood was not amused. "Why don't they have real chairs at this...*place?*"

Smallwood, no doubt, had a word other than *place* in mind but had caught himself at the last minute. He looked over at Crawford a few feet away from him. "Who are you?" He asked. "Sure ain't no client of Jack's."

"Mean 'cause he's white and only weighs one eighty?" said the other large black man next to Smallwood jovially.

"I'm a detective looking into Jack Rembert's death."

"What's to look into?" Smallwood said, lowering his voice. "Dude fell in the water and drowned."

"I'm not so sure about that," Crawford said. "Mind if I ask you fellas a few questions?"

"Nah, I gotta pay my respects to the family," Smallwood said.

"After that?" Crawford asked.

"Maybe...we'll see," Smallwood said dismissively, then to the other giant black man. "Thanks for nothin', homie."

The man gave him an amused look.

Crawford glanced at the other man. "How 'bout you, sir? Mr.— "

"Darnell Dove!" Ott said, stepping into the void just vacated by Robert Smallwood.

Ott's identification put a wide smile on the man's face.

"That's me, bro," Dove said to Ott, whom he towered above. He had to have a whole foot on the five-foot-seven inch Ott.

Ott smiled up at him. "You mind if we ask you a few questions?"

Dove shook his head. "Whaddaya wanna know?"

"You mind just stepping over here?" Crawford asked, pointing to a spot away from the crowd.

The three moved to a more secluded spot.

"You really think someone cacked ol' Jack?" Dove asked.

Crawford guessed that must mean 'killed.'

"We really think so," Crawford said.

"We got eyes on someone," Ott said. "But we could use your take."

"Well," Dove said, looking around, then dropping his voice, "ain't something I know a lot about, but the guy who just made kindling outta that chair might definitely make my list."

"Why do you say that?"

"You don't know the story?"

They did but wanted to hear Darnell Dove's take.

"Tell us?"

Dove looked around again to see if anyone was close. "So dude used to be a client of Jack's," he said. "Then when he got out of the game, he figured he could give Jack a run for his money. He's a smart fucker. Pain in the ass, though. Got a business degree and worked for Rosenhaus Sports for a while, Jack's big rival. Robert signed up a lot of ballers. Guys he knew, some of 'em teammates, others who just came to him." He stopped and eyed Crawford and Ott. "Sure you don't know the story?"

"A little," Crawford said. "That Rembert stole a couple his guys, right?"

"His three biggest guys, right after they became free agents, ready to sign big contracts," Dove said. "So Drew Rosenhaus, who figured he was just about to make a big time killing with them, fired Robert's ass. No more Rolls, no more Netjets plane, no more boat," he snapped his fingers, "just like that, everything was gone. And Robert wasn't much of a saver. You know what they say: how ballers end up without a pot to piss in. Well, sometimes it's true. 'Course he still had brains and he was never gonna starve, but it was like..."

"So why'd he come here?"

"The truth?" Dove said, eyeing Smallwood out of the corner of his eye as he talked to two men. "What's it look like to you?"

"Trying to sign guys up he can rep?" Ott asked.

"You ain't as dumb as you look," Dove said, clapping Ott on the back. "Just playing with you, bro."

"So, seems like what you're saying," Ott said, "is that Robert could have had two motives: taking out the guy who got him fired and messed up his life *and* getting to rep some of the players Rembert used to rep."

Dove shrugged. "Hey, you're the detectives. Last thing I'm trying to do is tell you how to do your job."

"Well thanks," Crawford said. "We might just have a few words with Robert."

"Go for it, man," Dove said. "Never know, if you got a good pair of hands, he might want to sign you up."

"You mean if I was twenty years younger and a hundred pounds heavier," Crawford said.

"And black," said Dove.

Crawford and Ott laughed and walked over to where Robert Smallwood had one big arm, that filled its sleeve to the bursting point, around a very tall black man. Smallwood saw them coming and waved them off with a raised hand and a shake of his head.

"Who's that?" Crawford asked Ott, meaning the man Smallwood was talking to.

"You don't recognize him?" Ott said. "'Big Dog' Jones. Seven-foot center for the Celtics."

Over Ott's shoulder, Crawford saw Christina Rembert coming toward them.

"Hello, detectives," she said, her voice just above a whisper. "Did you see anyone here who got you suspicious?"

"Hello, Mrs. Rembert," Crawford said. "No, can't say we did. But you certainly had a nice turnout."

She smiled. "Have you ever seen two more dissimilar groups? Palm Beach society and some of the most famous athletes in the country."

"I know," Crawford said. "Quick question. Were you surprised to see coach Daryl Boone here after what you said about him butting heads with your husband?"

Christina scratched her cheek and thought for a moment. "Not really, things change. Don't forget that Hilary Clinton went to Donald Trump's wedding."

Crawford nodded. "One man we were really hoping to talk to was Del Lewis, do you know why he isn't here?"

"Oh, that's simple, because he's on vacation out of the country. And my son-in-law said that he's unreachable. Otherwise, he definitely would have been here."

"Oh, I didn't know that. Do you happen to know when he returns?"

"Scott said he thought later today, as I remember."

"Well, again, it was a nice turn-out and thank you for letting us come," Crawford said.

"You're welcome," she said, smiling at Crawford. "Let me know if I can help in any other way."

Crawford nodded as Christina walked away. He saw Robert Small-wood walking toward his car.

"Come on," he said to Ott.

They followed Smallwood to his car.

"Mr. Smallwood," Crawford said as Smallwood had a hand on his car door.

Smallwood turned around. "Not now," he growled. "I got places to go, people to see."

"Come on, man," Ott said.

"Not now," Smallwood repeated.

Crawford and Ott turned and walked away. "Hey," Ott said, seeing Daryl Boone talking to a couple twenty yards away. "Let's see if we have better luck with him."

They walked over to Boone, as he turned away from the couple.

"Excuse me, coach," Ott said, and Boone looked at them.

"What's up, fellas?" Boone said.

"Hi, Mr. Boone," Crawford said. "We're Palm Beach detectives. Can we talk to you for a few minutes?"

"Sure, what do you want to know?"

"We're pursuing the possibility, actually the strong possibility, that what happened to Jack Rembert was not an accident."

"No shit," Boone said, then putting his hand up to his mouth as if he hadn't intended to let that slip out at a cemetery. "That's news to me. So what do you think happened?"

"He might have been drugged and become incapacitated when he was at the dock."

"Really?" Boone said, putting his meaty hand on his chin. "So, I'm guessing, you want to know who I think mighta done it?"

"Yes. Any thoughts at all would be helpful?"

"You're not looking at me—"

"No, not really," Crawford said. "Though we heard you and he had some pretty serious differences of opinions."

"Damn right we did. Lots. On me re-signing a contract I thought was too low. On him wanting a commission for my brother, an assistant coach, who negotiated his own deal with Dallas."

"What was the reason behind that?" Ott asked.

"Jack claimed he gave my brother Leon some advice," Boone said. "They had less than a five minute conversation."

"So, you knew the guy pretty well," Crawford said. "If you were us, who would you look at?"

Boone thought for a few moments. "You're catching me on something I never gave any thought to...but I'd at least have a conversation with Del Lewis."

"Why him?" Crawford wanted to confirm what he and Ott had talked about.

"The obvious. You got a guy who would stand to basically inherit Jack's roster of players, coaches, and owners. It would bump him up to a whole new level. A couple of levels, in fact. And, trust me, Del's ambitious. He was a good soldier, but with Jack out of the picture he gets to be a general. Know what I mean?"

"I hear you," Crawford said.

"Anybody else?" Ott asked.

"I don't know, maybe his son-in-law. Same deal."

"Scott Drexel, huh?"

"Yeah, but he's a whole different kettle of fish than Del Lewis."

"How do you mean?"

"Well, it's simple. Scott got his job because he was married to Jack's daughter. Otherwise, he'd be working at a car wash."

"Seriously?"

"No," Boone said. "That's not fair. He'd...be manager of the car wash. Maybe. He's not stupid, just not what you'd call highly motivated...unlike Del."

"Who else?" Ott asked.

"Oh, man, I don't know. It's not like a long list. And they're probably other guys I know nothing about. You know, Palm Beach guys," Boone said, looking around. They were the only three left at the cemetery. "Hey, fellas, if you don't mind, this is about as long as I want to hang out at a cemetery. Gives me the willies."

SIXTEEN

"Let's sit down and go over what we got," Crawford said as Ott pulled into the police station parking lot on County Road.

Five minutes later Ott sat opposite Crawford in his office.

"Ol' Daryl was a chatty one," Ott said.

"Yeah, I liked him. Kind of a no-bullshit guy."

"Something tells me you gotta be like that to be a coach," Ott said. "So Del Lewis, we really gotta talk to him."

"I wondered why he never got back to me."

"Until Christina explained?"

"Yeah, I must have put in five calls to the guy," Crawford said.

"Kinda strange nobody could reach him."

"I know, what if some big crisis came up with a player?"

Ott shrugged. "Exactly."

"Tell you what, I'm gonna put our resident bulldog on the job of tracking him down."

"Bettina?"

"Yup."

"She'll be able to do it if anyone can," Ott said. "You want to talk to Scott Drexel, or should I?"

"I'll do it. I already got his number from his wife."

"All right, who else?"

"Well, obviously Gretchen Bull. But Barber or Santiago woulda called us if they'd gotten a hit on the camera in Miami."

"Yeah, they said they'd monitor it every couple of hours."

"Obviously, the big question is, if it was Gretchen, who was she working for? Who was paying her to take out Rembert?"

"Tell you what," Ott said, "even though I spent practically a whole day at the docks, there're still a couple places I didn't check out. One of them was a hike from the parking lot. I figured it was less likely Rembert made it that far."

"All right," Crawford said. "Why don't you finish that up and I'll try to line up Scott Drexel. Meantime, if Bettina works her magic and finds Del Lewis, we should do him right away."

Ott nodded. "Sounds like a plan."

"Hey, also, what was your take on Darnell Dove? Seemed like he was trying to steer us to Robert Smallwood."

"Yeah, I got that loud and clear. Clearly no love lost there, what was your read?"

Crawford shrugged. "I don't know. Maybe he just wants it to be Smallwood. Maybe it's nothing more than that."

———

CRAWFORD GOT A CALL A HALF AN HOUR LATER FROM NATE BARBER, the Miami vice cop.

"Hey, Charlie, it's Nate Barber down in Miami, I got our girl Gretch on my iPhone camera. I wasn't having any luck with the security cam, so I went to Bull's house and just waited across the street. Over four hours of waiting, but I got the money shot."

"Nice goin'! I really appreciate it. Was she wearing a blonde wig, by any chance?"

"Blonde wig and showing a lot of cleavage. Like she was steppin' out on a hot date. You got anything new up there?"

"Just a couple more suspects," Crawford said. "But no question about it, Gretchen jumps to the top of our list. Big question is, who hired her?"

"I also got a shot of the Audi, too, complete with its plate."

"Well, thanks, really appreciate it."

"Do what you gotta, you know," Barber said. "What I was really hoping for was I might catch her in the act of doing something nasty. Like dragging some dude out of her house wrapped up in a rug or something."

SEVENTEEN

CRAWFORD CALLED OTT RIGHT AWAY. OTT DIDN'T PICK UP SO Crawford left him a terse message: *Call as soon as you get this.* Then he saw call-waiting. It was Ott.

"What took you so long?" Crawford said.

"You're not gonna believe this shit," Ott blurted. "I found another tape of Gretchen Bull right behind Rembert at the docks. She was only about twenty feet back and Rembert was clearly having a major problem staying on his feet. Then he went around a corner and that was all I could see."

"I'm assuming it showed Bull go around the corner too."

"Sure did."

"So sounds like a little shove would probably do it."

"Yeah, I mean the guy looked like he had no motor skills at all."

"Nice going."

Then he filled Ott in on the call he'd just had with Nathan Barber.

"We got plenty now. We gotta drop everything, get an arrest warrant, and go down there right away," Crawford said.

"I'm ready," Ott said, with no hesitation. "You at the station?"

"Yup."

"Pick you up in front in five."

Crawford and Ott had just gotten onto 1-95, when Crawford's cell phone rang.

It was Bettina, who was always bugging Crawford to give her even more challenging assignments.

"Well, that was child's play," Bettina said. "I got Del Lewis on my first try, second ring."

"Nice going. What's the deal?"

"Well, in fairness, as you know, he's been out of the country," Bettina said. "Just got back. Said he had no cell service on some little island in the Caribbean where he was. He also said he just heard about Jack Rembert when he got back. I said you'd call him right away. That you were a detective on the Rembert case."

"Good work...as usual."

"Well, this time I was just lucky," she said. "Not my usual persistence and hard work."

Crawford laughed. "Later."

"Later." They both clicked off.

Crawford called Lewis. He had the number memorized.

Lewis answered right away and was all business after Crawford identified himself.

"I know you've been trying to reach me. I got all your messages, detective. I've been out of the country, a place with no cell service."

"I heard. Can I meet with you tomorrow afternoon? We're looking into the death of Jack Rembert and have several questions. We're on our way out of town right now or I'd want to meet with you right away."

"Sure, I have a lot of catching up to do," Lewis said. "How 'bout 4:00?"

"That works."

"Come to my office at Phillips Point in West Palm. The penthouse. Sign says Rembert Sports Management."

"See you then," said Crawford.

Next, Crawford dialed the number that Muffie Drexel had given him for her husband.

The call went to voice mail. "Hey, this is Drex. Leave a message and I'll call you back after I reel in this three-hundred-pound marlin."

Odd, Crawford thought, why would Scott Drexel—Drex—want his clients to think he was out on a boat fishing instead of nose to the grindstone, negotiating a tough contract for one of them? And, just as curious, why would Jack Rembert let his son-in-law create the impression that he had gone fishing instead of tending to his clients' needs?

"Mr. Drexel, my name is Detective Crawford, Palm Beach police. Give me a call please, I'm looking into the death of your father-in-law and have a few questions for you."

He left his number.

A half hour later, when they were just south of Fort Lauderdale, Drexel called him back. "Yeah, hi, detective, my mother-in-law mentioned you were going to be at Jack's funeral. I saw you in the back. I figured it was you anyway since you and the guy you were with were the only two I didn't recognize. What can I do for you?"

"As I mentioned, I'd like to ask you some questions. Can we do it late tomorrow morning sometime?"

"Actually, I got golf then. Why don't you come by now?"

"I can't. On my way to Miami. How about early afternoon?" Crawford asked. "My partner and I are going to be meeting with Del Lewis at 4, how 'bout 1:30 or 2:00?"

"Um, yeah, I guess I could do that. I'm going to be working remotely. At home, not the office. Make it 1:30."

"That's good. I know where you live. See you then."

"Yup. See you then."

FOR THE REMAINDER OF THE RIDE SOUTH, CRAWFORD LOOKED INTO two men whom David Balfour had mentioned as—what seemed to Crawford, anyway—long-shot suspects. But he needed to check them out anyway because the truth was that anyone could have hired Gretchen Bull. All they needed was enough money for the job. The first one was Mark Shuman, the husband of the woman Rembert had brazenly escorted to the Red Cross Ball when Shuman was apparently out of town on business. Crawford was able to find his number. He called him and left a message for Shuman to call him back.

The second was the Russian oligarch, whose mistress was the six-foot-four black Russian basketball player who—in the words of David Balfour—Rembert represented and apparently had a 'dalliance' with behind the back of the oligarch. On showing Ott a photo of the Russian oligarch, Stanislav Dalyagin, back at the office, Ott had guessed the man was even shorter than himself.

"Kind of an unlikely-looking duo, don't you think?" Crawford said.

Ott nodded. "No shit. Guy woulda needed a step-ladder to have sex with her."

It took a while on Google and Wikipedia on Crawford's iPhone, but as they approached the outskirts of Miami, he had come up with some eye-opening information about Stanislav Dalyagin. The biggest discovery was that Dalyagin just happened to have a 278-foot super yacht, named the *Меркурий*, which just happened to be docked at the Palm Beach dock. Crawford got that information from an article in the *Palm Beach Post* after he Googled Dalyagin. In the article was a photo of the elegantly stream-lined super yacht. The article was about Russian yachts that had been seized by governments as part of a campaign, as U.S. Attorney General Merrick Garland explained it, to "hold accountable those who facilitate death and destruction in Ukraine." The article went on to say how authori-ties in Italy had seized a super yacht called the *Lady M* as well as a $440 million, 469-foot vessel called the *Sy A*, while Spanish law-enforcement officials seized a Russian yacht whose owner had close ties to Vladimir Putin. It went on to document other so-called super yachts seized in France, Great Britain, and as far-off as Fiji.

Crawford wondered why Dalyagin wouldn't be concerned about his own yacht being seized at the Palm Beach docks.

The oligarch had just leaped to the top of his list of people he wanted to interrogate, right below Gretchen Bull and Del Lewis. Crawford realized that getting a phone number for the man would be difficult, so he decided, as soon as he got back to Palm Beach, he'd go straight to the docks and try to get on board Dalyagin's boat and interrogate him.

———

At 6:25 p.m. and with moderate rush-hour traffic, Crawford and Ott arrived at Gretchen Bull's house at 16185 SW 136th Terrace.

They had decided they were just going to walk up to the house, ring the doorbell and confront Bull with the photos Nate Barber had emailed of him in a blonde wig, busty cleavage, and red high-heeled shoes. If he slammed the door in their face and refused to talk, their intention was to call Santiago Vasquez and Nate Barber and ask them to arrest Bull on suspicion of murder because in their haste to go to Miami they hadn't yet secured an arrest warrant from a local judge. They felt certain Vasquez and Barber would welcome the opportunity to arrest Gretchen Bull and let them join in the questioning of her.

But, when they arrived at her house, no one answered the door.

Crawford hit the doorbell again.

No answer.

"Why don't we hang around for a while and see if she shows up," Crawford said.

"Sounds good," said Ott.

They went back to their car, got in, and parked it across the street, a few doors down from Bull's house. They spent the next forty-five minutes watching cars come and go on the street, but none was a black Audi SUV.

"I'm hungry," Ott said, after a long stretch of uncharacteristic silence.

"I was just thinking the same thing," Crawford said. "I know a good place Dominica told me about. Plus, I'm thinking we spend the night down here unless we come back later and she's here. Might as well make a reservation."

"I agree," Ott said with a nod. "Get a bite, come back here afterward. If she's still not here, come back first thing tomorrow morning."

Crawford nodded, went to Google on his iPad and found the name of a place that had been recommended by Dominica.

It was called Astra and was a rooftop restaurant which, Dominica said, had 'great views of the city and amazing drinks.' Crawford called and made a reservation. 'Last table available' he was told.

They had an hour to kill and stuck around Bull's place, but still no Bull. Then they made the short drive to Astra. They arrived a little early for their 7:45 reservation, parked and took an elevator up to the top floor. It was indeed a breathtaking view in all directions and the place was packed.

They went to the bar to kill the ten minutes before their reservation.

"Case you hadn't noticed, Chuck," Ott said, flashing a big smile, "there're hotties galore in this place."

"Thanks, Mort. That was not lost on me."

"I figured."

"What you gents gonna have?" asked the tattooed bartender.

"Something tells me you got some pretty exotic drinks here," Ott said. "Got a drink menu?"

"Sure do," the bartender said, reaching under the bar and producing two small menus. "We got everything under the sun."

They took a look.

Crawford nodded and glanced at Ott. "Everything under the sun...with prices to match."

"So how would you feel about a Mojito pitcher for fifty bucks?" Ott asked.

"Hey, this isn't Friday night on the town," Crawford said. "It's Tuesday night on the job."

"That's what I figured you'd say," Ott said. "Good ol' straitlaced Charlie."

"I'm just not thrilled about arresting a guy when I'm hammered."

Ott's eyes drifted back to the menu. "Think I'm gonna have an Astra Mule."

Crawford read what the drink was. *Fig infused Belvedere vodka, freshly muddled raspberries & mint, ginger beer.*

'Muddled' was not how he wanted he and Ott to get.

"I'm okay with everything but a fig infusion." He turned to the bartender. "I'm gonna have a Mediterranean Old-Fashioned, please." It's description was *Makers Mark, demerara, orange & angostura bitters.*

Ott handed the menu to the bartender. "The Mule, please."

They paid for their drinks and ten minutes later went over to their 4-person table which had just been cleared.

"Cool place," Ott said, then pointed. "Looks like they got dancing later on."

He was pointing to an unmanned turntable and a partially enclosed booth.

Crawford laughed. "Don't get any ideas, Travolta."

"Forgot my dancing shoes," Ott said before leaning closer to Crawford. "Look hard right."

Crawford nodded. "I noticed."

There were two women at the next table over. Scantily-clad would be an overstatement, enticingly-clad would not be.

"I'll take the brunette," Ott said.

Crawford shook his head and mouthed, *We're on the job.*

They looked over the menus and Crawford said, "Jesus."

"What?" Ott asked.

"The prices."

Ott laughed. "Yeah, no kidding. Think Rutledge would have a problem okaying the Tomahawk."

Crawford looked down the menu. *36 oz. Tomahawk steak, grilled seasonal vegetables. $195.*

Ott held up his hands. "Don't worry, I'm going with the tuna," he said.

A few minutes later, they ordered and admired the views: Crawford of the city vistas, Ott of the women at the table next to them.

Their dinners were delivered and they ate. "Where do you s'pose she went?" Ott asked.

"Could be anywhere," Crawford said in between bites. "I just hope she's coming back. It would be tough tracking down someone who's a man one day and a woman the next."

Ott nodded, leaned forward, and lowered his voice. "The blonde with the boom-booms has been checkin' you out."

"Cut the shit," Crawford muttered.

"I'm not kidding," Ott said. "A couple of times."

"Eat your tuna."

They finished up and were having glasses of wine when one of the women next to them, a blonde, got up from their table.

Ott glanced over at the brunette who had caught his eye.

"You ladies care to join us for a nightcap?" Ott asked as Crawford gave him a kick under the table.

The brunette glanced at the blonde, and the blonde nodded.

Crawford and Ott stood up and introduced themselves as the women joined them.

The brunette was Jennifer and the blonde was Wren.

"You ladies from here?" Ott asked.

"Coral Gables," Jennifer said. "How 'bout you?"

"Up north," Ott said. "The Palm Beach area."

"What are you doing down here?" Wren asked Crawford.

"Business," Crawford said. "We're cops."

"*Uh-oh,*" Wren said, holding up her hands. "We'll behave."

Crawford laughed.

"You don't have to," Ott joked. "We're off duty."

"Well, until a little later," Crawford said.

Ott shot him a scowl.

They broke off into two separate conversations: Crawford with Wren and Ott with Jennifer.

Crawford saw Wren take a quick glance down at his ring finger after a few minutes. "How come you're not married, Charlie? A guy like you, I mean..."

Crawford saw Ott look over. He was tuned into their conversation as well as his own.

Crawford shrugged. "I was. It didn't work out."

"Sorry to hear that."

He nodded.

"Got a girlfriend?" she asked.

"Um, yeah, kinda." He saw Ott wince. "No, I do."

Wren leaned back in her chair. It was only a matter of time now, Ott realized, until the women were out of there.

Wren looked at Jennifer when there was a pause in her conversation. "Come on, Jen," she said, "time to go."

Jennifer frowned, but it melted into a smile. "Well, it was nice to meet you," she said to Ott. "Maybe we can have dinner some time."

"I'd like that," Ott said.

They said their good-byes and the women left as Crawford flagged down their waiter.

"What is wrong with you?" Ott hissed as soon as the women were out of ear shot. "Why'd you have to say—"

"You expect me to lie?"

"Absolutely...or maybe just have amnesia."

"Sorry. I don't do that," Crawford said. "And, by the way, did something happen between you and Dee Dee? I thought you two were hot and heavy?"

He was referring to Ott's girlfriend, Dee Dee Dunwoody.

"I never told you?"

"Told me what?"

"She got transferred to Hong Kong," Ott said. "Makes for a difficult relationship, know what I mean?"

"Yeah, I hear you," said Crawford. "Can't exactly hook up on weekends."

"No shit. It's nine thousand miles away."

"Sorry to hear that. I liked her."

Ott just shrugged. "So did I."

Crawford paid with a credit card, and they took the elevator down and got in their car. It was now 9:15. They had made a reservation at a hotel earlier not far from Gretchen Bull's house.

"I still can't believe you blew a lay-up like that," Ott said as they drove off.

"Mort, gotta get your head back in the game."

"Yeah, yeah. That Wren was totally into you, you know. Until you went and—"

"Told the truth?"

"Yeah, Charlie. In situations like that the best thing is to just be a little... forgetful."

Crawford laughed. "Sorry, ain't gonna happen."

Ott shook his head. "Putz."

EIGHTEEN

They drove to Bull's house, but there were no lights on inside the house or any other signs of life.

"I could still call Jennifer," Ott said. "She gave me her number."

Crawford shot Ott a look. "Give it up, for Chrissake."

Ott put up a hand. "Okay, okay."

They went to the hotel and with a minimum of conversation, checked in, then a short time later went to bed.

———

Crawford had asked for a wake-up call at 6:30 a.m. They got up, had a quick breakfast, and were on their way to Bull's house by 7:15.

Two blocks from the house, they heard the screaming of sirens which seemed to be coming from all directions. As they pulled up to SW 136th Terrace, they saw three police cars and an ambulance, all flashing their cherry lights, parked askew at different angles in front of Bull's house.

"Holy shit!" Ott said, as he skidded up in front of the house next door.

They bolted from the car and ran up to the front porch.

"Who are you?" a uniform at the front door asked.

Just then Santiago Vasquez walked out. "Hey, what are you guys doing here?"

"We came down here last night to question Bull," Crawford said.

"Too late," Santiago said, pointing at the twisted body of a tall woman with blonde hair and wearing a red blouse, short black skirt, and fishnet stockings.

"What do you know about it?" Crawford asked.

"Neighbor called a half hour ago, said she heard gun shots," Santiago said. "I came straight from home. She'd been hit at least five times. Bled out."

"What do you guess happened?" Ott asked.

"Well, it was still dark when it went down. Just starting to get light. My guess is whoever did it came to the door, rang the bell, Bull opened it, saw whoever it was, turned and ran."

"So all the shots were in her back?" Crawford asked.

"One in the neck, two in the legs, two in the back," Santiago said. "Maybe more."

"Hitter wasn't much of a shot?" Ott said.

"So it would seem, I mean he couldn't have been more than ten to fifteen feet away," Santiago said.

Crawford remembered the camera. "The good news is—"

"—I know what you're going to say. The camera," Santiago said, "I already checked it. As I said, it was still dark when this went down. All I could make out was a silhouette of a guy and a dark car. No help at all."

"That's too bad," said Crawford. "You got any problem if we go through the house? See what we come up with?"

"No. In fact, I was just about to myself."

"We'll do it together," Crawford said, taking out his vinyl gloves from his jacket pocket and putting them on.

"Did you search her clothes?" Ott asked. "I'm thinking a cell phone."

"Yeah, we did," Santiago said. "Nothing. My guess is the hitter found it and took it with him."

"We coulda used that," Ott said.

Santiago nodded. "Who knows, maybe we'll find it inside somewhere."

Santiago started out searching the living room while Crawford and Ott went through the master bedroom where Bull had a cluttered desk and chair in a far corner.

Crawford pointed at the desk. "I'm gonna check it out for a computer."

The three spent the next hour and a half searching the house. There was no computer and no cell phone to be found anywhere. There was a daybook, however, but it provided more questions than answers. One entry in the daybook got the same reaction from Crawford and Ott. It said, *Call SD*.

"Stanislav Dalyagin maybe?" Ott said.

Crawford nodded. "Maybe," he said. "I wish there was a number."

"Problem is they're a million people with those initials," said Ott.

"All right, well, there's nothing more we can do around here," Crawford said. "Let's go tell Santiago we're headed home."

They went and briefly compared notes with Santiago Vasquez, though there weren't many notes to compare. After that, they left the scene and headed north to Palm Beach. Santiago said he'd keep them in the loop on the murder and let them know if any new details came up.

"Shit," Crawford said as they got onto I-95, "a half hour too late."

"Yeah, maybe we'll have better luck with Del Lewis and Scott Drexel."

Crawford nodded. "We're due for a break."

NINETEEN

They got back to Palm Beach around noon. Ott went to get something for lunch and Crawford decided to go back down to the docks and look for Stanislav Dalygin's super yacht.

He parked at the lot for the marina and walked down one of the wooden docks. He had taken a screen shot of Stanislas Dalyagin's yacht, which he intended to show to the first person he came across. The first person, though, a man in a uniform, who Crawford guessed was either Greek or Turkish, seemed to know nothing about the boat. He smiled, shook his head, and said, 'no English' a few times. Crawford had more luck with the second person he encountered. He introduced himself and showed the man the photo. The tall, trim man, Crawford guessed, was an actual yacht owner, dressed expensively and with an aura that exuded worldliness mixed with a certain...superiority.

"Oh yeah, the Russian fertilizer king," the man said. "He left here yesterday. Much too nice a ship for that low-life thug."

"Do you know where he was sailing to?" Crawford asked.

"Sorry, no idea, maybe staying ahead of the U.S. government?"

"You mean because of the seizing of Russian ships?"

"Exactly," the man said. "In some cases, I read, they're selling them and buying tanks and munitions for those poor Ukrainians."

"Seems like a good cause."

The tall man nodded. "I agree. Speaking of low-life thugs..."

Crawford didn't understand at first. Then he got it. "Oh, you mean, Putin?"

The man nodded. "A notch above Hitler."

"Do you know anyone who might know where Dalygin's yacht is headed?" Crawford asked.

"Not offhand, but there's an easy way to find out."

"What's that?"

"There are these what-they-call *vessel tracking systems*," the man said, "I don't have one but you can go on-line and get one. The site is something like vessel.com, I believe."

Crawford first thought was...another job for Bettina.

"Well, thanks a lot, I really appreciate it."

"No problem," the man said. "The *Mercury*'s out there somewhere. You'll find it."

Crawford did a double-take. "The what?"

"The *Mercury*. That's the English translation of the yacht's name."

"Well, thank you again," he repeated, amped up with the revelation of the yacht's name. "I really appreciate your help."

He hung up and dialed Bettina right away. "Hi, Charlie."

"Hey, since I gave you such a lay-up last time, are you ready for a tougher one?"

"Charlie, you know me pretty well by now...am I not a girl in search of a challenge?"

"You are, and here it is," he said. "I need you to locate a boat. It left the Palm Beach dock yesterday and I have no idea where it's headed. North, south, or east, I don't know. There's this thing called a vessel tracking system, that supposedly can locate anything on the water—"

"Vessel tracking system?" she repeated.

"Exactly, so I need to know where it is now and where it's headed. For all I know it might have taken a short cruise—the Bahamas, the Caribbean, who knows, or maybe down to Miami. The guy who owns it is Russian, and as far as I know he might even be headed back to Russia. The boat is definitely big enough to cross the Atlantic comfortably." He gave her the ship's name, the translation, the info about vessel.com, and spelled out the oligarch's name for her.

"I'm on it, Charlie," Bettina said, almost as amped-up sounding as he felt. "Get back to you as soon as I have something."

"You're a doll," Crawford said and hung up.

TWENTY

CRAWFORD PICKED UP SOMETHING FOR LUNCH AT A SANDWICH SHOP, then drove back to the station. He walked in and saw Bettina at the front desk.

"Anything?" he asked.

"I didn't want to call you until I had as much info as I could get, so I'll tell you what I have so far. As of this moment the *Mercury* is off of St. Augustine headed north."

"Do you have any idea what it's final destination is?"

"That's exactly what I've been trying to find out, but I don't know yet."

"Okay, well let me know as soon as you do."

"Roger that. I've got a few more calls to make."

He gave her a big smile "I knew I picked the right one for the job."

"Or any job, Charlie."

———

HE WAITED AROUND FOR OTT TO TELL HIM ABOUT THE RUSSIAN'S boat, but when Ott had not returned by 1:20, he drove to Scott Drexel's house.

Muffie Drexel answered the door. "Oh, hello detective, you're every-where. My Mom's, the funeral, now here. Scott's in the den, I'll take you there."

"Thank you, Ms. Drexel."

"You can call me Muffie," she said, walking though the living room.

She led him into a darkened room where a TV was on.

"Scott," Muffie said to her husband, "you haven't met him yet, but this is detective Crawford."

Drexel stood up.

"Hi, I'm Charlie Crawford," Crawford said, extending his hand.

As Crawford guessed, Drexel had a handshake that was at the opposite end of the spectrum as the brawny jocks he represented. In fact, it reminded Crawford of when he took a six-pound grouper off the line while fishing on a dock with Dominica.

"Call me Drex. Everyone does," he said, pointing at an easy chair. "Have a seat."

"Thanks for seeing me," Crawford said, sitting down. Off to the side a golf tournament was playing on a massive high-def TV.

Drexel hit the mute button. "So, what did you want to ask me about Jack? Christina told Muffie you think it might not have been an accident."

"Yeah, the more we look at it, the more we know it wasn't," Crawford said. "So my first question to you is did your father-in-law ever mention anyone who he either feared or had reason to believe might—"

"—kill him?"

"Well, yeah."

"Have you talked to other people about this?" Drexel asked.

"I'm meeting with Del Lewis later on, as I mentioned on the phone. Also, I spoke to two men at the funeral, Daryl Boone and Darnell Dove."

"So Del is back from his little junket to no-tell island?" Drexel twisted his mouth in such a way that it looked like he'd just downed a bad oyster.

"He just came back from some island that apparently had no cell service."

Drexel put his foot up on the sofa next to him. "Oh, so that's his story," he said. "No cell service, you mean, so Marnie—that would be his wife—couldn't interrupt his days and nights with the Ford model."

"I don't know anything about that," Crawford said, wanting to return to his Q & A. It was beginning to seem like all sports agents did nothing but chase women and steal each other's clients. Crawford noticed Drexel's shoes and remembered seeing David Balfour wearing a similar pair. They were brown suede and had petite leather bows and were no doubt expensive as hell. He had been curious and asked Balfour who made them, and Balfour said they were called Belgian loafers. He wasn't curious enough to ask where he could pick up a pair. Drexel was also wearing a brilliant pink long-sleeved shirt, and Crawford bet, if he examined the label, chances were good it came from a Worth Avenue store called Maus & Hoffman. A simple polo shirt there, he knew, started around $250.

"So, ask away," Drexel said.

"I did," Crawford reminded him.

"Oh yeah, you mean, whether I could come up with anyone who might want to have killed Jack?"

Crawford nodded.

"I think, if it were me, I'd take a pretty close look at Lewis. But you sure as hell didn't hear that from me."

"Why do you say him?"

"Well, the obvious. He's got the most to gain."

"You mean, getting your father-in-law's clients. Taking over Rembert Sports Management."

"Wait, wait, wait, hold on a minute," Drexel said putting up his hands in protest. "Christina might have a little something to say about that."

"Could you explain what you mean?"

"Sure. Christina's the largest shareholder in R.S.M. now that Jack's dead. Lewis has twenty-five per cent and Christina has seventy-three per cent."

"And the other...two per cent?"

"That would be me."

Talk about a why-bother, Crawford thought. "But if I understand how it works, wouldn't Del Lewis be in a position to get—whatever it is—ten to fifteen per cent of what his clients make in new contracts?"

"Yeah, basically, unless Jack's guys opted to go with me instead," Drexel said.

From what Crawford had gleaned so far that was a less than likely scenario.

"Also, the fact that Del was conveniently out of the country when it happened," Drexel said. "Gee, what a great alibi, don't you think? Who could ever suspect him of having anything to do with it when he's a thousand miles away on some nude beach somewhere?"

Crawford had thought about that and was itching for his interview with Lewis. "Okay," he said, "I understand what you're saying. So is there anyone else who you think might have a motive?"

"Um, does the name Octavius Johnson ring a bell?" Drexel asked.

It did...vaguely. Crawford couldn't quite place it. "Remind me."

"Running back for the Cardinals. Had a little 'oops' with the law."

Crawford snapped his fingers. "Oh yeah, accused of assaulting his wife last year."

"Year before actually, and it was his girlfriend in a hotel in Atlanta," Drexel said. "Anyway, Jack dumped him like a hot potato when that happened. Said publicly, and kind of piously, something like, 'the league has no place for violent men like him.'" Drexel chuckled "Who's he kidding? As if football isn't a violent sport. This was a couple months after he signed Octavius to a five-year $125 million dollar contract and pocketed a twelve-million-five commission."

"Wow, and got to keep it?"

"Every cent of it," Drexel said. "But the point is, Octavius was loaded for bear. Showed up at our offices, screaming at the top of his lungs at Jack, saying stuff like, *how could you f-ing sell me down the river like that? You're supposed to f-ing fight for me. How the hell could you f-ing roll over like that?* Then he said he wanted a piece of Jack's commission 'cause the Cardinals weren't gonna pay him 'cause of a morals clause in his contract. Came around Jack's desk like he was going to pick him up and throw him out the window."

"What did Rembert do?"

"Hollered at Julie to call the cops."

"Julie is his assistant, I take it."

Drexel nodded. "Assistant...secretary, same thing," he said. "Then Octavius threatened to kick his f-ing ass and toss him into some f-ing swamp."

"That's a novel idea," Crawford said, stone-faced.

Drexel laughed. "I thought so too."

"How long ago did this happen?"

"Couple of months maybe."

"Oh, that's all?"

Drexel nodded.

"Any other...possible suspects?"

Drexel shook his head. "Not that I can think of off-hand."

"How was your relationship with your father-in-law?" Crawford asked.

"It was good. He gave me a couple of pep talks about not being hungry enough, but hey, that's just not me. I get the job done, though."

"How did you feel about the two per cent equity interest he gave you?"

"What exactly are you asking? Did I think it was an insult or something 'cause it was so little. Is that what you're asking?"

"It's not really much of an inducement to get you 'hungry,' as you would say."

"Our deal was I was going to get another two per cent in three years."

Wow, big whoop, thought Crawford.

"Do you know the name Gretchen Bull?" Crawford asked, carefully watching Drexel's reaction.

He showed none. "No."

"You're sure?"

"I said no, didn't I?"

Crawford got to his feet. "Well, I appreciate your time, Mr. Drexel."

"Drex."

TWENTY-ONE

BACK IN HIS CROWN VIC, CRAWFORD SAW A VOICEMAIL ON HIS CELL phone, which he had muted for his interview with Scott Drexel. It was from Bettina. He played it.

"So I think I know where Dalyagin is headed. Charleston, South Carolina. Give me a call and I'll explain."

He called Ott first.

"So how'd it go with the son-in-law?" Ott asked.

"To hear him tell it, it's either Del Lewis or a baller named Octavius Johnson. Lewis...'cause he wanted Jack's job maybe."

"And Octavius Johnson's the girlfriend-abuser, right?"

"Yup. Rembert repped him and cut him loose the moment the girl-friend thing came out."

"Aren't agents supposed to jump to their client's defense?"

"That's what I would have thought, but apparently not this time," Crawford said. "All right, I gotta give Bettina a call. She's got some info on that Russian oligarch. I'll fill you in about that on the way over to Del Lewis."

"Okay."

He dialed Bettina. "Hey, Charlie," she said. "You'll be proud of me. I sacrificed my lunch break to try to find out where the Russian's headed. I went down to the docks and asked around a little and ran across this British guy who's got a friend on Dalyagin's crew. He said, 'Yeah, yeah, my mate Yuri'—that's what the Brits call each other, mate—'he's headed up to Charleston, South Carolina. He's all excited about going there 'cause he's heard so much about the town.'"

"Nice goin'. Very resourceful of you. I tell you what, take another break, you earned it."

"Thank you, Charlie, that's very nice of you."

"I'm gonna tell Ott to look out because you're after his job."

"Oh, no, where would the PBPD ever be without Mort?"

Crawford chuckled. "Oh, so I guess that means you're after *my* job."

TWENTY-TWO

THE PENTHOUSE AT THE PHILLIPS POINT OFFICE BUILDING AT 777 South Flagler Drive in West Palm Beach had one of the best views Crawford had ever seen. Anywhere. The only problem was that you had to look almost straight down to see the Intracoastal from the 18th floor, and you didn't get the same overwhelming perspective of the occasional super yacht floating by as you'd get from eye level. Still, the views of Palm Beach and the endless ocean were breathtaking.

Del Lewis, seated in a cream-colored leather chair, was a tall man who looked to be in good physical shape and had a helmet of white Mike Pence hair and, curiously, a diamond earring. Crawford guessed he was around forty and probably wore the earring so his players would think he was one of them. The diamond earring was not that big. So, Crawford speculated again, his players wouldn't think he was making too much money off of their broad shoulders, massive thighs, and flypaper hands.

"Thanks for seeing us," Crawford said to Lewis, "I'm sure you're very busy with all that's happened so we'll try to make this relatively brief."

Lewis nodded.

Crawford glanced over at Ott. "Why don't you go first?"

"Okay. Mr. Lewis, what was your first reaction when you heard the news about Jack Rembert?"

Ott always had good openers, which was the reason Crawford often let him lead off.

"My first reaction...hmm, well, that I was going to miss him. I mean Jack started this business from nothing. He was one of the masters of it, one of its pioneers, and made a lot of men very, very rich. Jack was also a very decent human being, a man of character." It was like he had cribbed the notes off the priest at Rembert's funeral. "He'd give his right arm for you." Unless maybe you were Octavius Johnson, Crawford thought. "He taught me everything I know, and like I said, I'm gonna miss the son-of-a-bitch."

"And what about when you heard he might have been murdered?" Ott asked.

"I couldn't believe it," Lewis said. "I mean Jack had enemies. You can't avoid having a few if you've been in this game thirty-five years, but the way it happened..."

"It seems like he had more than a few enemies," Ott said.

Lewis thought for a moment. "Hey look, there's a big difference between enemies and guys who want to kill you. I'd say the latter's a very, very short list."

"Okay," Ott said, "so who's on it?"

"Oh God, I don't know. I haven't really had time to think about it much."

"When did you first get the news?" Crawford asked.

"When I landed at PBI, and got a million messages on my cell phone," Lewis said.

"But not before that?" Crawford asked.

"I told you, I had no cell service where I was."

"So nobody on that island is able to communicate with the outside world?" Crawford asked.

"I wasn't."

"Do you know the name Gretchen Bull?" Crawford asked without warning.

"Never heard that name," Lewis said.

There was a pause.

"So, as you said, you haven't had much time to think about it, but now, who do you think might have been capable of killing Mr. Rembert?" Ott asked.

Lewis didn't hesitate. "Nobody I can think of. I know you've been talking to the family and other people and I'm sure you've heard the names Robert Smallwood and Stanislas Dalyagin bandied about..."

"But, are you saying, you don't think either one could have done it?" Crawford asked.

"Not Robert, I don't think anyway. The Russian guy...I don't know... maybe. I know he threatened Jack."

"How do you know that?" Ott asked.

"And what did he say?" Crawford added.

"I know because Jack told me," Lewis said. "You know about Anoushka, right?"

Crawford and Ott nodded.

"Well, Dalyagin actually showed up here—I wasn't here at the time— and told Jack to stay away from Anoushka."

"How could he?" Ott asked. "He was her agent."

"He meant in a...sexual way."

"Or what?"

"Jack told me Dalyagin got very colorful about what he'd do to him."

"Which was?"

"You really want to know?"

"Yes."

"Something about cutting off his cock and feeding it to the sharks."

"Ouch!" said Ott. "So did Rembert stay away from her then?"

"That I don't know. Jack typically wasn't one to take orders or be intimidated by anyone. Especially from a Russian in the fertilizer business."

"So you just made a pretty good case for Dalyagin being the killer."

Lewis shrugged. "I don't know. Obviously, it's up to you to get to the bottom of it."

"Mr. Lewis, I'm just gonna come right out and say it," Crawford said, "It's been speculated that you have the most to gain by Rembert's death."

"Is there a question there?"

"Yeah. Did you have him killed?" Crawford asked.

Lewis shook his head as if the question was an insult. "No, I didn't. I make a ton of money here at R.S.M. I'm not one of those *more, more, more* people. In fact, I'm the last person who wanted him dead. 'Cause it would mean I'd have to work a hell of a lot harder. I work hard enough, plus I have two boys at Rosarian and a girl at the Greene School. I like going to their games, and my daughter wants to be an actress, so I go to her plays. If I were to have to take on all of Jack's guys, in addition to mine, I'd never have time for any of that stuff. I'd never see my family. I've already spoken to a headhunter about hiring a big gun to come to R.S.M. and take over Jack's guys. I don't want them. Well, maybe one or two."

Crawford glanced at Ott, then nodded. "Sounds like you got your priorities straight. Not often you hear a man say, *I don't want any more money.*"

Lewis laughed. "Well, I didn't exactly say that. I just don't want to work anymore for it."

"What about Scott Drexel?" Crawford said. "Instead of bringing in a new guy, why not give some of Rembert's guys to him?"

Lewis nodded. "Matter-of-fact, that's a battle about to be fought. Scott's already pitched that. Plus, Chris, his mother-in-law, chimed in on that subject, too."

"But?"

"How do I put it? Let's just say, Scott's definitely *not* a chip-off-the-block of his father-in-law."

"What exactly do you mean?" Crawford asked.

"I think you get the idea."

Ott was tapping the side of his chair. "We have one last guy," he said. "Octavius Johnson."

"Hmm, now there's someone I never thought of. But now that you mention it...you obviously know it didn't end well between Jack and him."

"So we heard," Ott said. "He's not playing anymore, right?"

"Yeah, no, last I heard is he's up near Savannah somewhere, working on his father's farm. Trying to get back into the league."

"Working on a farm? That's a long fall from a couple million a year."

Lewis nodded. "His first year signing bonus was five million."

"Wow," Ott said, shaking his head, "Just curious, what's the average number of years players are in the league?"

"You won't believe it."

"How many?"

"Three point three years, to be exact."

"You're kidding."

Lewis shook his head.

"Nope. All you hear about are the guys like Brady and Brett Favre. But a lot of guys don't make it two years."

Ott turned to Crawford. "Charlie here was an MVP running back in college."

Crawford face reddened. "Stop, please. Our front line averaged under two hundred pounds."

"Where was this?" Lewis asked with a straight face. "Palm Beach Atlantic or something?"

It was a diss.

"Worse. Dartmouth College."

TWENTY-THREE

"GUY HAD ALL THE ANSWERS," CRAWFORD SAID ON THE ELEVATOR ride down.

"You ain't buyin' it," said Ott.

"I don't know. Slick, very slick."

Ott nodded.

The elevator stopped at the ground floor. "So I'd say it's time we pack up and go talk to Stanislav Dalygin."

"Gotta be a little careful with this guy, you know," Ott said with a smile.

"What do you mean?"

"Just thinkin' about what he warned Rembert he'd do to him."

———

CRAWFORD AND OTT WENT AND PACKED A FEW THINGS FOR WHAT they expected to be a one-or two-day stay and got on I-95 for the drive up to Charleston, South Carolina. Just past Daytona, Crawford pulled out his phone and scrolled for a number.

"Who ya calling?" Ott asked from behind the wheel, doing the driving as usual.

"You remember that detective up in Charleston I told you about?"

Ott shook his head. "Refresh my memory."

"I was trying to track down an art dealer in Charleston who screwed David Balfour."

"Oh yeah, now I remember. Never found him though, right?"

"Yeah, never did. Anyway, the detective's name is Nick Janzek. Good guy, I had breakfast with him once," Crawford said, as he dialed a number.

"Hello?" A voice answered.

"Is this Nick?"

"Yeah, who's this?"

"Charlie Crawford, Palm Beach, Florida."

"Yeah, sure, I remember you. How's it going, Charlie?"

"Good, man. So me and my partner are heading in your direction. We want to talk to a Russian billionaire who's headed there on his boat. And I mean a big, big, big boat."

"Oh, yeah, I heard a 400-footer just pulled into one of the marinas here," Janzek said. "I just assumed it was that guy, David Geffen. He had one here that was supposedly longer than three football fields."

"I'm guessing the owner's our guy. Ever heard the name Stanislav Dalyagin?"

"Can't say as I have," Janzek said. "What did he do?"

"Well, we don't know for certain he did anything," Crawford said. "But we're looking into him for a murder in Palm Beach."

"You need me to do anything?"

"I don't have anything specific yet," Crawford said. "Maybe we could just meet up. Me and my partner expect to get in around 6:30 or so—" Ott held up six fingers. "Ah, my partner's saying six."

"That's cocktail hour in Charleston," Janzek said. "I'll buy you guys a drink."

"Thanks. Got a place in mind?"

"Yeah, I do, it's called the Last Saint, 472 Meeting Street. Put it in your GPS," Janzek said. "We'll be hitting it at Happy Hour, so I can afford it."

"Sounds good," Crawford said. "See you then."

"See ya," Janzek said. "In the meantime, I'll take a run down to the marina and see if the boat is owned by your guy Dal...what is it again?

"Dalyagin."

"Okay, catch you later."

LAST SAINT WAS IN A MODEST-LOOKING TWO STORY WHITE HOUSE sandwiched between a UPS Store and a T-Mobile shop. Ott parked across the street, and they walked in at 6:10. Across the room, Crawford saw Janzek in a booth with one woman beside him and another across from him.

Janzek saw him and waved.

Janzek was an inch or two shorter than Crawford and a solid 175 pounds. He had

emerald green eyes and dark hair, he wore a little on the shaggy side. A three-inch scar from below his left eye ran down the side of his face and stopped just above his sturdy chin that had taken a few shots over his forty years of hard living.

Ott's eyes lit up when he saw the women Janzek was with because both were even better-looking than the ones at Astra. "Hot dog," Ott said enthusiastically as they walked across the bar.

"Calm down, big fella," Crawford muttered under his breath.

"Hello, Nick," Crawford said as they approached the three.

"Hey, Charlie," Janzek said. "So I invited some friends." He gestured to a dark-haired woman across from him. "This is Ryder." He indicated the woman on his right. "And this is Jackie."

"Hi, I'm Charlie Crawford, and this is my partner, Mort Ott," Crawford said.

"Have a seat," Jackie said, and Ott slid in next to her while Crawford sat next to Ryder.

"I asked the ladies to join us because they're two of the most brilliant gumshoes in Charleston and Savannah," Janzek said.

Ryder laughed. "I liked it better when you called us the Sleuth Sisters."

"Oh, so you're sisters?" Crawford said.

"Sisters in crime...solving," Ryder said.

"Same mother, same father," Jackie clarified.

"So I checked out that boat and it's definitely the Russian's," Janzek said. "Name's something unpronounceable that starts with the letters, *Mepk,* then some letters that don't exist in the English language."

Crawford nodded. "It translates to *Mercury.* Owner's name is Stanislas Dalygin."

"The fertilizer king of Russia," Ott added.

"Got it," Janzek said. "So who'd this guy kill?"

"Him personally, no one," Ott said. "But we're looking into him hiring a guy...who, by the way, was found shot dead in Miami yesterday morning."

"Oh wow," Ryder said, rubbing her hands together. "This is a juicy one."

Jackie shook her head and rolled her eyes. "Don't mind her."

"So what are you planning on doing?" Janzek asked.

"Well, since this is not our jurisdiction," Crawford said, "how would you feel about going to his boat with us and seeing if he'll let us question him?"

"Sure, I got no problem with that," Janzek said.

Ryder's' eyes got big. "Can we go?"

"No, that's probably not a good idea," Janzek said. "You can't be in on every case."

Ryder glanced at Crawford next to her. "Please?"

"Don't be a beggar," Jackie said. "We've got our hands full anyway."

"Yeah, but this sounds *so* good."

"How 'bout this," Janzek said, "you can be a consultant. We pick your brain if we've got questions on how to play it."

"You're no fun," Ryder said, in full pout mode.

Janzek eyed Crawford. "You didn't say who the guy killed?"

"Oh, yeah. This big-time sports agent."

"He reps Darnell Dove, Amari White, and Glendennon Jones, among others," Ott added.

"Who's that? Glendennon Jones?" Janzek asked.

"Better known as Big Dog Jones, center for the Celtics," Ott said.

"Oh, I know who you mean, the agent," Janzek said, "saw him interviewed on ESPN once."

"Name's Jack Rembert."

"Right," Jackie said. "I remember reading about it. He drowned, right?"

Crawford nodded. "Under very suspicious circumstances."

"Tell you what I'll do," Janzek said. "In case we have trouble getting on board, first thing tomorrow morning I'll try to get us a search warrant. I have a good relationship with a judge, should be no problem."

"Hey thanks, we'd appreciate that," Crawford said. "I'd like to go check out this boat after we leave here."

Janzek nodded. "Good luck with that. You'll need to take a rest going from one end to the other."

"What is this boat, the QE2 or something?" Jackie asked.

"Funny you should ask," Ryder said, who had Googled Dalygin's ship. "It goes just as fast as the QE2. Top speed is 31 knots or around 35 miles an hour. And get a load of these features: it has the standard billionaire's helipad, not to mention a putting green that's an inch-for-inch replica of the 10th green at the Masters, a casino that's a scaled-down version of the old casino in Monte Carlo, a glass bottom pool that looks down at the casino, an indoor tennis court...oh and listen to this...oh wow, this is my favorite, and I quote, 'known alternatively as underwater observatories, Nemo lounges or Neptune lounges, these rare interiors give guests a view of life below the water as they cruise past fish-filled coral reefs and, in deep water, dolphins, sharks and killer whales.'"

"You're kidding," Jackie said.

"No, wait there's more...just to make sure blood-thirsty terrorists don't come after you, it comes fully equipped with bomb-proof glass and anti-missile systems," she paused for effect, "and last but not least, a driving range where you knock eco-friendly golf balls out into the water which are made from fish food and dissolve completely in just a few days."

Jackie and Ryder laughed as the others shook their heads in complete disbelief.

"Gotta be kidding me," Janzek echoed Jackie,

"I'm guessing our guy, the fertilizer king, must be a pretty avid golfer," Ott said with a straight face. "I've heard they've got some really nice courses out there in the Gulag."

TWENTY-FOUR

Despite Nick Janzek's offer to put them up at his house and cook them breakfast the next morning, they kept their reservation at the Mills House, a hotel in downtown Charleston. After drinks, Crawford and Ott went down to the dock where Dalyagin's boat was moored. Janzek had exaggerated its size, but not by much.

"Sucker's the longest thing I've ever laid eyes on," Ott said.

"I don't get guys and their boats," Crawford said matter-of-factly.

"It's simple. It's to compensate for their short—"

Crawford nodded. "Okay, I should have expected that."

"What else would it be? I read somewhere that it costs somewhere around ten grand a day just to maintain one of these, which doesn't even include gas."

"What do you mean? What's to maintain?"

"*What's to maintain?* How 'bout everything...from scrubbing the damn barnacles off the bottom, swabbing the decks, repainting the thing constantly, paying a crew of twenty, insurance...guarantee you that ain't cheap—"

"Okay, I got the idea," Crawford said. "Just for the record, I wasn't planning on getting one anytime soon. How do you know all this stuff anyway?"

"Back when I was up in Cleveland, I looked into getting this 22-foot piece of shit boat called a Pacemaker."

Crawford smiled. "What? Were you going to take it out on that burning river up there?"

"Why do you always give me shit about the beautiful Cuyahoga River... and for that matter, Cleveland in general."

"'Cause it's easy."

"And New York isn't?"

Crawford cupped his chin. "Hey, just going through a little rough patch at the moment, but it's still the greatest city ever."

Ott sighed as he looked up at the monster boat. "Can we talk about something else? Like those hot Farrell sisters...? By the way, that Jackie had her eye on you."

Crawford shook his head. "Why do you always come up with bullshit like that?"

"Because it's true. It was obvious."

"Okay, enough. Next subject?" Crawford said.

"That other one, Ryder—"

"Who was clearly Janzek's squeeze."

"Yeah, I know," Ott said, with a smile, "but I might just have to snake her away from him."

TWENTY-FIVE

CRAWFORD'S FIRST CALL THE NEXT MORNING WAS TO SANTIAGO Vasquez in Miami.

"Hey, Santiago, it's Charlie Crawford. Just wondered if you got any new details on the hit on Gretchen Bull?"

"Nah, nothing yet. I'm waiting to hear back from the medical investigator. I'm also looking at security cameras in the area but haven't found anything new. As I told you, the one I set up across from his house was no help, but maybe another one might catch a look at the hitter's face or his license plate. Something."

"Understood. Well, let me know. In the meantime, would you have a problem if I sent down a crime-scene tech from Palm Beach? I don't want to step on your toes."

"No problem. Send him on down."

"It's a her. Dominica McCarthy's the name. I'll have her give you a call if that's all right."

"Of course."

"Thanks. We'll be in touch."

His next call was to Nick Janzek. They agreed to meet at Dalyagin's boat at 9:00.

Crawford and Ott had breakfast together at the hotel at 7:45.

At just before 9:00, they parked at the dock and walked to Dalyagin's boat, where Janzek was waiting for them.

"Makes you feel pretty small," Janzek said, greeting them.

"Sure does," Crawford said.

"How the hell do we even get on the thing?" Janzek asked, looking up at the five levels of the boat.

"We go to the stern," Ott said.

"Then just hop on?" Janzek asked.

Crawford laughed. "Something tells me there's a little bit more to it than that."

The three started walking toward the stern of the boat. It was clearly where you boarded, but there was a problem, a big problem.

A large man with a bushy beard and above it a very pale face and above it a ball cap on which the ship's name was written in Russian along with another line also in Russian stood guard.

The man had his arms folded across his vast chest. To Crawford, he looked as big as Robert Smallwood, the chair-crushing ex-football player at Jack Rembert's funeral.

"We are police officers and would like to speak to Mr. Dalyagin," Crawford shouted up to him.

The man lashed back at them with a long string of Russian words. The only thing they understood was the physical motion of his hands. He thrust them away from his chest several times. A translator's words, Crawford was certain, would be something like, *get the hell out of here!* Then he went silent and just glared at them. Another man joined him and stared at them as if they were the lowest of vermin.

"I'd say it's time for Plan B," Janzek said to Ott and Crawford.

"We need to speak to Stanislav Dalyagin," Crawford told the guard again.

This time there was no reaction, except a third man came up beside the two Russians with what Crawford thought he recognized as a PMB-93 Russian-made pump action shotgun.

"Plan B?" said Ott.

"How long do you think it'll take to get a warrant?" Crawford asked Janzek.

"I put a call into the judge. We can probably be back here within three hours," Janzek said.

"I think it would be wise to have a few more armed men with us," Crawford said. "Intimidate these assholes."

"I agree," Janzek said, then to the bearded man with the ball cap, he shouted. "We'll see you later, comrade."

The bearded man remained motionless.

They turned and walked away.

"He's got some set of balls," Ott said. "A Russian telling us to fuck off in the heart of America."

"Oh, so now you understand Russian?" Crawford said.

"Guarantee you that's what he said," said Ott.

"Probably right," Crawford said. "It was pretty ballsy—his attitude—especially with the possibility that his ship could be seized by the government at any moment."

"We should get in touch with the feds, tell 'em the boat's here," said Ott. "They could sell it and get more tanks and bullets for Ukraine."

TWENTY-SIX

TRUE TO HIS PREDICTION, JANZEK WAS ABLE TO GET A SEARCH warrant from a cooperative judge, and they were back in just over two and a half hours. But this time, it was the three of them and behind them twelve of Charleston's finest, all fully armed, locked-and-loaded. Janzek had also managed to dig up a Russian-born barmaid he knew from one of his haunts on King Street, who had agreed to act as translator.

The bearded man with the baseball cap was facing them, his stone-faced expression the same as before.

"What's it say on his cap?" Janzek asked the Russian-born woman, whose name was Ulyana.

"The name of the boat, *Mercury* and *First Mate* under it," Ulyana said.

"Well, you tell, Mr. First Mate, that we want to see his boss in the next few minutes or we're coming aboard per the search warrant." Janzek held it up and showed it to the Russians.

Ulyana rattled off a few sentences in Russian.

The First Mate didn't move at first, then he said something.

"He said, 'I'll be back,'" Ulyana translated as the man walked inside.

"So we'll see," Janzek said with a shrug to Crawford.

"World War 3's gotta start somewhere," Ott muttered under his breath to Crawford.

"Not funny, Mort."

They heard footsteps and a short man wearing tight black jeans and a black T-shirt that said 'BALMAIN Paris' on it appeared. He looked supremely bored at the sight of thirteen armed men and one woman.

"What do you want?" he said in accented English.

"Are you Mr. Dalyagin?" Janzek asked.

"Who the hell else would I be?"

Crawford took a step forward. "Mr. Dalyagin, I'm detective Crawford from Palm Beach, and this is my partner, Mort Ott. Detective Janzek here, from Charleston, has a search warrant for us to come aboard the *Mercury*. We'd like to ask you some questions."

"About what?"

So far the man had answered three questions with three questions. It was getting tiring.

"We are investigating the murder of Jack Rembert, which occurred near where your boat was moored at the Palm Beach docks. We want to question you about it."

"I know nothing about that."

"Mr. Dalyagin, I'm getting tired of shouting at you," Crawford said. "I need you to let us come on board your boat."

"All of you?" Dalyagin said, taking in all thirteen of them. "You have got to be kidding."

"Tell you what," it was Janzek this time, "just the three of us. These other men will wait for us to come back ashore."

And at that exact moment, ten men walked out onto the stern of the *Mercury*. All of them cradling, what appeared to Crawford, assault rifles and light machine guns.

"I count seven AK-47's and three RPK's," Ott said out of the corner of his mouth.

"I'd say they got us beat in terms of firepower," Janzek added.

"Hey, it's not like we're really gonna have a shoot-out," Crawford said.

"I hope the hell not," Janzek said. "I'm not real keen on being the cause of an international incident. Things are jittery enough between us and the damn Russians."

Crawford glanced over at Dalyagin. "Mr. Dalyagin, as I said, we need to ask you some questions. It won't take more than a half hour maximum."

"I've already said to you, I know nothing about what happened to that man, Jack Rembert. I have never met him, and I've only heard about him by name."

"My partner and I have come all the way from Palm Beach to speak to you and we're not going home empty-handed."

"And again," Ott said, "we have a court order from a judge. And since you're in America, you will obey it."

Dalyagin shook his head and shot him a disdainful look. "Your piece of paper means nothing to me. I am not American citizen."

"Listen, Mr. Dalyagin, I can tell you this," Janzek said, "you're not going to leave this town without answering the detectives' questions. This is a murder case we're talking about—"

"Probably two," Crawford added.

"So don't even think about leaving here until you've met with these detectives," Janzek continued.

Dalyagin didn't acknowledge Janzek, but just turned to his right and walked inside the boat. The other ten men followed him.

"What do we do?" Ott said to Crawford.

Crawford shrugged. "Live to fight another day," he said, turning to Janzek. "Unless you got a better idea, I think we should go talk it over, weigh our options."

Janzek nodded. "I agree. There's nothing more we can do at this point." He turned to the twelve men behind him. "All right, boys," he said. "Let's call it a day."

Several of his men had looks of disappointment. Slowly, they turned and made their way to their vehicles.

Janzek shot Crawford a what-more-can-we-do shrug. "Why don't we go back to my office and talk it over?"

Crawford looked at his watch. It was just past three. "Yeah, let's do that," he said. "You sure you don't have anything better to do?"

"I'm all yours. Charleston is murder-free at the moment."

———————

THEY DROVE TO THE CHARLESTON POLICE STATION ON LOCKWOOD Drive, parked, went into the station, and took seats in Janzek's office.

Janzek shook his head as he looked over his desk at Crawford and Ott. "You do realize this could turn into a major incident?"

Crawford smiled and nodded his head. "Yeah, we were talking about it on the drive up."

"We've never been the lead story on CNN before," Ott said to Crawford.

"Or any story except on local news," Crawford said, "and I sure as hell want to keep it that way."

"I get it," said Janzek.

"So what are we gonna do?" Ott asked.

Crawford exhaled deeply. "I don't know if there's a perfect solution, but I was thinking about trying to intimidate the guy even more."

Janzek nodded. "I think I know what you mean, instead of twelve guys with guns, a hundred guys with M-20 bazookas."

"You have those?" Crawford asked, impressed.

"Nah," Janzek said with a laugh, "just giving you a hypothetical."

"Gotcha. So what I was thinking was...what if we had fifty of your guys on either side of Dalyagin's boat, plus a helicopter or two overhead, plus maybe a gunboat in the water beside him?"

Janzek nodded excitedly. "I like it."

"I think if it were me, and I was in Dalyagin's shoes, I might agree to a sit-down, wouldn't you guys?"

Janzek and Ott both nodded.

"Yeah, definitely," Ott said. "'Especially since he knows we probably don't have the goods to arrest him for anything anyway because we got no proof at this point."

"Right," Crawford said to Janzek. "You want to give it a shot?"

Janzek nodded. "I'm just thinking about the most impressive show of force I can muster…I think I can do all those things you mentioned. I could even station a couple of very visible snipers on top of a 10-story building not far from the marina."

Crawford gave him a thumbs-up. "Nice touch," he said. "So I'm thinking what if we did it first thing tomorrow morning?"

"I'm good with that," Janzek said. "But I better get working on it. Hey, you guys want to do an early dinner tonight?"

"Yeah, that sounds good," Crawford said. "Tell us when and where and we'll be there."

"Well, in this town there aren't a hell of a lot of places a cop can afford," Janzek said. "Let me think about it and get back to you."

"Sounds good," Crawford said. "But it's on us."

"Yeah, and how 'bout you invite along your friends Jackie and Ryder?" Ott said.

"Sure, why not? I'll see if they're free."

Crawford and Ott stood up and Crawford reached across Janzek's desk to shake his hand. "Pleasure workin' with you, Nick."

"Likewise," said Janzek.

"Hey, Charlie, it's Nick," Janzek said, "let's meet at a place called Taco Boy, up on Huger Street at six tonight. Great tacos and margaritas and a nice outdoor vibe. I think you'll like it."

Crawford had the call on speakerphone. "Sounds good," he said. "Mort and I are just cruising around the city. Hell of a nice place you got here."

"Yeah, I like it. Only downside is getting stuck behind one of those horse-drawn carriages. The Boston driver in me wants to horn 'em but…I hold back."

"Know what you mean," Crawford said, "got stuck behind one already. Mort's lovin' it too."

Ott nodded and spoke into the speaker. "Awesome houses and architecture."

"Oh, also," Janzek said. "Ryder and Jackie are gonna be joining us."

"Cool," Crawford said, "see you in a couple of hours."

"Yup, later."

A few minutes after he clicked off with Janzek, Crawford got a call on his cell.

He looked down at the display. "Dominica," he said.

"Hey," he answered, flicking on the speaker phone, "what's up?"

"So I'm down in Miami, been here most of the day," Dominica said. "And I've got something. I'm just not sure how helpful it is."

"Let's hear. I got you on speaker."

"Hi, Mort," Dominica said.

"You're back in your hometown, huh?"

Dominica had grown up in Miami.

"Yeah, but I liked it better twenty years ago," she said.

"That's true about most places," Ott said. "So whatcha got?"

"I didn't find anything in Bull's house, so I've been checking out security cams. That guy you put me in touch with—"

"Santiago?"

"Yeah, he showed me the tape from the camera across from Bull's house which was no help except it showed a dark SUV. But when I took it and blew it up, I noticed something that he must have missed."

"Which was?"

"A bike rack, think they also call 'em hitch mounts, you know? On the back of the SUV."

"Nice catch," Crawford said.

"Yeah, but I'm not sure where it gets us," she said.

"Hey, it's more than we had before," Crawford said. "Keep digging, will ya?"

"I'm gonna keep at it for the rest of the day," she said. "Then I'm gonna have dinner here with my Mom and Dad."

"Nice," Crawford said.

"How's it goin' up there?" Dominica asked.

"Oh, man, it's a long story," Crawford said. "Tell you when we get back."

"I hear that town is famous for single women," she said. "You boys stay out of trouble."

Ott laughed. "As you know, Dominica," he said, "trouble is my middle name."

Taco Boy was in a big converted industrial building on Huger Street north of downtown Charleston. Altogether, including a big parking lot and a back outside area, it sat on several acres of land. The decor in back consisted mainly of brightly-colored picnic tables and wide-open spaces where, Janzek explained, dancing took place usually with a DJ spinning tunes. At the table next to the five of them—Jackie and Ryder Farrell had arrived a little after the men—was a table full of young women and men along with three dogs on leashes. Janzek explained that Taco Boy was a favorite of college students from the nearby College of Charleston.

"That's a pretty good school, I hear," Crawford said, as all five nursed tall margaritas.

"Oh, yeah, beautiful school," Jackie said.

Ryder smirked. "Top ten of party schools in the country."

"Is that right?" Ott said. "I bet we've got a few contenders for that title in Florida."

"Oh yeah, which ones?" Ryder asked.

"Well, Florida State and I'll bet University of Miami's right up there too," Ott said.

"Good to know," Ryder said with a laugh. "If I ever have kids, I know where *not* to send 'em."

"Come on, Ryder," Janzek said. "Be a sport."

"Not at 80 grand a year. I want my kids to study, not turn into boozehounds."

"So maybe when you have kids you should be looking at places like Brigham Young or Liberty University in Virginia," Janzek said. "No booze allowed."

"Or Baylor's another one," said Ott.

"Hmm, there must be a happy medium," Ryder said.

"You got a problem with dry colleges?" Janzek asked.

"No, not really, it's just—"

"You're such a hypocrite," Jackie said to her sister.

"What do you mean?" Ryder said, ratcheting up a fake irritated tone.

"That time I visited you in college, you were the queen of beer pong," Jackie said.

"You should talk," Ryder said. "As I recall you were a master of Drunk Jenga at Chapel Hill."

Jackie laughed. "Now that you mention it, I was pretty good."

The waitress stopped by their table, and they ordered food and more margaritas all around.

"Cut me off after this one," Crawford said, hoisting his margarita glass.

"Yeah, cut me off after two," Ott said.

"You guys are no fun," Ryder said.

"We got an early one tomorrow," Crawford said.

"What's going on with the Russian?" Jackie asked.

Crawford glanced at Janzek. "You want to answer that?"

"Let's just say he was not very hospitable when we went to pay him a visit."

Crawford nodded. "But we expect him to be more hospitable tomorrow morning."

"I can't wait to hear the end of this story," Jackie said.

A DJ, who had been setting up behind them, spun a tune by Lady Gaga called *Just Dance*.

"Come on," Ryder said, grabbing Janzek's hand.

They stood up and walked over to where a few other couples were dancing and joined in.

Jackie looked across the table at Crawford. "Shall we?"

"Sure," Crawford said, "if you don't mind dancing with a guy with two left feet?"

Jackie laughed and eyed Ott. "You gonna be all right if we leave you alone, Mort?"

"Not the first time I've been a fifth wheel," Ott said, glancing over at a table next to them.

Crawford and Jackie got up and went to the dancing area. Ott stood up, walked over to the table next to theirs, and asked a single woman in a yellow short skirt to dance. She smiled, nodded, and stood up. They walked out to the dance area and started dancing.

It turned out that Ott was the best dancer of them all. Not too much motion, just enough. Not a thrasher or a *look-at-me* show-off, not a strutting peacock, but just a smooth operator.

The man, no doubt about it, had rhythm.

"You from around here?" his dancing partner asked.

Ott had close to twenty years on her.

"Florida," Ott said. "Just up here...visiting...with my partner."

She furrowed her brows. "Your partner? You mean—"

"No, no, my work partner."

She smiled. "Oh, gotcha."

The DJ spun another tune. It was Beyonce.

"I love this song," Jackie said to Crawford.

Crawford, at best a game dancer determined not to embarrass himself or his partner too much, just smiled and nodded.

A few minutes and two songs later, he and Jackie went back to their table and sat down. Shortly after that, Janzek and Ryder joined them. "You guys got some pretty good moves...for cops," said Ryder.

"That was a back-handed compliment if I ever heard one," Crawford said to Janzek. "But I'll take it."

"Yeah, me too," Janzek said, glancing out at Ott still on the dance floor. "But 'ol Mort's got us beat by a mile."

"A man of many talents," Crawford said, watching his partner.

Jackie leaned toward Crawford. "So how long are you guys going to be up here?"

"'Til we get some answers from the Russian. Probably leave tomorrow."

"But what if he won't talk?" Ryder asked.

Crawford sighed. "I don't really know."

"Is he your primary?"

"Well, tell you the truth, we don't really have a primary at this point," Crawford said. "We know who actually did it, but she was a hired hitter."

"She?"

"Yeah, actually a him and a her. Depending on the day."

"Transgender, you mean?" Ryder asked.

Crawford nodded.

"Got it," Ryder said.

Ott followed the woman in the yellow skirt back to the tables.

He smiled and thanked the woman, who sat down at her table, then Ott joined the other four.

"Lookin' good, Mort," Ryder said, shooting him a thumbs-up.

"Thanks. For an old guy, you mean?" Ott said.

Ryder shook her head. "For any guy."

"Well," Crawford said, "I think me and Mort better hit it. I expect we could have a long day tomorrow."

Jackie looked at her watch. "What? It's eight o'clock, the night's still young."

Crawford laughed. "Yeah, but we ain't."

He and Ott stood up. "Nice to have met you again," Crawford said, first to Ryder, then to Jackie. "It's been fun."

Jackie leaned forward and gave him a kiss on the cheek. "Maybe when you wrap things up," Jackie said, "we can have a little celebration dinner."

Crawford nodded. "That would be nice."

TWENTY-SEVEN

CRAWFORD AND OTT GOT WAKE-UP CALLS AT 6:30.

They met in the breakfast room at 7:00.

"Time to nail that Commie fuck," Ott said as Crawford walked up to his table.

"I agree. It's gonna be interesting to see what troops Janzek mobilizes."

"I'm guessing he's not gonna screw around," Crawford said.

"I'm guessing you're right."

HE *WAS* RIGHT.

At 7:50 a.m. when Crawford and Ott showed up at the docks, they first saw forty uniformed cops and ten more plain clothes officers lined up on either side of Dalyagin's boat. After that, Crawford heard the chopping of engines overhead, and soon two helicopters appeared and started circling the *Меркурий*. And quietly idling at the stern of the *Меркурий,* was a 25-foot SAFE boat with twin 300-horsepower engines and *POLICE* inscribed on its hull in big blue letters and two uniformed cops inside the cabin.

Ott pointed up at a nearby building where one man was standing with a rifle on a sling on his back while another man aimed a long sniper rifle at the *Меркурий*.

"As promised," Crawford said as he looked up at the building.

"Do you s'pose Dalyagin has a clue?" Ott asked, shifting his gaze back to the *Меркурий*.

"Oh yeah, guarantee he does. You don't really think this build-up has escaped his attention, do you?"

Just as he spoke, the First Mate in the ball cap and beard walked out onto the stern of the boat. He glanced over at Crawford and Ott's Crown Vic and dialed up an exaggerated scowl.

Ott flicked his head at him. "There he is again, Mr. Happy," he said as Nick Janzek rolled up next to them in his Charger.

"I wish we had Chargers instead of Vics," Ott said.

"What's wrong with Vics?" Crawford asked as Janzek got out of his car.

"Chargers are just cooler," Ott said as Crawford lowered his window.

"Morning, boys," Janzek said. "Are you ready to rumble?"

"Ready," Crawford said, opening the door and getting out as Ott did the same.

"I see we got the head of the welcoming committee waiting for us," Janzek said as he gave the bearded first mate a wave.

The bearded man, of course, did not wave back.

The three walked up to the stern of the *Меркурий* until they were ten feet away.

As they got there, the bearded First Mate glanced to his left and Stanislav Dalyagin appeared.

One of the helicopter pilots lowered his craft so it was only 100-feet above the

Меркурий. Something told Crawford that Janzek had instructed him to do that.

"I am going to give you one half-hour of my time," Dalyagin said, raising his voice to be heard above the helicopter. "That is all."

Janzek glanced at Crawford. Crawford nodded.

"All right," Dalyagin said. "Come aboard."

The bearded First Mate opened the gate so they could step onto the

Меркурий. Janzek led the way. They filed onto the ship past the First Mate. If looks could kill, they'd be dead. The three walked up to Dalyagin. There were no handshakes or *nice to meet you's*.

"Follow me," Dalyagin said.

The three followed him down a hallway with rich mahogany walls on either side and a bright Calcutta Gold marble floor. Then they walked into a room that quite literally made Crawford's jaw drop, and he heard Ott's mumbled *holy shit* behind him. The room, he thought they were referred to as salons, had a double height ceiling—25-feet high, he guessed—with tinted floor-to-ceiling windows on three sides. It was truly breathtaking. In the center was a semi-circular white leather sofa that could probably seat 10 people. It faced three white leather chairs with a glass-topped table in between. On the table was a massive bouquet of fresh flowers in practically every hue in the color spectrum. Above, seeming to float in the air, was a massive, disc-like circular light that looked like a flying saucer preparing to alight. At the far end of the salon, separated by two columns, was what appeared to be a glistening silver-sided jacuzzi that sat five feet above the white marble floor.

The First Mate, who had followed them in, posted himself by the door and just stared straight ahead like a Buckingham Palace guard.

They followed Dalyagin over to the white leather sofa and sat in the three chairs facing Dalyagin.

"Nice room," Janzek said to Dalyagin.

"It's called a grand salon," Dalyyagin said, imperiously.

"Okay," Janzek said. "Nice grand salon."

"What are your questions?" Dalyagin said.

Crawford was ready. "You don't deny knowing Jack Rembert, do you?"

"I know who he is," Dalyagin said.

"You said before you'd never met him, but I was told by his business partner you actually came to his office in Phillips Tower in West Palm Beach."

"That's his story."

"So you didn't?"

Dalyagin shook his head but not as forcefully as he might have.

Crawford pursued it. "His partner said you threatened to kill Rembert."

Ott nodded. "Yeah, using very colorful words."

Dalyagin shrugged and smiled. "Mr. Lewis has...what is your expression? A vivid imagination."

"Oh, so you do know *him*? Del Lewis?"

"I know of him."

Ott tapped his fingers on the glass table. "Because of them representing Anoushka Novokov, we assume." Ott plowed right in. "We've been told that Rembert had an...intimate relationship with Ms. Novokov, who is said to be your girlfriend."

Dalyagin eyed him like he was a repugnant cockroach. "Listen, little man," he hissed in his accented-English, "Rembert was her agent and that's all he ever should have been. But he crossed a boundary."

At that moment, Crawford heard footsteps and looked toward the door to see a tall black woman in sweatpants and a T-shirt taking long, purposeful strides in their direction.

"That man," she shouted in almost-perfect English, "was a pig!"

It occurred to Crawford that she must have been hearing their conversation somehow. There had to be a microphone hidden somewhere. Possibly in the bouquet of flowers.

Dalyagin stood up and stepped in front of Anoushka Novokov. He said something to her in Russian, but she was clearly unwilling to be denied and demanding to be heard. She pushed him aside and loomed above Crawford, Janzek, and Ott.

"Stanislav had nothing to do with what happened to Jack Rembert," she said to them.

"How do you know that, Ms. Novokov?" Crawford asked.

"Because he is not like that. He does not kill people," she said, stabbing with a long finger to make a point. "Despite what you may think of Russians, we are not all like Putin."

"We would be happy to go away and not bother you," Crawford said, softening slightly, "if Mr. Dalyagin could just answer our questions instead of evading them."

"Let me tell you something," Anoushka said, forcefully. "Despite what you may have heard, Jack Rembert tried to rape me. Tried…unsuccessfully because I was stronger than him and it was never going to happen. After that I fired him as my agent. You probably don't know about that."

Dalyagin stepped between Anoushka and where the detectives were sitting and, holding his hands up to her, rattled off something in Russian. She replied in a tone of agitation, then glanced back down at the detectives.

"I apologize for bursting in here, but…" she turned, marched out, taking long, athletic strides across the grand salon, and never finished her sentence.

Dalyagin sat back down, checked his watch, and said calmly, "You have ten more minutes."

Ott spoke first. "We are sorry to hear what Rembert tried to do to Ms. Novokov, of course, but wouldn't that give you even more reason to do harm to him?"

"'Do harm to.' You mean kill him?" Dalyagin said. "Listen, as she said, I don't kill people. Despite what you Americans may think, we're not all thugs and assassins. Our people do not all have automatic weapons like all your people do, we don't kill children in our schools, we don't have gang shoot-outs."

That was a conversation stopper and none of the detectives replied at first.

Then Crawford glanced at Janzek and Ott. "Anything else?" he said to Ott.

Ott shook his head.

"Okay, Mr. Dalyagin," Crawford said. "That does it," he looked at his watch, "and it only took twenty-five minutes."

The three detectives got to their feet.

"Thank you," Crawford said to Dalyagin. Janzek and Ott just nodded at him. They walked out of the grand salon past the stone-faced First Mate and into the hallway back toward the stern.

"Dude's only got one expression," Ott said of the First Mate. "I'd really like to see that putting green and the casino."

"Not today, Mort," said Crawford.

They got to the stern and went down the gangway to dry land.

"So what do you think?" Janzek asked the other two.

"Guy made a few good points," said Crawford.

"I know," Ott said. "It's kinda hard to admit."

"All right," Janzek said. "I'm gonna call off the dogs."

He first looked up at the helicopters and made a circular gesture with one hand. He did the same with the fifty men flanking Dalyagin's boat, then to the SAFE boat, and finally to the two snipers up in the nearby building.

"I don't know, man," Crawford said to Janzek. "It's still possible he could have done it, but I'm just not getting that vibe at all. What about you?"

"I don't think he's your man, but that's just my gut," Janzek said, then to Ott. "What about you, Mort?"

"Nah, I don't think so," Ott said. "But if he did, he's probably gonna skate 'cause we got nothing on him anyway. What do you think of the name, *Mercury?*"

"I've thought about that and think it's just a coincidence," Crawford said. "No significance."

"Yeah, me too."

"All right, well, we might as well hit it," Crawford said to Ott, then he extended his hand out to Janzek. "Thanks for all your help, Nick. We really appreciate it. It's been good seeing you and your city again. Hey, give our best to Jackie and Ryder and tell 'em it was great meeting 'em."

"Yeah," Ott said. "I second that. And if y'all want a little fun in the sun, come on down to the Sunshine State and pay us a visit."

TWENTY-EIGHT

CRAWFORD HAD FIGURED HE AND OTT COULD KILL TWO BIRDS WITH one stone: question Stanislav Dalyagin in Charleston and Octavius Johnson in Savannah. Bettina had Googled Johnson and after wading through a number of articles about him being arrested for putting his girl-friend in the hospital and, subsequently being dropped by the Philadelphia Eagles, she came across an old article in the *Savannah Morning News*. The headline, below the fold on the front page read *From Pro Football Player to Peanut Farmer,* and it showed side-by-side photos of Johnson in uniform and more recently on a John Deere tractor in overalls. The article said the farm was located in a little town outside of Savannah called Riceboro. Effi-cient as Bettina was, she included a map of where Riceboro was located and directions how to get there.

It was just over two and a half hours from Charleston to Riceboro, where Octavius Johnson was apparently engaged in a new line of work made famous by Jimmy Carter. He was, for now anyway, a peanut farmer. But, Crawford guessed, if he had his druthers, he'd much rather be a foot-ball player. Ott was at the wheel as they approached Savannah, and Craw-ford had just Googled Riceboro and read to Ott what he learned from

Wikipedia. "The city of Riceboro, population 941, has historic beginnings and is the oldest existing city in Liberty County, Georgia, home of many successful rice plantations."

"How can they call it a city if only 941 people live there?"

"That's a very good question, Mort, and I don't know the answer."

"Maybe Octavius can shed some light on that. And also, why he's in the peanut business instead of the rice business?"

"You'll have to ask him that, too," Crawford said. "Here's something else: I go to this site that says, '10 Best Things to Do in Riceboro' and all there is is an ad for a place called the Chitlin' Factory and another one for the Himalayan Curry Kitchen."

"Yum," said Ott.

"Which one?"

"I don't know about you, but I've always had a hankering for Himalayan Curry."

Crawford laughed. "I'll wait for you in the car while you go pig out."

Twenty-five minutes later, Ott pulled into a gas station. As Ott filled up, Crawford went inside the station's small convenience store. A short, bald man with a red bandanna around his neck was behind the counter.

"How ya' doin'?" Crawford said.

"Hey," said the man.

"I was wondering if you knew where the Johnson peanut farm is?"

"Sure do. You're only about a mile from it," said the man and gave Crawford directions. "You know, Octavius Johnson, the football player works there. For his papa."

Crawford nodded. "I heard that."

"We also got another celebrity from here."

"Is that right? Who's that?" Crawford asked.

"DeLisha Milton-Jones."

"Ah, can't say I know that name."

"She was an Olympic Gold Medalist and WNBA player. Don't live here no mo'. A coach up at some big college."

"Is that right? Pretty good for a small town, two big athletes like that."

"Not bad," the man said. "Get you anything?"

"Ah, yeah," Crawford said pointing at a shelf. "I'll have a box of those Moon Pies, please."

The man smiled. "You got good taste."

Crawford paid for them, thanked the man, and walked back out to the car.

"Whatcha got there?" Ott asked, pointing at the bag.

Crawford pulled the box out of the bag. "Moon pies, I understand they're a great dessert after Himalayan Curry."

Ott laughed. "I've heard that."

They pulled up to the Johnson farm five minutes later. There was a one-story house just off the road and a large barn behind it. A woman was sitting on the porch of the house shucking corn. Crawford and Ott got out of the Vic and walked up to the porch.

"Hey, ma'am," Crawford said. "We wondered if Octavius is around?"

She looked at them suspiciously. *Like what do two white guys want with my boy?*

"He's in the barn, what do you want him for?"

"See, ma'am, we're detectives. Just need to ask him a few questions."

Her eyes narrowed and her whole body seemed to stiffen. "My boy's been through enough."

"It won't take long," Ott said. "Just a few quick questions."

"Like I said, he's in the barn." She practically spat it out.

"Thank you," Crawford said, and the two started toward the barn.

It was an open barn with two big beams ten feet apart that they walked through. No one was in sight. They heard a clanking noise from one corner and walked toward it. It was a smaller room with a dirt floor. In it was a large black man wearing overalls and no shirt on a bench lifting what looked-like several hundred pounds of barbells. He saw them approach and frowned.

"Who the hell are you?"

"Hi, Octavius," Crawford said, taking out his wallet. "We're detectives from Palm Beach, Florida. Crawford's my name and my partner's is Ott."

Just then an older man, dressed also in overalls but wearing a sweat-drenched white T-shirt walked in. He had a shotgun in his hands, but it was lowered.

"Put that down, please," Crawford said. "We're just here to ask Octavius a few questions...Mr. Johnson?"

"What about?" Octavius asked.

"Is he your father?" Crawford asked, flicking his head at the older man.

"Yeah."

"Mr. Johnson, we need you to put that shotgun down," Crawford said.

"Put it down, Daddy, we don't need no trouble," Octavius said.

The older man took a few steps and leaned the shotgun up against a wall of the room.

"Okay now, what's this about?" Octavius demanded.

Octavius was standing now, sweat glistened on his massive biceps and chest. "I'm sure by now you know about the death of your former agent, Jack Rembert," Crawford started. "Well, we're the detectives on the case. It started out looking like an accident, but we now know it was a murder."

"And you think 'cause of my scrap with him, I mighta did it?"

Ott cocked his head. "We're just askin'. Like we've asked nine other people before you. And like we might ask nine more before we're done."

"Look," Octavius said, slowly shaking his head. "Before what happened to Rembert, I got me another agent. He's in the middle of negotiating a new contract. So my days as a peanut farmer are gonna be over soon." He glanced at his father and smiled. "Sorry, Daddy, I'm not much good at it anyway."

His father smiled back.

"Good for you," Crawford said.

"So you know nothing about what happened to Rembert then?" Ott asked.

"Not a damn thing. I been right here for the past month," Octavius said.

"My son hasn't even been outta the city limits," said his father.

"We heard something about a fight you had in Rembert's office," Ott said.

"That was a long time ago," Octavius said. "And I had a right to be hot."

"You never threatened him? Nothing like that?" Crawford asked.

Octavius didn't hesitate. "Yeah, I mighta. So what? Never meant a word of it."

"Look, the only thing my son ever did wrong was hookin' up with the wrong woman," Johnson's father said. "Always steppin' out on him, stealing money from him, pickin' fights with

him—"

"Okay, Daddy, okay," Octavius said, going over and putting his huge arm around him.

"Don't let it get you crazy."

But the older man wasn't done. "Bitch got arrested, ya know."

"What for?" Crawford asked.

"I don't know, for makin' all that shit up."

Octavius laughed. "No, Daddy. The charge was extortion and falsifying documents."

"Really?" Crawford said.

"Really," said Octavius. "Plus all the charges against me been dropped."

"She started it in the first place," the older man said.

"How?" Ott asked.

"Hit my boy on the head with a vodka bottle," the older man said.

"Bourbon," Octavius said, fighting a smile.

"What?"

"It was a bottle of bourbon. Half full."

Crawford glanced at Ott, then turned back to Octavius. "Well, Octavius, we wish you well with your new team. Who you gonna be playing for?"

"The Cleveland Browns."

Ott's eyes lit up. "All right, that's my team," he said. "Maybe with you they'll have a winning season for once."

"Count on it," Octavius said with a big smile.

"Okay, well thanks," Crawford said, putting out his hand. "Thanks for your time."

Octavius nodded.

Crawford turned to Octavius's father. "Thank you, sir."

"Sorry 'bout the shotgun," the older man said. "You fella's want a couple bags of peanuts for the road."

"Hell, yeah," Crawford said. "I never turn down peanuts."

TWENTY-NINE

THEY GOT BACK ONTO I-95 AND MADE GOOD TIME DRIVING DOWN THE long state of Florida.

They arrived back at the station by mid-afternoon and immediately went to work on the things they'd talked about during the uneventful seven-hour trip back to Palm Beach. First, Crawford called Robert Smallwood, the ex-football player and current agent, who Jack Rembert had sniped several high-salaried football players away from, at his office in Boca Raton. Simultaneously, Ott called Mark Shuman at the number he found for Shuman's home in Palm Beach. His wife Sally Shuman then gave him her husband's office number.

Crawford left a message for Smallwood while Ott reached Mark Shuman, yet another man whose wife allegedly had an affair with Jack Rembert, on his first try.

"Mark Shuman," the man answered.

"Mr. Shuman, my name's Mort Ott. I'm a detective with the Palm Beach Police Department looking into the death of Jack Rembert," Ott said. "I'd like to set up a time, sir, for me to come ask you a few questions."

"What about?" Shuman asked.

"I'm speaking to a lot of people who knew Rembert and you're on my list."

"I have absolutely no idea why, but I guess I have no problem with a few questions."

"Fine, how's ten tomorrow morning? I'll meet you wherever you'd like."

"Make it eleven and come to my office," Shuman said and gave him the address.

Remembering how tough Robert Smallwood was to even engage in a brief conversation, Crawford called him again, then a third time, and finally got him on the fourth try.

"You're a persistent man, detective," Smallwood said.

Crawford thought, *and you're an evasive one.* Instead, he said, "I'd like to ask you a few questions face-to-face as soon as it's convenient, Mr. Smallwood."

"I'm busy as hell as the moment," Smallwood said.

"Turns out I'm going to be in Boca for most of the day tomorrow," Crawford improvised. "What time would work for you?"

Smallwood sighed. "I'm telling you, nothing I say is gonna—"

"How's ten or eleven?"

Smallwood sighed again. "Okay, okay, make it eleven," he said, gave Crawford his address and cut the call short.

Then, just because he had missed talking to her, Crawford called Dominica McCarthy.

"Hi Charlie, how was Charleston?"

"It was a trip, literally and figuratively," he said. "How 'bout dinner tonight?"

"You're on. The usual?"

"Well, actually I have two 'usuals,'" he said.

"I know. Malokor and Cafe Centro."

"Exactly. You game for Cafe Centro? Copeland's playing tonight."

"Of course, I love that place. Him too."

"Good. Pick you up at seven," Crawford said. "Did you get anything more on the shooter in Miami?"

"No, sorry," she said. "Just what I told you, a black car probably in the Mercedes/BMW family with a bike rack on the back."

"Okay, thanks. that's a start."

"See ya at seven."

As Dominica walked to Crawford's car, she noticed the dent on his bumper. She slid into the passenger side seat, leaned into him, and gave him a kiss on the lips. "You still haven't fixed that dent from Cam's accident?"

She was referring to when his brother borrowed his car and clipped a homeless man after five too many drinks. "Nah, never seem to get around to it."

"You'd better. It'll get rusty after a while. The salt air."

"I know. I'll get on it."

They drove up to Cafe Centro, in the Northwood section of Palm Beach, parked and walked into the restaurant.

The owner, who doubled as the maître d', was at the front door.

"Hello, Sal," Crawford said. "How's everything?"

"Couldn't be better," Sal said, "now that Ms. Dominica's in the house."

"Thank you, Sal," Dominica said.

"What about me?" Crawford said.

Sal laughed. "Oh, yeah, you too," he said, pointing at a table. "You're at your usual table next to the window."

As they walked into the large room fronting on Dixie Highway, a black man playing the piano caught Crawford's eye and gave him a nod.

"My man," Crawford said, so only Dominica could hear. "Tickling the ivories."

She smiled, nodded, and sat down as Crawford held her chair.

A trio of jazz musicians—called the Copeland Davis Trio—played several nights a week at Cafe Centro in one room, while in another room—separated by the kitchen and restrooms—a Motown band of spirited seasoned musicians played on other nights. It was the best of both worlds for Crawford, who loved all music with the possible exception of hip hop and bluegrass.

They ordered drinks and, ten minutes later, dinner, while they listened to the music and Crawford filled in Dominica on his trip to Charleston.

"He actually gave you that lecture on why Russia's so great and America's so bad?" Dominica asked.

"No, it wasn't so black and white as that, and some of it was valid. I mean when was the last time you heard about a school shooting in Russia where twenty-five kids got killed?"

"Okay, true," Dominica said. "But when was the last time we invaded a country and killed and kidnapped children?"

"Good point."

"So I'd call it a tie. Both countries have a long way to go."

Crawford gave her a fist bump. "But I'll still take this one."

"Me too...in a heartbeat."

Coleman Davis, the eponymous leader of the jazz trio, came up to them on a break. "How y'all doin'?"

Crawford pointed at a chair in between them. "Good, man, have a seat."

"Just for a minute," Coleman said, then to Dominica, "wish one time you'd just come up alone. Lose your cop friend."

Dominica laughed. "Still the biggest flirt in West Palm, I see," she said. "Bet you say that to all the ladies."

"Um, I might be guilty as charged," he said, then to Crawford. "Got any juicy murders cookin', Charlie?"

"I wouldn't call it juicy, but yeah, I got one."

Coleman turned to Dominica. "So, tell me, what you do again?"

"I do the hard part, come up with all the evidence, so Charlie can just go arrest the bad guy. You know, make him look good."

Crawford laughed. "Actually, that's kinda true."

"Well, not really," Dominica said. "So how'd you get started in the music business, Coleman?"

"Wow, it's been so long I kinda forgot, but they had this old, beat-up Korg piano at this orphanage where I grew up in New Orleans."

Dominica nodded. "Well, there you go, the birthplace of jazz. No wonder."

"Yeah, it was a pretty good town for music," Coleman said, as their food arrived.

"Well, you two, enjoy your dinners," Coleman said, getting up.

"We will," Crawford said. "And your music."

Coleman nodded. "Thanks for coming."

They watched him walk away, then wave at another couple and sit down at his piano.

"Nice guy," Dominica said, scratching her head. "What were we talking about?"

"The U. S. of A...how we preferred it over the U.S.S. of R?"

"Oh right...that Anoushka sounds like one hell of a tough cookie."

"Yeah, I liked her. Particularly after what she went through with Jack Rembert."

"You believe her?"

Crawford nodded. "Rembert was a taker. A guy who felt entitled to take whatever he wanted. I'm not quite sure why David Balfour was a friend of his."

Dominica cocked her head. "Was he? Maybe just an acquaintance?"

"I'm not too sure. But enough of a friend that he had a hunch Rembert didn't get drunk, fall off the dock, and drown."

"And without him you probably never would have suspected murder, right?"

"Yup. Absolutely."

"Geez, Charlie, without homicides what would you and Mort do for fun?"

"Drive each other crazy," Crawford said. "We don't do well when we have nothing to do."

They ate, talked, and listened to the music for another forty-five minutes. Then he paid the check.

Dominica looked him in the eye, smiled. "Well, shall we?"

"Shall we what?"

"Don't be coy, Charlie....have a sleep-over."

He didn't answer, he just got to his feet.

THEIR USUAL MODUS OPERANDI WAS TO START WATCHING SOMETHING on Amazon Prime, Netflix, or Apple TV then just ease into it. Crawford once told Dominica he liked the kissing almost more than the sex itself. She frowned at him and said, *Why? What don't you like about what I do?* He had put up his hands and said, *no, no, no, don't get me wrong, that part is fantastic, but the kissing is much more than just a prelude, a starting point, because you are so amazing at it.* She seemed appeased by that and, shortly after, the kissing began and went on for a good—really good—ten minutes. Finally, she pulled back, smiled at him and said, *I see what you mean, I really am a good kisser.* Amused, he said something like, *But it takes two to tango.* She said, *I wasn't saying you were a bad kisser. Jeez, Charlie, don't get all offended.* He laughed and said, *I wasn't offended, I just want to know you feel I'm pulling my oar here.* She laughed, *Pulling your oar? How romantic. Is that what you think it is?* He put up his hands again and said, *Just a figure of speech meaning... well, doing my part in the kissing depart-ment.* She shook her head. *Relax, Charlie, you're definitely doing your part, pulling your oar, however you want to say it, you are an amazing kisser. Now, can we please move on?*

Gladly, he'd said.

And with that he had slipped a hand behind her and unclasped her bra, then moved his other hand down to her panties. She smiled up at him and whispered, "And you're not too shabby at bra and pantie removal."

This time it was a similar sequence of events...but without all the chatter.

THIRTY

Dominica was a Starbucks girl, so Crawford had to make stops both there and at Dunkin' Donuts. If it was the weekend—instead of a workday—he'd go whole hog and prepare grapefruit or honeydew melon followed by eggs, toast, and bacon. At 7:30, he arrived back at his condo at the Trianon with the two bags from Dunkin' Donuts and Starbucks.

Dominica was in her usual early morning garb—a long-sleeve dress shirt of Crawford's and a pair of black lacy panties—which never failed to get Crawford in the mood all over again.

They had their coffee and donuts, or in the case of Dominica, some kind of breakfast wrap, in front of Crawford's wall-mounted TV watching that blathering morning couple on MSNBC.

"I think she's got a 'daddy complex,'" Dominica said of the blonde member of the blather team.

"And he's got a 'I-just-love-to-hear-myself-talk' complex," Crawford said.

"So why, may I ask, are we watching this then?" Dominica said.

"'Cause the alternative has two minutes of news or talk, then five minutes of commercials."

"That is true," Dominica said. "But there's always CNBC."

"Yeah, but stocks and bitcoin get old."

"Also, true," she said, "what about the Cartoon Channel?"

Crawford's eyes got bigger. "I didn't know there was such a thing?"

"There must be," she said, popping half of a bacon slice in her mouth. "You got a busy day today?"

"Don't talk with your mouth full," he said, teasing.

"Sorry, you got a—"

"Yeah, more follow-up on Rembert. I'm going down to Boca to talk to a man who weighs four hundred pounds."

"A football player, I'm guessing?"

"Ex," he said. "What about you? What are you up to?"

"I've gotta go back to the scene of those burglaries in the estate section."

"No good leads yet?"

"Not really."

No hesitation "Feel like making love before that?"

"After I finish my bacon."

ROBERT SMALLWOOD'S OFFICE IN A LOW-RISE OFFICE COMPLEX IN Boca Raton was a shrine to his glory years as a Buffalo Bills and Kansas City Chiefs NFL football player. There was a Bills jersey and a Chiefs jersey in large glass frames both with the number 65. Similarly, there were two helmets, one from each team on the top of a four-tiered shelf. Below were various trophies which, Crawford guessed, commemorated the big man's exploits on the football field from high school through college and on into the pros. In one corner was a life-size cut-out of Smallwood standing in a Bills uniform, his arms crossed over his chest, but without a helmet. He seemed to be smirking, as if to say, *your quarterback's about to be in big, big trouble!*

"I guess I owe you an apology for blowing you off at Rembert's funeral," Smallwood said. "To be honest, talking to cops isn't really one of my favorite things. Plus I was doin' a little business."

"What? You had some bad experiences...with cops?" Crawford asked, again noticing—he couldn't miss it—the bicycle-chain size gold necklace around the man's massive neck.

"Yeah, you could say that. Had some bad experiences when I was a kid. But hey, not like that's an unusual thing."

"I hear you," Crawford said. "So I'm just gonna skip the small talk and get right to it. On paper, you look like a perfect suspect. As I hear it, Rembert stole a bunch of free agents from you who were on the verge of signing hundred million dollar contracts—"

"More than that for two of 'em."

"Okay, so you would stand to make millions, I'm assuming?"

Smallwood nodded.

"Then when it didn't happen, you got fired and lost everything."

Smallwood nodded again.

"So that's motive one, to get the guy who screwed you. And motive two, by taking him out, maybe get those players back plus other players of his."

"All of that's true, but I was raised by a mother who taught me you don't sit around and lick your wounds when you get knocked down. You get back up, stay in the game, and kick ass,"

"Which, it looked like, you were doing at Rembert's funeral."

"Yeah, well, I got a guy out of that. Signed him yesterday, in fact."

"Nice goin'," Crawford said. "Okay, the thing your mother told you sounds pretty good, but men don't always do what their mothers say."

"Look, man, all I can tell you is I had nothin' to do with what happened to Rembert," Smallwood said, throwing up his hands. "If you don't believe me," he shrugged, "you don't believe me. You're probably gonna ask me for an alibi for when it happened."

"No, I'm not actually. 'Cause whoever did it hired someone to do the job."

"I didn't know that," the big man said, shifting in his chair. It was a whole lot sturdier than the one he broke into smithereens at the funeral.

"Well, obviously, I wasn't expecting to come down here and get a full confession out of you even if you did it."

"I didn't."

"Okay, so who do you think did?"

"Del Lewis maybe. Scott Drexel maybe. They'd stand to gain the most."

"Who else?"

"You've ruled those two out?"

"I didn't say that."

"I heard about some woman he had a kid with who stood to gain a lot, too."

Crawford's head snapped to attention. "'Some woman?' Who's some woman?"

"I don't know her name. You just hear stuff in this business. A lot of stories and rumors, maybe ten percent of it's true."

"Okay, so who'd you hear it from then?"

"I really don't remember."

"You sure? You strike me as a man with a pretty good memory."

"Not always. Those helmets we used to have didn't always do the job."

Crawford nodded.

"Okay, those three. Anyone else?"

"Nah, man, I'd take a good look at Del Lewis and the Coffee Boy, but I'm sure you probably have already."

"Wait a minute, the Coffee Boy, who's that?"

"Drexel. That's what some of the players called him 'cause Rembert was always telling him to go fetch coffee in their meetings."

"He must've loved that. I just have to ask you one last thing," Crawford said, pointing. "Is that chain around your neck real gold?"

Smallwood frowned. "Whaddaya think, man? I'd wear fake gold? Shit, it's as real as that tie around your neck is." He zeroed in on the tie. "Just for the record, detective, paisley ties ain't happening anymore...if they ever were."

Crawford smiled and got to his feet. "Well, thanks for the fashion tip, Robert, and I appreciate you taking the time to see me."

They shook hands.

"Don't know if I was any help. And you probably still gonna keep me on your suspect list, right?"

"Yeah, but pretty far down."

"Yeah, bet you say that to all your suspects."

THIRTY-ONE

MARK SHUMAN CALLED OTT AND SAID HE'D LIKE TO CHANGE THEIR meeting from his office to his home and Ott said that was no problem. Shuman lived in a Mediterranean style house on Onondaga Avenue, up on the North End of Palm Beach. It was a mystery to those who lived on Onondaga where the name came from, but the consensus seemed to be that someone named it after where they originally came from which, they guessed, might be Onondaga County in upstate New York, best known for the location of the city of Syracuse.

Shuman answered the door when Mort Ott pressed the buzzer. He was a slim man with white eyebrows and a sizable nose that probably inhaled more air than most. He was wearing a V-neck sweater that was curious to Ott because it was eighty-eight degrees outside. However, when Shuman ushered Ott in, Ott understood. The air conditioner had to be set at sixty-five degrees or less.

"Thanks for seeing me, Mr. Shuman, I appreciate your time," Ott said, following Shuman into a living room where the color brown was prominently featured: chocolate-colored walls and brown furniture which had been all the rage fifty years ago.

"No problem," Shuman said. "Obviously, you're trying to get to the bottom of what happened to Jack Rembert."

Shuman sat down and Ott sat opposite him.

"Yes, I am, and I'm just going to get straight to the point," Ott said.

"Have at it."

"What we've heard, and let's just call it through the grapevine, was that it seems Dick Rembert had a fairly recent affair with your wife."

"Well, yes, that's absolutely true," Shuman said, "but my wife has had a lot of affairs with men."

Whoa! What?

"Ah, can you explain that please?"

"Sure," Shuman said, hiking up his socks, "fact of the matter is Sally and I have what you'd call an open marriage. Are you familiar with what that is?"

"Yes...I think so, but can you explain it for me?"

"Absolutely. So we agreed some years back that our sexual relationship had gotten a little...um, I think 'stale' is the best way to describe it, or maybe a tad 'unfulfilling', know what I mean?"

"I think so," Ott said, doing his damnedest not to blush.

"So we decided to seek out other lovers. We just felt that it was much more honest than, well, sneaky affairs on the side...if you know what I mean? So since then, we have both had a number of, let's call them, paramours."

Ott was fascinated. How many? More than ten? Less than fifty? How do you go about meeting them? Chat groups? Dating web sites for swingers? What?

"I understand," Ott said while he thought how he would pose his next question. "So...and I'm just speculating now, does that mean that you harbored no ill will against Jack Rembert for, well, sleeping with your wife?"

"Hell, no. He was just another guy. Just like Sally never, as you say, *harbored any ill-will* about any of the women I, um, had sexual relations with."

Ott nodded. "Okay, well, thanks for explaining all that. So did you and your wife ever talk about any of your, um, paramours?"

"You mean, specifically Jack Rembert?"

"Yes."

"Not really...oh wait, I remember one time she did mention that she found him to be a rather 'selfish' lover."

Ott's first instinct was to poke that subject with a follow-up question but realized he was now heading down the proverbial rabbit hole, which wasn't going to get him even remotely close to finding his murder suspect. He also realized he had heard all he needed to hear to cross Shuman off his list.

"Well, thank you, Mr. Shuman," he said, rising to his feet. "As I said before, I appreciate you taking the time to meet me. And I wish you well in all your future...endeavors."

As he walked out of the living room toward the front door, a million questions about the sex lives of Sally and Mark Shuman flooded his brain. But none of them, not one, had a damn thing to do with his homicide case.

THIRTY-TWO

As soon as Crawford got back from Boca Raton, he called David Balfour. "Hey David," he said, when Balfour answered, "it's Charlie, I have a question for you."

"Ask away."

"I heard something about Jack Rembert having a child, and I don't mean with Mrs. Rembert?"

Balfour laughed. "I knew what you meant, and I know all about it. None other than my Scavenger Hunt partner Silla Vander Poel. But this goes way back to the dark ages."

"I could use whatever details you have."

"Sure, okay. So quite a while back Jack had an affair with Silla. I mean, literally, a one-night stand, according to him. But she got pregnant, and he tried to get her to have an abortion but she said no. And nine months later along comes little Truxton."

"I've never heard that name before."

"I know, me neither," Balfour said. "Anyway, the poor kid was handicapped somehow. I'm not quite sure what it was. Jack paid all the bills because Silla always lived beyond her means—still does for that matter. Anyway what I heard, and I never talked to Jack about it, was that at one point Silla went to him and tried to get him to give her a lot of money. Five million, I heard. Ostensibly for the care of Truxton, but really to spruce up her wardrobe and allow her to rent a villa in Cap Ferrat for the summer."

"Wherever that might be?"

Balfour chuckled. "The Riviera. *Tres cher*...anyway Jack apparently said that he'd give Truxton everything he needed but Silla was on her own," he said, then snapped his fingers. "I see where you're going on this, Charlie. Maybe if Jack was dead, she's have a shot at claiming a chunk of his estate on behalf of Truxton."

"We both got there at the same time actually," Crawford said. "But sounds like I should put Silla on my list of people to talk to. Particularly since she was with Rembert the night he was killed."

Balfour shrugged. "Oh yeah, absolutely. It never occurred to me up until now. Seems like you got a hell of a lot of candidates with motives."

"Yeah, I know. Instead of narrowing down the field, Mort and I seem to be expanding it."

"But is that the way it usually works?"

"Well yeah, pretty often. Although there's no real pattern to it. But I'd say this case has a lot more possibles than most."

"So you actually think Silla might be behind it?"

"I haven't had any time to think about it. But who knows? The sense I'm getting from you, though, is that she's kind of a long shot. I mean, murder-for-hire...might be above her pay grade?"

"She's a friend so I'm sure as hell not about to point the finger at her."

"I understand," Crawford said.

"But, when you think about it, who'd ever suspect that a respected lawyer from a good family down in South Carolina would kill his wife and son in cold blood."

"Yeah, I saw that on Netflix too," Crawford said. "Well, thanks for the information about her. Guess I'll be paying Silla a visit."

"Watch out for her."

"What do you mean?"

"You look up cougar in the dictionary, there's a picture of her."

BASED ON WHAT ROBERT SMALLWOOD HAD MENTIONED ABOUT SCOTT "Coffee Boy" Drexel, Crawford figured he'd do a routine background check on the man. He didn't expect to find much because Drexel seemed so mild-mannered. Meek almost. Like all he needed to do was stay married to Muffie and it would be one long, slow ride down Easy Street. So he was surprised when he found out that a year before, Drexel had been involved in a fender-bender in West Palm Beach, which lead to a charge of drunk-driving and second-degree assault. It seemed that Drexel had gotten into a shouting match with the other driver, which resulted in Drexel punching him and breaking his nose. It was a misdemeanor, but Drexel got a five hundred dollar fine and had to take a course in anger-management. Mild-mannered and meek...um, maybe not so much.

Then Crawford phoned the number that David Balfour gave him for Silla Vander Poel. It went straight to voicemail, and he left a message asking her to call him back. He was surprised when she did fifteen minutes later.

"Hello."

"So you're that marvelously attractive policeman my friend Rose Clarke told me about the other day," Silla gushed.

"Hello, Ms. Vander Poel, thanks for getting back to me," he said. "Would it be possible to meet with you sometime soon? I'm one of the detectives investigating the death of Jack Rembert."

"Sure. How about you come over for a drink tonight?"

People questioned while drinking sometimes produced unexpected results, Crawford thought, so why not?

"Yes, if that's good for you. What time were you thinking?"

"Say, 6:30?"

He looked at his watch. It was just past five. "That would be good. What's your address, please?"

"It's 242 Kawama Lane."

"Thanks. Look forward to it."

"Me more. Bye-bye, handsome."

Well, Balfour warned me.

H E PULLED UP TO THE HOUSE ON KAWAMA AT 6:30 AND RANG THE
doorbell. A minute later a young Filipino woman came to the door.

"Oh, you are the policeman that Ms. Vander Poel is expecting?"

"Yes, hi," Crawford said.

"Well, she is in back and asked me to escort you out there."

Crawford nodded and followed her through the house. She opened the
back sliding door and Crawford saw a dark-haired woman in what looked
like a hot tub off of a wide stone porch.

The woman spotted them and gave a big wave to Crawford who went
up to her as the Filipino woman walked away. Silla was wearing a string
bikini not usually seen on women her age, which Crawford guessed to be
around fifty to fifty-five, and had a glass of wine in hand.

"Thank you, Bernila," Silla said, then smiled at Crawford. "Rose was
not exaggerating. So glad to meet you."

"Nice to meet you, too, Ms. Vander Poel."

"Please, call me Silla," she said. "Why don't you join me in here, Charlie? I have some men's bathing suits in the pool house over there. Um, I
think there's a 40-inch waist and a 36... no, both too big, I can see. I think
also a 32."

"Thank you, but no," Crawford said. "My boss frowns on me swim-
ming on the job."

She laughed. "Are you sure? It's so refreshing in here."

"No, thanks, I'm happy standing."

"Well, in that case, I insist that if you're going to stand you have a drink
in hand," she said. "Bernila!"

The Filipino woman came bounding outside onto the porch. "Yes,
ma'am?"

"I'll have another rosé, and...Charlie?"

"A Coke, please."

"Oh, come on, be a sport."

"Just a Coke, please."

"Glass or bottle, sir?"

"Bottle, please," he said.

Silla smiled. "Just like all *real men*."

He nodded a bit uneasily. "So...do you mind if I ask you a few questions about Jack Rembert?"

"No, not at all. Fire away."

"Well, this is a little ticklish," Crawford said, brushing hair out of his eye, "but I know that you and Mr. Rembert have a son—"

"That blabbermouth David, right?" she said. "Doesn't matter. Everyone knows anyway."

"And so my question is...well, I'm actually talking to people who stand to gain if Rembert was no longer alive?"

"Wait? How did I stand to gain?" Silla asked and polished off the rest of her wine.

"Well, I would guess that your son, Truxton, might have a partial claim on his estate. Along with his two daughters and Mrs. Rembert."

"I don't know how you figure that. I would assume Christina would get everything."

"Except apparently he left a, ah, *lady friend* several million dollars."

"That bastard. How'd you find that out?"

"Sorry, I'm not at liberty to say."

She laughed. "That sounds so much like police-talk," she said. "Did whoever-it-was happen to say how much Truxton got?"

"Sorry, it didn't come up."

Bernila came out with Silla's wine and Crawford's Coke on a silver tray.

"Thank you, dear," Silla said, raising her glass. "Cheers." They clinked drinks.

"Are you married, Charlie, Rose didn't say."

"No, I'm not."

"Well," she said with a coquettish smile, "just so happens, neither am I."

He was beginning to think that was not her second glass of wine. Probably more like her fourth. He was also beginning to wonder why he had made the decision to interview her in the first place. Because he was becoming increasingly more desperate? That was the only answer he could come up with. He was also kicking himself for having put himself in this position of talking to a "cougar," as Balfour described her, who wanted him to jump into a hot tub with her...and quite possibly more. He started wondering if he had missed something, a suspect he or Ott had already talked to who was Jack Rembert's killer. Instead of this clearly innocent but lonely woman. Someone who had glibly or cleverly not aroused their suspicions. It wouldn't be the first time. It had happened before. But he prided himself on having a reliable read on liars and dissemblers, almost always able to sniff out the guilty ones. The trick, of course, was to come up with unassailable evidence. As Chief Norm Rutledge, not one to dole out compliments lightly, had once said to him, in a moment of weakness perhaps, *You got the best gut in the game, Crawford.* Or maybe it was *best nose in the business*, but whatever it was, it was unlike Rutledge, who was much more at home skewering his men than complimenting them.

"My final question—" Crawford started.

"Aw, does it have to be," she said with a pout, leaning forward slightly to give Crawford a peek at her ample breasts, "I'm so enjoying this."

"Have you heard any of your friends talking, or speculating, about who may have had a reason to want Jack Rembert dead?"

What the hell, it was worth a try. He had nothing else.

"Hmm," she said putting her hand on her chin. "No, I really haven't. Most people loved Jack. I don't know anything about his business, of course, but I guess you have to step on a few toes to become as successful as he obviously was."

Crawford slowly nodded. "Well, thank you very much. I appreciate you seeing me on short notice like this. And thank you for the Coke."

"You barely touched it." He had taken two sips. "Are you sure you have to leave?"

He nodded and smiled. "I'm sure. It's been a long day."

She smiled and cooed. "We could make it a long night."

Get me out of here, he thought, *fast.* "Well, good night, Ms. Vander Poel, thanks again," he said and slinked away.

THIRTY-THREE

THE MORNING AFTER CRAWFORD'S DRINK WITH SILLA VANDER POEL, all hell broke loose on the Palm Beach wild-and-wacky front.

Crawford got a call at just past nine from Bettina, out at the front desk of the station.

She was talking in a whisper. "Charlie, there're three men here who'd like to speak to you. They claim they know something about the Rembert murder but...there's something funny about them."

"What do you mean by 'funny'?"

"I mean, they strike me as kind of...odd. They look a little odd, they—"

"All right, I'll be out in a second."

After all, he and Ott had very little—too little—going at the moment. What was another couple of odd jobs?

One of the men had a long, grey ponytail which stopped just above a belt that had a buckle with a big Q on it. The second one had a shaved head and wore baggy jeans and a loose black T-shirt. The third man wore cargo shorts and in one of the pockets was the outline of something that looked to Crawford like a pistol.

"Gentlemen," Crawford said, walking up to them, "my name's Detective Crawford. Bettina said you fellas might have some knowledge about the Jack Rembert case. Is that right?"

"Yeah, ah, can we talk in private?" the pony-tailed man said, looking around like he was worried people might overhear their conversation.

"Sure," Crawford said, waving his hand for them to follow him, "come on back. I'll get my partner to join us."

On the way back, Crawford swung by Ott's cubicle. They all introduced themselves. The three men were Gary, Chuck, and Manny. They followed Crawford into his office, Ott dragged in another chair, and they all sat down.

"So, we're all ears," Crawford said. "What can you tell us about the Rembert murder?"

The three glanced around at each other to see who was going to lead it off.

The one with the big Q belt buckle, Manny, spoke. "You mentioned the Rembert murder," he said earnestly. "It was actually the John Fitzgerald Kennedy, Junior, murder."

Chuck with the long gray ponytail nodded emphatically.

"Excuse me?" Crawford said, as Ott's eyes bored into Manny's.

"Your guy Rembert was actually John F. Kennedy, Junior," Gary chimed in.

Then it hit Crawford. About hearing something on his car radio about a man who a group of people were saying was actually young Kennedy in disguise. About how the plane crash that had reportedly killed him, his wife, and his sister-in-law was all a hoax. How there was never a crash at all and that the three had gone off and lived in some remote island somewhere off of Canada.

"Okay," Crawford said to Manny. "Let's hear your details."

"I can see you're a little skeptical," *a lot more than a little,* "so I'll fill you in on the whole thing. "So at first everyone said John-John, that was his nickname you remember, was actually a guy by the name of Vincent someone," Manny glanced at the other two, "you remember his last name?"

"Sorry," Gary said shaking his head.

Chuck just shrugged.

"Well anyway, they checked it out and it turns out that this guy Vincent was actually born six years after Kennedy."

"And also didn't look like him at all," Gary said. "Actually had this red birthmark behind his ear which John-John definitely didn't have."

"But if you go to our website," Manny said, "you'll find that John-John was born on November 25th, 1960. And guess who else was born on November 25th, 1960?"

"I'm going to take a wild guess," Crawford said. "Jack Rembert?"

"Bingo," said Manny with a nod.

"Wait a minute," Ott said. "What is your website?"

Manny pointed down at his belt buckle. "QAnon.friends.com," he said with pride.

"You want to hear something else?" Gary asked.

"Sure."

"Guess what that guy Rembert's middle name was?"

This time it was Ott. "Fitzgerald?"

"Bingo again," Manny said. "You guys are pretty smart."

"So you fellas are the ones who, ah, came up with that Pizzagate thing, right?" Ott said, his head cocked at an inquisitive angle, knowing that was a QAnon hoax.

"Not came up with it," Manny said. "Exposed it."

"Wait, refresh my memory on that?" Crawford said.

"It's simple," Gary said. "See, we discovered that certain high-profile politicians were sexually abusing children at a D.C. pizza parlor."

Chuck nodded excitedly.

"Oh yeah, now I remember," Crawford said. "And weren't the Clintons involved in it somehow."

"So our research found out," Gary said, "involved in it up to their eyeballs. So was that guy, George Soros."

"Is that a fact?" Crawford said.

Chuck nodded vigorously.

"Seems like that guy Soros gets accused of just about everything," Crawford said.

"That's 'cause the man's got his fingers in every pie," Gary said.

Crawford glanced at Ott who seemed to be doing his damnedest to stifle a grin. "So just to make sure I got this straight, are you saying that John F. Kennedy Junior, John-John, was actually a big sports agent and that Jack Rembert never existed?"

"And that he was married and had two daughters," Ott said, "who actually would be president JFK's grandchildren, right?"

"Yup. And Teddy's nieces," Manny said.

"Wow," Crawford said. "That's some story."

"And why are you coming to us with this?" Ott said. "I mean, instead of going to the newspapers or TV reporters?"

"Why? Because we're law-abiding citizens and we wanted to give you a heads-up," said Manny.

"Yeah, that's how we roll," said Gary.

Chuck just nodded eagerly. That seemed to be his role in the three-some. The nodder. And occasionally, the shrugger.

"But also because of the reward," Manny said.

"The reward? What reward?" Crawford asked.

Manny frowned. "The three hundred thousand."

"Dollars?"

"Yes, dollars," Manny said. "You don't know what I'm talking about?"

"No clue."

"We heard it on the radio," Manny said. "We assumed it was the Palm Beach Police Department who put it up."

Crawford looked over at Ott, who raised his shoulders. "Sorry, we don't know anything about any reward."

"But we can guarantee you it's not coming from Palm Beach Police Department," Ott added. "We're not real flush here."

The three men looked totally deflated.

"Well, we thank you guys for stopping by," Crawford said. "We'll see how all of this factors into our investigation." He might as well ask, he figured. He asked everyone else, after all. "So do you fella's have any idea just who might have killed...John-John?"

"No, not really," Manny said. "But we got our researchers on the case... workin' overtime."

"Well, if they come up with anything, tell 'em to get in touch with us," said Ott.

Crawford stood up and shook hands with the three Q men. "You know how to get out, right?"

"Yeah, sure, no problem," Manny said. "You don't need to walk us out."

"Okay, well then, take it easy fellas," Ott said, and the three men walked out of Crawford's office.

Ott closed the door to Crawford's office and burst out laughing.

"What?" Crawford said, straight-faced. "You don't think there's anything there?"

"Gee, Charlie, I don't know. If I did, I'd probably think that O.J. was innocent and the moon is made of green cheese."

"You mean, it isn't?" Crawford said, still in full straight-face mode. "I think we better find out more about this big reward."

THIRTY-FOUR

CRAWFORD CALLED BETTINA AT THE FRONT DESK. "YOUR POWERS OF screening people are slipping."

"Sorry, Charlie, I didn't really know what to make of those guys. What did they say?" Bettina asked.

"That our victim Jack Rembert was actually John-John Kennedy."

"JFK's son?"

"Yup."

"I am really sorry, I—"

"You're forgiven, but what I need you to do is run down a rumor, or whatever it is, that three hundred thousand dollars is being offered to whoever provides information leading to the capture of Rembert's killer."

"I'll get right on it."

"Thanks."

Five minutes later, his cell phone rang. The number popped up and it looked vaguely familiar. At first, he was going to let it go to voice mail, but then he decided to answer it.

"Hello?"

"Hi Charlie, it's Silla." He wished he had let it go to voicemail. "After you left I started thinking about your question about who I thought might have killed Jack."

"Yes?"

"And I had a thought. One of the men on the other scavenger hunt team—you know about the scavenger hunt, right?"

"Sure. Jack was looking for a clue when he died."

"Yes. So one of the men on the other team, Charles Stockley, had a big wager with Jack that his team would beat ours."

"What's a big wager, Silla?"

"A quarter of a million dollars. Two hundred and fifty thousand," she said, just in case Crawford didn't know what a quarter of a million was.

"I think I see what you're suggesting. That this man Stockley might have been worried that your team was going to win and killed Rembert so he wouldn't have to pay the bet."

"Well, it's pretty logical, don't you think?" Silla said.

Logical or not, he just wanted to get her off the phone.

"Um, I suppose maybe it is," Crawford said. "Thank you for the tip, Silla. I'll look into it."

Her voice got husky, as if she was working up to a sexy purr. "Do I get a reward, Charlie?"

He tried to laugh it off. "Yes, my heartfelt appreciation."

———

It didn't take Bettina long. She called him fifteen minutes later.

"Whatcha got?" Crawford answered.

"The three-hundred-thousand-dollar man," she said. "It's a baseball player named Shohei Ohtani."

"You mean, the seven hundred-*million*-dollar man."

"What?" Bettina said. "I'm not following."

"Ohtani just signed a ten-year contract for seven-hundred million," Crawford said, doing some quick math. "So that reward he's offering, for him it's chicken feed. Three hundred thousand is, if my math is correct, less than five hundredths of one percent of the contract Jack Rembert negotiated for Ohtani two months ago."

"You're kidding. How much is that a year?"

Crawford did some more math. "Um, somewhere in the neighborhood of thirty-five to forty million a year. If it was a straight ten-year pay-out, which I don't think it was. I remember reading there was some pretty big deferred payments."

Bettina whistled. "I guess I could get by on that."

Crawford laughed. "How'd you find out about it?"

"The usual, Wikipedia, plus my hairdresser. She hears every rumor between here and New York, as well as all the juicy gossip that's floating around out there."

"Thank her for me," Crawford said. "So I gotta hand it to Ohtani, that's a pretty good way of showing your thanks to a guy who just made you the richest baseball player who ever lived."

"Is he single?" Bettina asked.

Crawford laughed. "What do you mean? You're not."

"No, but I could change that."

———

CRAWFORD OPENED UP HIS MACBOOK AIR, WENT TO GOOGLE, AND typed in Shohei Ohtani. As he expected, his offer was all over the internet. He clicked on a *USA Today* link. The headline read, *Shohei Ohtani, Star Baseball Player, Offers Big Reward.* The article went on to say that *Future Hall-of-Fame Dodgers Pitcher, in a stunning act of gratitude to his former agent, is offering a reward of three hundred thousand dollars to the person or persons who provides a tip that leads to the arrest and conviction of sports agent Jack Rembert's killer.* Ohtani was quoted as saying, "The man was very good to me, treated me right, and I want to make sure that the person responsible for his death is brought to justice." The story stated how, originally, Rembert's death looked like it was an accident but that "*it was later ruled a homicide by the Palm Beach County medical examiner*" and how *"celebrated Palm Beach homicide detectives, Charles Crawford and Morton Ott, are assigned to the case."* After finishing the story, he skimmed several other stories from Axios, CNN, and *The New York Times*.

Then he called Ott. "Hello, *Morton*, did you happen to read about Ohtani's reward?"

"Sure did. And I think I'd rather be called 'eminent' or 'venerable' instead of 'celebrated.'"

"Hey, take what you can get," Crawford said. "But I gotta tell you, I'm not too thrilled about this thing at all."

"What do you mean?" Ott asked. "Because it'll turn into amateur hour now?"

"Already has with Eeny, Meeny, and Manny. We better get ready for a lot more like those three clowns."

"I hear you. But what can we do?"

"Not a lot," Crawford said. Then he told Ott about Charles Stockley, the man who Silla Vander Poel had mentioned, who was on the other scavenger team against her, David Balfour, and Jack Rembert, and his two hundred fifty-thousand-dollar bet. He hung up with Ott, found Stockley's phone number, and dialed him. He was calling him not because he sounded like a viable suspect but more because he thought you never knew when someone totally innocent might come up with a scrap of information that might be useful in breaking a case. On the other hand, you never knew when someone who seemed innocent on paper could turn out to be a more viable suspect after you interviewed him. In any case, Crawford had run out of people to interview, though he thought he should at least give a cursory look at Chloe, the onetime mistress of Sumner Redstone and later Jack Rembert. Often times, he went back to interviewing people a second time around when he had second thoughts about them or when new information surfaced which warranted further questioning. He didn't feel the necessity to do that at this point.

Charles Stockley's phone just rang and rang. There was no voicemail, and no one picked up.

He looked at his watch. It was 5:30. He thought about going to his gym in West Palm a little earlier than usual just as his cell phone rang. It said *Savannah Investigations* on the display.

"Hello?"

"Charlie?" said a woman's voice that sounded familiar.

"Yes?"

"Hey, it's Jackie Farrell," she said. "Of Jackie and Ryder sleuth sister fame."

"What a nice surprise, good to hear from you, Jackie," Crawford said.

It had only been a day or two since he and Ott had last seen the sisters.

"So after we saw you we went back to our office in Savannah, having wrapped up our case in Charleston, but nothing much is happening here," Jackie said. "So lo and behold, Ryder told me about that football player who put up three hundred grand to solve that case of yours."

"Yeah, how 'bout that, but he's actually a baseball player."

"A very rich baseball player apparently," Jackie said. "So Ryder gets in my ear and starts talking about how her wardrobe could use some upgrades and her Jeep's on its last lap and yada-yada—"

"So, let me guess, you guys want to come down and solve the sucker? Make us look bad."

"No, hardly, and we'd never do it unless you guys were good with it. We just thought—"

"Hey, happy to have you, come on down."

"Are you sure you're okay with that?"

"Definitely, we'd love to have you guys on it. A couple of pros instead of a stampede of amateurs we're expecting. When were you thinking?"

"Tomorrow, if that's all right."

"Sure. It's only a little over a five-and-a-half-hour drive, but, of course, that's with lead foot Mort at the wheel going like a bat out of hell."

"You mean *Morton*."

Crawford laughed. "Oh, so you read that article in *USA Today* too?"

"Yup. 'Celebrated,' huh...nobody's ever called us that."

"When you've been at it as long as we have, guarantee you they'll call you something like that."

"Hope so." Jackie said. "Why don't we give you a call when we're an hour outside of Palm Beach?"

"Sounds good. Look forward to seeing you ladies."

"No one's ever called us that either."

THIRTY-FIVE

"Yeah, but Charlie, what if they solve it?" Ott asked after Crawford told him about his conversation with Jackie Farrell.

"You mean 'cause it would make us look like pikers?"

"Yeah, of course. I can just hear Rutledge now. 'So, let me get this straight, a couple of girls from Savannah come down here—'"

"It ain't gonna happen. It's not like we're gonna give 'em every little detail of the whole thing. You and I are gonna solve it."

"Well, then why'd you tell 'em to come down?"

"'Cause I liked them. Fun to have around."

"That's it?"

"Mort, I got a girlfriend."

The next morning Crawford called Charles Stockley again, the man on the opposing scavenger hunt team from Jack Rembert, David Balfour, and Silla Vander Poel, and this time Stockley answered.

"Good morning, Mr. Stockley," he said. "My name's Detective Crawford, Palm Beach Police, and I'm investigating the death of Jack

Rembert. I wondered if I could meet with you and ask you a few questions."

"What about?" Stockley asked, defensively.

"Well, we know that Mr. Rembert was killed during the scavenger hunt which you were a part of—"

"Killed. I thought he drowned?" Stockley said.

Crawford had assumed that by now word had gotten all around that it was definitely a homicide. The stories in the papers and on TV news had all made that clear.

"He did, but we know for a fact it was a homicide. Would you be available this morning?"

"Yes, but no more than fifteen minutes."

"That's all it will take. Say 11:00?"

"Okay. I live at 1197 North Lake Way."

"Okay, see you then."

An hour later Crawford drove up a brick driveway to a large grey-shingled house owned by Charles Stockley. A tall, skinny man wearing a New York Yankees ball cap was pruning a rose bush to the left of the front door. He turned and walked toward Crawford's car as Crawford got out.

"You the detective?"

"Yes, Detective Crawford," he said, putting out his hand.

Stockley made no effort to shake it. "Let's go inside, get out of the sun. I want to make this quick."

"That's fine," Crawford said, following Stockley inside.

Stockley led them into a vast family room off of a large immaculate kitchen where he sat down at a white granite-topped table. Crawford pulled up a chair opposite him.

"Go ahead," Stockley said, all business, glancing at his watch.

"I was told that you had a two-hundred-fifty thousand dollar bet with Jack Rembert that your team would win the scavenger hunt last week."

"Yes, why? Is that illegal or something?" Stockley asked with a frown.

"That's no concern of mine. It's been suggested, however, that the possibility of losing your bet might be a motive to stop Rembert from finding a game-winning clue at the docks."

Stockley's beady eyes zoomed in on Crawford. "Wait a minute...you're not really suggesting that to stop them from winning I had something to do with what happened to Rembert, are you?"

"No, I'm not," Crawford said, holding up his hands. "Look, Mr. Stockley, all I'm trying to do is solve a murder. To do that I ask a lot of people a lot of questions. You're just one of many, so please don't get defensive."

"Defensive? You come into my house and suggest I had something to do with what happened to Rembert and you expect me not to react," Stockley said, looking down at his watch. "You've got twelve more minutes."

"What was your first thought when you heard about the death of Rembert?"

"That's a stupid question. Of course, I was sorry about it, then felt terrible for his wife and his family."

"No thoughts about someone who might have wanted him dead."

This time Stockley actually stopped to think before he answered.

"Actually, something did occur to me now that I think about it."

"And what was that?"

"Well, I remember hearing about one of Jack's daughters going out with a...cop, or a fireman, or a mailman maybe. From Jupiter, I think. She met him on one of those dating sites that all the kids go on these days."

Crawford nodded.

"Anyway, after a while supposedly, the daughter told Jack that the guy asked her to marry him, and she accepted. Jack hit the roof and said no way in hell was his daughter going to marry a cop, or fireman, or mailman, whatever the hell he was. Threatened to cut her off. So what I heard was the guy—"

"The cop, fireman, mailman, or whatever."

"Yeah...that he threatened Jack."

"Threatened him? How so? What did he say?"

"I don't know exactly, but here's a guy making, whatever they make—forty, fifty thousand a year—and he sees his chance of marrying the daughter of a man worth hundreds of millions slipping away...I mean, hell, maybe he threatened to kill him?"

"But you don't know that for a fact?" Crawford said, amazed that it apparently hadn't dawned on Stockley that Crawford was, in fact, a cop himself. "You're just speculating?"

"True, I don't know it for a fact, but I can just imagine."

Crawford cocked his head. "I don't know, Mr. Stockley, that sounds like a bit of a reach, but I'll check it out."

Stockley shrugged. "Hey, you never know. Men in those professions looking at this as the big score, maybe" he said, then checked his watch. "Oh, wow, it's been fifteen minutes, but I must say this is kind of interesting. Trying to help you get to the bottom of this."

"And I must say, Mr. Stockley," Crawford said, tongue firmly in cheek, "how grateful I am to have you assist in my investigation."

"You're very welcome. I've actually got a little more time if you need—"

"Thanks, but I better be on my way...us cops gotta earn our forty or fifty thousand. Can't loaf on the job, you know."

CRAWFORD GOT A CALL FROM JACKIE FARRELL SHORTLY AFTER HE GOT back to the station at 11:45.

"Hey, Jackie," he answered. "Where are you guys?"

"About an hour away. We got going first thing this morning."

"Tell you what, why don't we meet you for lunch. You got GPS?"

"Sure do."

"Plug in 151 North County Road."

"What's that?"

"A place called Green's. Nothin' fancy, but I think you'll like it. I'll bring Mort."

"See you in an hour."

"See you then."

CRAWFORD CALLED OTT ON HIS CELL PHONE AND TOLD HIM ABOUT their lunch date. Ott said he had something else planned, but he'd break it.

Then Crawford called Dominica McCarthy. "Hey, you got any lunch plans?"

"I was planning to go to Publix and get a sub."

"Do that tomorrow. I got some new friends from Savannah I'd like you to meet."

"Sounds good. When?"

"Meet out back at 12:40."

"I'll be there."

DOMINICA, OTT, AND CRAWFORD GOT TO GREEN'S FIRST, AND TEN minutes later, the Farrell sisters showed up, with surprised looks on their faces when they saw Dominica.

Crawford made the introductions and the five looked at the menus and ordered.

"So Charlie told me on the way over that you're private detectives up in Savannah," Dominica said to Jackie and Ryder.

"Yup," Jackie said. "Also have an office in Charleston."

"I love those two cities," Dominica said.

"Oh, so you've been?" Jackie said.

"Yes, last year," Dominica said. "I loved the old houses and so many great restaurants."

"Which ones did you go to?" Ryder asked. "Do you remember?"

"Well, in Charleston there was one called High Cotton and then one in Savannah that was called Mrs....Somebody's Dining Room, do you remember, Charlie?"

"Oh sure," Jackie said. "Mrs. Wilkes Dining Room."

"Yes, exactly, that's it. We loved that place."

"Can't beat it," Ryder said. "So how long have you been a crime scene tech, Dominica?"

"Well, I started down in Miami and I've been here for a little over four years."

"It must be nice working with 'celebrated' detectives like Charlie and

Mort," said Ryder.

"Please, Morton," said Ott with a grin.

"Sorry, Morton," Ryder said.

"Yeah, they're pretty good," Dominica said.

"*Only* pretty good?" Ott said.

"I don't want to puff up your ego."

"So that guy putting up the reward, that was pretty amazing, huh?" Dominica said to Jackie and Ryder.

"Yes," Ryder said, "the money in gumshoeing isn't all it's cracked up to be. So we figured we'd come down here and go back home rich. I'm kinda kidding, but hey, it would be nice."

Dominica nodded as the waitress showed up with their food.

"Ew," Ryder said, frowning down at Crawford's sardine platter. "You really did order those greasy little fish, Charlie."

"You believe it?" Dominica said.

"Omega-3 fatty acids," Crawford said. "Really good for you."

"That's what he always says," said Dominica.

"I'm down with the tater tots," Ryder said, looking at his plate. "But, those smelly little things, yuck."

The five ate and swapped stories for the next forty minutes, then Jackie and Ryder said they wanted to explore Palm Beach a little since they'd never been there before. Ott said he wanted to walk off some of the Philly Cheese Steak bomb and extra fries he'd had, so Crawford and Dominica rode back to the station together.

As soon as they got in the car, Dominica turned to him with a quizzical look. "Are you totally clueless, Charlie?"

"What? What do you mean?"

"Any idiot could see that Jackie has a sneaker for you," she said. "And here you show up with me. I mean, *really*."

Crawford shrugged. "I had no idea."

"And you call yourself a detective. A 'celebrated' one at that."

"Okay, I'm getting a little sick of that 'celebrated' thing."

"Okay, well then how about *oblivious*."

That shrug again. "If the shoe fits, I guess."

THIRTY-SIX

"That was a bit of surprise," Jackie said getting into the passenger seat of Ryder's Jeep.

"What? All he did was dance with you once," said Ryder.

"I know but..."

"You know, but what?"

"I thought we made some kind of...connection."

"My dear, sweet naive sister," Ryder said, "guys like Charlie make connections with *all* women without even realizing it."

"I guess, I just..."

"*Just* what, you seem to be having problems finishing your sentences these days, girl."

"Fuck off."

Ryder laughed. "Good job, you finished that one just fine."

Gary, Chuck, and Manny found the address of Scott and Muffie Drexel, Jack Rembert's daughter and son-in-law, and drove up to their house.

Gary rang the doorbell and the three waited. Muffie opened the door and looked out at the three, unimpressed at what she saw. "Yes?"

"Mrs. Drexel?" asked Gary.

"Yes. Who are you?"

"My name is Gary Volynets, and these are my associates, Chuck and Manny. We're investigating the death of your father. May we come in?"

Muffie glanced down at Manny's big Q belt buckle and put up a hand. "No. Who are you?"

"We're working undercover, as I said, to try and solve your father's murder."

Muffie looked slightly more persuaded. "So you mean along with the Palm Beach detectives, Crawford and I-forget-the-other-one's name?"

"Ott," Manny said. "Mort Ott. Yes, we're working very closely with Charlie and Mort. Sharing leads and that kind of thing."

"Okay, well what do you want from me?" Muffie asked.

"May we come in?" Gary asked. "Maybe ask you some things Charlie and Mort may have neglected to ask."

"Ah, okay, I guess so," Muffie said. "My husband's working in the study. We can go into the living room. Do you have any badges or papers?"

"No, ma'am, as Gary said we're working undercover."

"Okay, well...come on in, I guess."

The three men followed her into the living room and sat down facing each other.

"Okay," Muffie said. "Go ahead and ask your questions."

Gary glanced at Manny. "You go first."

Manny, with his droopy face and clusters of nose hairs, mustered a lopsided smile. "Mrs. Drexel, sometimes we need to ask what you might consider personal questions, so please don't be offended if I ask you one."

"Ah, o-kay, go ahead."

"What year were you born?"

She frowned. "What year was I born? What does that have to do with anything?"

"You'll see. What year?"

"1998. Why is that relevant?"

Manny glanced at Gary who nodded. The nod seemed to have a secret meaning.

"It's relevant because in the year 1996 your mother, Carolyn Bessette, married your father, John Fitzgerald Kennedy, Junior."

Muffie's frown was immediate.

"And in 1998 you, their daughter, was born. Though it was kept secret."

Muffie looked like she wanted to either run or scream for her husband. "What in God's name are you talking about? That's the craziest thing I've ever heard. My father is not, was not, John Fitzgerald Kennedy, Junior."

"We expected you might deny it," said Manny.

"But your father, masquerading as one John Fitzgerald Rembert, died under mysterious circumstances which we believe might be at the hands of a cabal headed by George Soros and Bill Clinton."

Muffie sprang to her feet. "I've heard enough. Get out of here right now. Scott!"

Scott Drexel came out of the study with headphones on and eyed the three strangers. "What is it, Muffie? I'm on a call to one of my players..." He eyed the three men. "Who the hell are you?"

"We're here getting to the bottom of what happened to your father-in-law, John F. Kennedy, Junior," Manny answered.

Scott Drexel looked from one to the other in abject bewilderment and shook his head. "I don't know why you're here or why my wife let you lunatics in, but you must have dropped some mighty powerful drugs on the ride over," he said, then pointed to the door. "Now get the hell out of here and go back to the looney bin you escaped from."

———

Muffie Drexel called Crawford right away. "Hello, Mrs. Drexel."

She was livid. "Detective Crawford, three of your *associates* just left here and I want you to make sure they never, ever come back. Do you understand?"

"Calm down, Mrs. Drexel. 'Associates?' What do you mean by that? Who were they?"

"They said something about working with you. One's name was Gary, another one was Chuck, and I forget the third."

"Oh my God, and Manny. Had a long gray ponytail, right?"

"Yes. What is wrong with those men? They claimed I was John F. Kennedy, Junior's daughter."

"Mrs. Drexel, I assure you those men have nothing to do with the Palm Beach Police Department or law enforcement in general. I'm sorry they came to your house, and I assure you I will do whatever I can to have them cease and desist what they're doing."

"Thank you. The whole thing was just crazy."

"Do you happen to remember what kind of car they were driving, by any chance?"

"They parked on the road, not in my driveway," she said. "Come to think of it, I do remember now, they were in a white pick-up."

Uh-huh, thought Crawford, with a gun-rack in the back of the cab, no doubt.

THIRTY-SEVEN

CRAWFORD CALLED CHIEF NORM RUTLEDGE AND TOLD HIM WHAT Muffie Drexel had just reported. He suggested that Rutledge send a couple of uniform cops right away up to the area where the Drexels lived and see if they could find a security camera that caught an image of the license plate of the white truck. He also suggested that Rutledge put out a few patrol cars to be on the lookout for the truck, and if they found the men, to charge them with impersonating police officers, but more importantly, get them off the island of Palm Beach.

He called Muffie Drexel back and assured her that the three men would not bother her anymore and inferred they might be arrested when they were tracked down. Then, he asked her about the man her sister had almost married until her father stepped in and put an end to it.

"Oh, Bruce, he was such a lovely man. He would have been a great husband, but Sally told me he moved away after what happened. Somewhere out west, she said."

"And what did he do, for a job, I mean?"

"Um, let me think, either a carpenter or a plumber, as I recall. Why?"

"I was just curious."

OTT GOT THE CALL FROM A UNIFORMED COP WHO HAD JUST PULLED over the three men in the white pick-up.

"Oh, you mean, Larry, Moe, and Curly," he said, referring to the Three Stooges. "I'll be right there."

He thought about calling Crawford but didn't think they both needed to waste their time on the trio of nutters.

Ott saw a Crown Vic up ahead on South County Road with the white Ford truck in front of it. He pulled over behind the Vic, got out, and went up to the uniform behind the wheel of it.

"Hey, Jerry," Ott said. "What'd the Three Stooges have to say?"

The uniform rolled his eyes. "That they were within their rights and under Florida law could even go so far as to perform a citizen's arrest," he said, shaking his head.

"Oh, Christ, really?"

"What do you want me to do?"

"Nothin', man, I'll take it from here," Ott said, leaning forward and patting the uniform on the shoulder. "Nice collar."

The uniform laughed and started his engine. "Good luck."

Ott nodded and walked up to the white pick-up. Manny was at the wheel, Gary was smoking a cigarette, and Chuck was asleep and snoring.

"We meet again," Ott said.

Manny looked up at him, all beady eyes and abundant nose hairs. "Hi, Mort."

"All right, boys," Ott said, motioning to Chuck. "Hey, wake doofus up, will ya?"

Gary gave Chuck an elbow. "Huh, what?" said Chuck, blinking his eyes.

"Listen up, all three of you," Ott said. "From now on there's gonna be no more asking anyone questions, no harassing people, no citizens arrests, no nothin' in this town 'cause you clowns are going over the Southern Bridge right now and never coming back to Palm Beach. I ever see you again you're gonna spend a few days in jail. Maybe longer. You got it?"

The three nodded their heads almost in perfect unison.

"Okay, now get the hell out of here. I see you again and you're in big trouble."

Ott walked away, got back in his car, and went back to the station.

AT JUST PAST SIX, OTT HEADED HOME TO WEST PALM. HE REGRETTED not telling Manny, Gary, and Chuck that he didn't want to ever see them in West Palm either. Ott made a right off of Dixie Highway onto Edgeworth Drive where he lived in a one-story, cement block ranch-style house. He wasn't much of a gardener, but he kept his patch of grass on the front and rear nice and green and took great pride in his healthy sea grapes, Carolina jessamines, and Southern wax myrtles. He noticed as he drove in that they could use some water. He parked, went to the side of his house, and turned on the hose. He hit the spray nozzle and started to give his plants and flowers a good watering. He had noticed, or thought he had noticed, how some of them seemed to respond almost immediately. How some would go from a little limp and droopy to straighter and taller.

Out of the corner of his eye, he saw a black car pause in front of his driveway, then suddenly it drove in just as Ott saw something emerge from the driver's side window. In a hail of gun fire, bullets ripped into the ground in front of him, his plants and finally hit him several times. He went down, the hose still in his hand.

CRAWFORD GOT A CALL FROM A WEST PALM COP HE AND OTT HAD worked with once. He knew by how the cop shouted his name, then loudly identified himself that something was wrong. Really wrong. "Charlie, it's Randy Gilder, your partner's been shot. They're taking him to Good Sam."

Crawford could hear a siren in the background.

"How bad is he?" Crawford asked, tensing up.

"I don't know for sure," Gilder said. "He took one to the gut and another in the neck or shoulder. I'm not sure which. Ambulance to Good Sam just left."

"Happened at his house?"

"Roger that."

"I'm on my way," Crawford said. "I'll call you later to get details."

"You got it," Gilder said. "Hope he's gonna be okay."

"Me too," Crawford said.

Crawford was still at the station. He ran out of his office to the back where his car was parked, got in, and started the engine. Then, tires burning rubber, got onto South County heading for the middle bridge. He put his flasher on the top of his car and hit the button for his siren. He was going sixty by the time he got to the bridge. He skidded around the corner after the bridge and turned onto Flagler Drive. There was still a lot of post-rush-hour traffic, so he had to pick his way around cars, at one point going into the southbound lane and narrowly missing a car coming straight at him.

Three minutes later he wheeled into the Emergency Room driveway of Good Samaritan hospital. He had been here more times than he would have liked in the past. When Rose Clarke had been intentionally mowed down by a hit and run driver. When his brother, Cam, had clipped a home-less man accidentally after too many drinks. When Ott's girlfriend, at the time, had been tortured mercilessly and left for dead.

And now Ott himself.

Crawford slammed on the brakes, jumped out of his car, and ran in the Emergency Room door. He held up his wallet to two women at the desk. "Crawford, Palm Beach Police, where's the gun shot vic who just came in?"

One of them pointed and Crawford saw an open room with four or five doctors or emergency rescue medics clustered around a table.

He rushed over to them. One of the medics held up her hands to Craw-ford and headed him off.

Crawford flashed her his badge. "He's my partner. How's he doing?"

"He sustained two bullet wounds, one to the stomach, another to the shoulder. Somehow, he's still conscious."

Crawford stepped to her left, trying to bypass her, and get closer to where Ott lay.

"Detective! Stop!" the medic said.

Crawford was just a few feet from the table and looked down at Ott. Ott saw him and started to smile but winced in pain suddenly.

A doctor turned to Crawford. "Please," he said sharply, "you have to leave *now!*"

Crawford looked down at Ott and could have sworn Ott winked at him.

Then his eyes shut, and he was out cold.

THIRTY-EIGHT

CRAWFORD DIDN'T KNOW WHO TO CALL FIRST. ALL HE KNEW WAS, HE wasn't going anywhere for a while. Good Samaritan Hospital was going to be home for the foreseeable future. He knew Ott had an older sister, who he was very close to. She had never married or moved away from Cleveland. Her first name started with a K. Katherine, no, Karen, no, Kimberley... shorter. Then he remembered. It was Kay. Kay Ott. It was about the shortest name one could have, a close second being Mort Ott. Their parents apparently believed in brevity. He was going to try to track her down first because, though he knew Ott's mother was still alive, he was pretty sure she had remarried, and he didn't know her new name. He just remembered, having heard Ott mention it once, it had a lot of Z's and C's in it. But when he reached Kay, she'd, of course, know. He glanced back at where Ott lay in the middle of all ten hands that were ministering to him.

Crawford shook his head. *Poor bastard.*

He went back to the emergency room desk, where the two women were seated.

"Excuse me, is there any place where I can talk privately and not disturb people?" he asked.

"Yes, sir," one of the women said. "Halfway down the hallway," she pointed, "there's a couch and two chairs. No one's there at the moment."

He smiled and nodded. "Thanks."

He walked there, sat in one of the chairs, and glanced at his watch. It was 6:45 p.m. He went to Google and typed in Kay Ott, Cleveland. Five minutes later, by process of elimination, he was sure he had found the right Kay Ott. There was only one other. He dialed the number and a woman picked up after the third ring.

"Hello?"

"Hi, this is Charlie Crawford. Are you the Kay Ott related to Mort?"

"Yes, Charlie, I know you work with Mort. Is he okay?"

"I'm sorry to say, Kay, but Mort's been shot. Twice actually. But I think he's going to be all right." He decided not to tell her he had winked at him. After all, Crawford wasn't a hundred percent sure he actually had.

"Oh my God, oh my God. Where? Where was he shot?" she asked.

He wasn't sure if she was asking what part of his body or what was the location of where he was shot, so he answered both. "He was shot in the stomach and shoulder, at his house in West Palm."

"Is he in a great deal of pain?" Kay asked.

"I'm sure they gave him sedatives or painkillers."

"I want to come see him right away...with my mom."

"I would wait a bit. You don't want to come if he's going to be unconscious the whole time. And Kay, do you have your mom's phone number?"

She read it to him. "She should be there now unless she's out grocery shopping."

"Thank you," Crawford said. "You know Mort as well as just about anyone. He's a tough old bird."

"Thank you, Charlie," Kay said. "I really appreciate you calling."

"Just give me ten minutes on the phone with your mother, then I'm sure you'll want to give her a call."

"Will do. See you in Florida," Kay said. "Mort's told us a lot about you."

"Don't believe a word," Crawford joked. "Tell me you mother's name again, please?"

"Marie. Marie Kowalczyk."

"Thanks." He clicked off. Sounded like maybe only one C and one Z. He dialed the number. She answered quickly too.

"Hi, Mrs. Kowalczyk?"

"Yes?"

"This is Charlie Crawford, Mort's partner in Palm Beach," he said. "I'm sorry to have to tell you but Mort's been shot. I think he's going to be okay, but he was shot in the stomach and the shoulder."

The poor woman started howling, shouting *no, no, no* over and over. Then, "Oh my poor boy, are you sure he's going to be all right?" Then she burst into another round of wailing.

"I think he is. I'll know more soon. This just took place a short while ago."

"I have to come see him. Right away," she said, gasping in short breaths.

Crawford guessed she probably was not much of a traveler and might be lost in an airport. "Can I make you a reservation, ma'am? And I might be able to arrange for you to get a ride to the airport. Maybe first thing tomorrow morning?"

"Oh, no, tonight. I must see my boy right away."

Crawford thought for a moment. "Let me see what I can come up with. I'm going to hang up now, but I'll call you back as soon as I have something."

"Please, Charlie, I need to see my son."

"I understand, Mrs. Kowalczyk. I'll call you back as soon as possible."

"Thank you."

Crawford first dialed Bettina on her cell as she'd have gone home by now.

"Hey Charlie," she answered, perkily. "What's up?"

"Mort's been shot. I need you to see if you can get a flight from Cleveland to here for two. For his mom and sister. Probably too late for tonight but first thing tomorrow morning."

"I'm on it. Oh my God, how's he doing?" Bettina said calmly.

"Shot twice. I think he'll live."

"Oh, the poor guy."

"I know. Gotta go."

His next call took a lot longer. Actually, it was a series of calls.

He knew that all cops—and undoubtedly Cleveland cops—responded quickly to the phrase, *officer down*, and would do their damnedest to accommodate a fallen brother. He got bounced around a little when he called what seemed like a main Cleveland Police number, but after fifteen minutes or so got on with a take-charge Sergeant named Barnes, who said he knew Ott when he was on the force there and could arrange transportation to get his mother and sister to the airport, even if he had to drive them there himself. Crawford thanked him and said he'd get back in touch a little later that night with a solid plan.

His third call was to Chief Norm Rutledge. "Have you heard about Mort yet?" Crawford asked when Rutledge picked up.

"Yeah, just heard. How's he doing?"

"As good as a guy with two slugs in him can be doing."

"Stomach and shoulder, right?"

"Yeah, I'm at Good Sam."

"I'm on my way," Rutledge said.

"See you here."

That was a surprise since ostensibly Rutledge and Ott had a somewhat strained relationship. Though sometimes, Crawford thought, Rutledge faked it—that is, gave the impression of being just barely able to tolerate some of Ott's somewhat unorthodox ways of performing certain police procedures. Not to mention, Ott having a somewhat loosey goosey style. And sometimes seeming to be kind of a wise-ass, and certainly not as serious as Rutledge might like him to be. But Rutledge also knew—though he might not admit it—that Ott was every bit as smart, intuitive, and hardworking as Crawford. He valued him for that and the fact that he was one of his men.

A few minutes later Crawford got a call on his cell. The display said, *Trianon,* which was the condominium building where Crawford lived.

"Hello?"

"Hey Charlie, it's Mel Purcell at the Trianon."

Purcell was the manager.

"Hey, Mel, what's up?"

"Hey listen, there was a guy here at the building a little earlier I thought you should know about."

"What about him?"

"He was parked in a car near the front entrance. Just sitting there, his engine idling for like an hour. Finally, Donny," a member of the building staff who manned the front desk during the day, "went out and said something like, 'Can I help you?' Guy had on shades and one of those bucket hats pulled down low. Donny said it was like he was trying to hide his identity. Guy said, 'I'm a friend of Charlie Crawford. Just dropped by to see him.' Donny told me, the guy just seemed kind of suspicious to him, and a couple minutes later, he drove off. I just thought you'd want to know."

"What time was this, Mel?"

"Around six-fifteen, six-thirty."

Right around the time Ott was shot, Crawford thought. So maybe what happened was the man went from the Trianon to Ott's house on Edgeworth Street. It was no more than five minutes away.

"And what color was the car?"

"Black."

"Thanks, Mel, I appreciate it," Crawford said. "Will you tell the staff that if that guy, or anyone suspicious looking, comes around again to call me right away? And also, try to get a shot of his license plate."

"You got it, Charlie. Will do."

"Thanks," Crawford said and clicked off.

The shooter could only have one motive, Crawford thought: Take out the cops who were hot on his heels and maybe, getting closer to taking him down on the Rembert case. That MO had been around for a long time, but it came with a big-time risk. That cops would redouble their efforts if one of their own went down. Fact was, a psycho in New York, back when Crawford was on the job up there, had laid in wait for him on a stoop under his Upper West Side apartment back in 2015. It was the first guy he ever shot. Come to think of it, in the gut, just like Ott. He lived.

Bettina called back to say that she had booked Ott's mother and sister on an early morning flight on Spirit Air that landed in Fort Lauderdale just after 10:30 a.m.

"I'll pick 'em up," Crawford said.

"I can, if you want," Bettina volunteered.

He thought about how busy he'd be.

"You know what, I might just take you up on that."

"Good. 'Cause that way I get to see Mort."

"I hope he'll be conscious by then," Crawford said, as call waiting clicked in on his phone. He recognized the Cleveland number. "I gotta hop."

"Sergeant Barnes?"

"Yeah, it's me. I'm off tomorrow, so I can give those ladies a lift to Hopkins Airport."

"You're a good man," Crawford said and gave Barnes the flight information Bettina had secured.

"How's he doin'? Your partner?"

"I've been on the phone since I got off with you," Crawford said. "I'm going to go check on him now."

"Tell him his hometown is pullin' for him," Barnes said. "I don't know if you knew, but he was like cop-of-the-year up here."

"I knew that, and I'll definitely tell him what you said."

Crawford put his phone in his pocket, stood up, and walked to where Ott was being cared for by the medical team. This time he wasn't going to attempt to get close up but try to get someone to give him an update on how Ott was doing.

Just as he got to the Emergency Room door, in front of the reception desk, the sliding glass door opened and in walked Dominica McCarthy and Rose Clarke. Dominica looked like she had come straight from work and was wearing her blue nylon jacket that said *Forensics* on the back and a ball cap with *CSI* above the brim. Crawford had once bought her a T-shirt that he found on an internet site that said in big bold letters, *BASI-CALLY A DETECTIVE*, which she wore with pride, everywhere but at the station.

Rose Clarke, real estate agent to the stars and billionaires, was dressed in a stylish beige designer suit which accented her curves as much as Dominica's bulky outfit did not. But most people knew, especially Crawford, that Dominica had a Ms. Universe figure. Rose was not only a good friend of Dominica, but of Crawford and Ott as well.

"Hey, Charlie," Dominica said, deep concern in her voice. "How's he doin'?"

Crawford gave both women kisses on the cheeks. "I was just about to try to find out," he said, then to Rose. "Thanks for coming."

"Of course," Rose said, then pointing at the emergency room off the main lobby. "Is that him over there?"

Crawford nodded. "I got a feeling they got their best people on it."

"They better," Rose said.

A nurse turned and saw the three coming toward the room where Ott was being cared for.

"Excuse me," Crawford said, raising a hand to her.

She frowned but walked over to them. "You can't get any closer. Would you please wait in the visitors' room?"

"Sure," Crawford said. "But can you just give us a quick update?"

"We're all good friends of his," Rose said.

"Well, he's lost a lot of blood," she said. "The bullet in his shoulder passed through, the one in his esophagus is still there."

"But he's going to be all right, right?" Dominica said. "I mean, his life's not in danger, is it?"

"No," the nurse said. "He strikes me as a very strong-willed man."

"Oh, you can say that again," Crawford said.

"Phew," said Rose as the nurse walked away.

"Thank God," Dominica said, smiling at Crawford. "We need that guy around...to make you look good."

"Amen to that," Crawford said.

Next came Norm Rutledge in one of his trademark brown suits looking solemn as he approached Crawford. "How's he doing?" He asked Crawford, nodding at Dominica and Rose.

"He's definitely gonna make it. One bullet passed through his shoulder, another one still in his esophagus."

Rutledge nodded, looking relieved. "What do we know about how it went down?" he asked Crawford.

"Just that he got ambushed in front of his house," Crawford said. "I'm gonna call back the first cop on scene and get details. I think the shooter might have been targeting me too."

"You're kidding?" said Rutledge.

"No. Tell you about it later."

Rutledge nodded. "You get a chance to speak to any family members yet?"

"Yeah, his mother and sister. They're flying in tomorrow morning."

Rutledge nodded. "So you think the shooter thought you were getting too close?"

"I don't know what else it could be."

Rutledge shook his head. "I never really understood that motive."

"What do you mean?"

"Well, they take you out, then there's gonna be twice as many men on the case."

"Yeah, I hear you."

Rutledge looked over at the cluster of bodies around Ott. "Is he conscious?"

"Last thing I knew he was out."

"I just hope he's not in a lot of pain when he comes to," Rutledge said.

That was quite a statement coming from Rutledge.

"Yeah, me too," Crawford said, and the two women nodded. "Well, I'm gonna give that cop a call."

Rutledge nodded.

"We'll go into the visitors' room," Dominica said and pointed to the room that was one-third filled with anxious-looking people.

Crawford nodded and walked to a corner where he could get some privacy. He looked up the number for Randy Gilder, the West Palm cop who had called him on an hour earlier and dialed.

"Hey, Charlie," Gilder answered. "How's he doing?"

"He's gonna make it," Crawford said. "So tell me what you know."

"Okay, a call came in from the next-door neighbor who saw the whole thing," Gilder said. "A black car pulled into Mort's driveway and a few seconds later the neighbor saw Mort go down while he was watering his plants. I got there two minutes later, and he was on his back on the lawn, a bunch of people around him. One was pressing a towel or something up against his stomach. He had a hose still in his hand when I got there, bleeding like a son-of-a-bitch. I took my shirt off and shoved it up against his shoulder. A few minutes later the emergency response team got there and took over. So I got the name and number of a woman who saw it happen if you want it."

"Yeah, sure do."

Gilder gave him the information. "So that's about it. Any clue who it might have been?"

"If I knew, I'd know who did my murders."

"I hear you...well, give him my best, will you?"

"Sure will. Thanks."

Crawford dialed the woman who had witnessed the shooting.

"Hello," answered a woman.

"Mrs. Colucci?"

"Yes."

"My name is Detective Crawford, your neighbor Mort Ott's partner."

"Oh, yes, how is he?"

"I think he's going to be all right. He's at Good Samaritan Hospital now. Officer Gilder gave me your name and number. Can you tell me exactly what you saw?"

"Yes, of course. I was looking out my window doing dishes and saw this black car pull into Mort's driveway as he was watering his flowers. I saw something in the driver's side window, which I figured later musta been a gun, and a few seconds later Mort fell to the ground."

"Did you, by any chance, see the car's license plate?" Crawford asked, knowing that was a very long shot.

"Sorry."

"What about...do you know what kind of a car it was?"

"No, I don't really know cars, but it looked like a nice one, a fancy one. An SUV. When the driver put it in reverse, and turned back onto Edgeworth, I did notice something on the back of it."

"What was it? Do you know?"

"I think it was one of those bicycle rack things. But there was no bicycle on it."

Crawford flashed back to when Dominica had told him the same thing.

"And what color was it?"

"Black," she said. "When I saw that Mort was bleeding, I grabbed a towel from my bathroom and ran out to try to help."

"Thank you for that, Mrs. Colucci," Crawford said. "Is there anything else you can remember?"

"Um, I don't think so," she said. "Tell you the truth, the whole thing was kind of a blur. But, thank God, the policeman and the medics got there so quickly."

"Well, thank you very much. If you have any more thoughts on it, don't hesitate to call. In the meantime, if I have any more questions, I'll ring you back."

"Okay, Detective. I'll be praying for Mort. He's such a nice man."

THIRTY-NINE

THAT BIKE RACK AGAIN, CRAWFORD THOUGHT AS HE JOINED THE other three in the visitors' room.

Rutledge looked up at him. "Anything?"

"Yeah, I think so. Probably was the same shooter who killed that guy I told you about down in Miami," Crawford said, then to Dominica. "It was a black SUV with a bicycle rack on the back."

She nodded. "Gotta be the same guy."

"So what's your next play?" Rutledge asked.

"I don't know yet. There's a lot to process."

"Is there anything I can do?" Dominica asked.

"Maybe," Crawford said. "I'm sure the West Palm crime scene techs are at Mort's house now. Maybe you could contact them later. I'm curious to know how many shots there were. Down in Miami, the shooter fired about twenty shots from pretty close range and just hit the vic five times."

"Sounds like a real shitty shot," Rutledge said.

"Yeah, that's what I'm thinking," Crawford said.

"So probably not a pro?"

"That's my guess. But I don't know where it gets us."

Rutledge shrugged. "I don't know either."

"I bet Mort would have a theory."

RUTLEDGE AND CRAWFORD TALKED SHOP WHILE DOMINICA AND ROSE
went to get the four something to eat from a nearby Thai restaurant.

"So who do you want to sub for Mort?" Rutledge asked Crawford.

They were seated next to a Hispanic family, which consisted of a man
and a woman and two young sons. The mother had what looked like dried
tears and smudged make-up below her eyes and the husband had been
locked in a 1000-yard stare ever since they got there. The boys were
huddled together playing a computer game. The rest of the people in the
room were quietly talking or napping fitfully.

"I haven't had time to give that any thought," said Crawford.

"Well, you're going to need somebody."

"I agree. Maybe Shaw."

"He'd be good," Rutledge said. "Or what about Alarcon?"

Crawford nodded. "I don't know what it's going to be like without Ott."

"I hear you...something tells me he's gonna want to get back on the case
as soon as he can walk. Something also tells me I'm going to have to tell him
to sit it out for a while."

"Yeah, but he could work from the station."

Rutledge shook his head. "You know Ott. The man can't sit still."

"All right. I think I'll go with Shaw. You want to tell him or want
me to?"

"I'll tell him. Then I'll have him give you a call to coordinate things."

Crawford nodded. "You do know that Ott's size eight and a half
Skechers are going to be impossible to fill, right?"

"Yeah, I know. But don't tell him I said so," Rutledge said grudgingly.

A few minutes later Dominica and Rose came in with bags of food.

Rose held up one of the bags. "Best Thai food in Florida."

"I never had their stuff before," Rutledge said.

"You're in for a treat," Dominica said as she sat down and opened
the bag.

"Here you go, Norm, one Unagi Don for you," Dominica said, "whatever that may be."

"Sushi," Rutledge said.

"And one duck pad thai for you," Rose said to Crawford, taking the cardboard box out of her bag.

"Thanks," Crawford said, glancing at the Spanish man whose faraway gaze had shifted to him.

"Smells so good, doesn't it?" Rose said.

Rutledge nodded, took off the plastic top and dug in with his chopsticks.

"You know, I'm not really that hungry," Crawford said, standing and walking over to the Spanish family. He handed the box to the mother. "You guys look hungry. This is really good."

The woman looked up at him, as the two boys smiled in anticipation. "Are you sure?"

"Come on, ma," the older of the two boys said.

"Well, thank you very much," the woman said, and Crawford handed her the box.

"Maybe you guys would like some spring rolls, too?" Dominica said holding them up.

The older boy nodded and smiled.

Dominica stood, walked over to him, and handed him the spring rolls.

"What do you say?" the mother said.

"Thank you very much," the older boy said, and his younger brother nodded eagerly.

"One for each of you," Dominica said.

———

RUTLEDGE WOLFED DOWN HIS SUSHI, THEN GOT TO HIS FEET.

"Okay, well, you guys hold down the fort," he said. "If Ott comes to when you're here, tell him I expect him at his desk tomorrow morning at eight."

Crawford looked at Dominica and rolled his eyes.

"I saw that," Rutledge said, taking out his wallet, "who do I owe for the food?"

Rose held up a hand. "It's on me, Norm."

"You sure?"

Rose nodded.

"Well, thanks, that's very nice of you," Rutledge said, turning to Crawford and Dominica. "I'll see you at the station."

Crawford nodded. "You're gonna call Shaw, right?"

Rutledge nodded and walked away.

"What's he gonna call Shaw about?" Dominica asked.

"Filling in for Mort."

"Nobody can."

"He knows that."

AN HOUR LATER, AROUND 9:30 P.M., DOMINICA AND ROSE GOT UP TO leave.

"How much longer are you gonna be here?" Dominica asked Crawford.

"I don't know, a while."

"All right," she said, bending down to give him a kiss. "See you tomorrow."

Rose did the same. "If you see him, give him my love," she said.

"I will."

"Thank you for the food," the Spanish woman said with a wide smile.

"You're very welcome," Rose said.

The two walked toward the sliding glass doors. Dominica turned and gave him a wave.

A few minutes later, Crawford went up to the reception desk and asked where Ott had been moved to.

The woman said he was in a room on the third floor but was still unconscious and couldn't be visited yet.

He thanked her and went back to where he had been sitting.

He looked at his watch a little later. It was just past 10:30. He closed his eyes, trying to take a nap but couldn't fall asleep. His mind flashed back to a series of incidents in cases that Ott and he had worked. A few of them brought smiles to his face. He looked at his watch again. It was 11:15. He had an idea. Probably a bad one. But, what the hell.

He walked up to the reception desk again. This time just one woman was there.

He smiled at her. "This may be a dumb question, but if I paid you, could I get a room for the night? Preferably on the third floor."

She shot him what was, unmistakably, an *are you out of your mind?* look.

"Are you—" she started. "No, sir, we can't do that, but the Ben is just down Flagler."

The Ben was an upscale hotel that had opened a few years ago.

"I'll pay you three hundred dollars," he said, knowing his offer was essentially a bribe.

"Sir, are you trying to get me fired?" she said, the heat rising. "That is completely unauthorized."

He put up his hands. "Okay, okay," he said, "just thought I'd ask."

He walked away. He could imagine the woman telling her co-workers, *You'll never believe what this guy tried to get me to do....*

He sat down and the Hispanic woman smiled at him. He smiled back.

Then he stood and walked to the sliding glass doors. He got into his car and drove back to his condominium at the Trianon. As he drove in, he looked around for the black SUV with the bicycle rack even though he knew it was highly unlikely its driver would be there again. He went up to his seventh-floor condo, stripped off his clothes, and got into the shower. He stayed in the shower longer than usual, toweled off, and got into a new set of clothes. He took a pillow off his bed along with his white comforter, walked out of the condo, got on the elevator, stopped at the ground floor, and went to his car.

He drove back to Good Samaritan Hospital and went through the sliding glass doors with his pillow and comforter in hand.

The woman from before looked at him suspiciously.

"This isn't unauthorized, is it?" He said, holding up the pillow.

"You're fine, sir," she said. "Sweet dreams."

He went back to the chair where he had been sitting. The Hispanic family was no longer there.

He didn't have sweet dreams, but instead he had one, in particular, that was quite disturbing.

He and Ott were in their Crown Vic going over the bridge at Southern when suddenly, with no warning, the bridge collapsed. They splashed into the Intracoastal and started to sink. Crawford had hit his head on the dashboard and was woozy. Next thing he knew, Ott had his arm around him and was pulling him out the driver's side window. They came to the surface gasping for air and, a few minutes later, washed up on a beach on the east side of the Intracoastal.

"You okay?" Ott asked him and Crawford noticed a large bandage around his shoulder.

"Yeah, I'm fine," Crawford said, though he had swallowed a couple mouthfuls of dirty Intracoastal water. "Where are we?"

"I don't know," Ott said, getting to his feet and looking around. "Holy shit, you're not going to believe this."

"What?"

"We're at fucking Mar-a-Lago."

Crawford woke up at that point and just shook his head.

He looked at his watch. It was 3:30 a.m. He was tempted to sneak up to the third floor and check on Ott, but the woman at the desk was giving him the suspicious eye again. He adjusted the pillow and pulled the comforter over him and went back to sleep.

HE WOKE UP TO THE WELCOME SIGHT OF DOMINICA LOOMING ABOVE him. She had just tugged at his sleeve.

"Come on, big boy, rise and shine."

"Jesus, what time is it?" he said, looking down at his watch. It was 7:05. "How'd you know—"

"I just knew," Dominica said, raising a Dunkin' Donuts bag. "And I got you your breakfast of champions."

He didn't need to ask: an extra dark large coffee with two blueberry donuts.

"I got you three since you didn't have dinner," she said. "So how'd you sleep?"

He smiled at her. "I'll take a bed with you in it, any day of the week."

She laughed. "So eat your breakfast. In the meantime, I'll see if we can check on Mort."

"He's on the third floor," Crawford said, then lowered his voice, "let's just go up there."

Dominica frowned. "Are you sure?"

He nodded. "They're not gonna give us permission and I gotta see him."

CRAWFORD ATE THE THREE DONUTS RAVENOUSLY AND DRANK THE coffee, then looked up at Dominica. "You ready," he asked, flipping his head to his right, "let's take one of those elevators over there."

The elevator bank was on the opposite end of the large open area and quite far from the reception desk. Crawford waited until a man came in and started talking to the receptionist at the front desk.

"Let's go," he said, and the two walked quickly to the elevator.

They got into the elevator and Crawford pushed the button for the third floor. "Let's hope at this hour they don't have a full nurse crew."

Dominica nodded as the elevator stopped at the third floor. The door opened and Crawford stuck his head out. No one was in sight. He motioned for Dominica to follow him down the hallway. They looked at the handwritten names on cardboard rectangles on the closed doors. *Brown... Lelchuk...Sanchez...*he wondered if Sanchez was related to the Hispanic family from last night...then *Ott.*

Dominica's eyes brightened, as Crawford glanced down the hallway and pushed the door open.

And there was Ott, flat on his back, his eyes were open, staring up at the ceiling. He had a drip bag next to his bed and it led to his right arm where the IV was taped. There was a tube going down his throat and another one in his nose.

Crawford and Dominica walked over to him and looked down at him. "Oh, my God," Ott said, then coughed, clearly in pain.

"Don't talk," Crawford said to Ott's smiling face.

Ott nodded.

"How you doin'?" Crawford said. "Hand signals or just nod."

Nothing at first, then Ott slowly raised his hand and gave him a thumbs-up.

"That's what we want to hear," Dominica said.

Ott half-nodded.

"They get that bullet out of your old carcass yet?" Crawford asked.

Ott did his best to shrug.

"Well, look, we just wanted to see how you were doing," Crawford said, then decided to steal Rutledge's joke. "We expect you back at the station later today."

Ott smiled.

Crawford leaned down and was about to pat Ott on his good shoulder but thought better of it. "Good luck, old buddy. We just wanted to see you."

A tear appeared in Ott's eye as he slowly nodded.

Dominica leaned down and kissed him softly on the cheek. "Get better, Mort."

FORTY

Rob Shaw was in Crawford's office facing him.

"So he didn't know whether they took out the bullet in his gut or not?" Shaw asked.

"Esophagus to be exact," said Crawford. "I think it's safe to say that he was pretty drugged up when we saw him."

"Tough old bastard probably be back before we know it."

Crawford just nodded. He hoped so.

"All right, so I'm gonna give you the down and dirty on our subject," Crawford said, seeing Shaw's iPad in his lap. "You're gonna want to take some notes."

"Okay, fire away, I'm a fast typer."

"So, in no particular order, our suspects..."

Suspect number one: Scott Drexel, Rembert's son-in-law and agent at Rembert Sports Management, not the sharpest tool in the proverbial shed or the most ambitious guy around. But maybe looking to assume some of Rembert's jocks and take a giant leap up in tax bracket. Plus, he got cited for punching a guy over a fender bender. Anger management issues?

Two: Del Lewis, Rembert's right-hand man. Obvious motive—take over the whole operation and Rembert's prized list of athletes whose salaries add up to close to two billion dollars. Claims he was happy making the money he was making with Rembert running the show, but I'm not sure I buy that.

Three: Weezie Gifford, Rembert's girlfriend who thought he was going to divorce his wife and marry her. Also, motive would be a big jump in bank account balance and lifestyle, not to mention jewelry, wardrobe, you name it. Told me she'd be fine without all that stuff. Once again, not sure I buy it. Oh, also, almost forgot, she's got a rock on her finger that Rembert gave her and was trying to get back after he cut her loose. Supposedly worth 750K.

Four: A very long, long shot. Daryl Boone, head coach of the Jacksonville Jaguars. Rembert repped him and supposedly they had a pretty rocky relationship. Among other things, Rembert claimed he was due two and a half million for getting Boone's brother a big job with the Green Bay Packers. Boone said it was bullshit, that his brother already knew top management there and Rembert had nothing to do with it. I'd call him one in a hundred, if that.

Five: Rembert's other daughter, Sally Hemmes, who secretly blames Rembert for her whole unhappy life. What happened was, she was going to marry a guy, a plumber or something like that, and Rembert put the kibosh on it. Said he'd disinherit her. So she called it off and has had a series of bad relationships ever since. But hiring a hitter for her father, then killing the hitter, then shooting Mort, probably way above her pay grade.

Six: Robert Smallwood, ex-player for the Chiefs and the Bills and now an agent down in Boca. Rembert stole a bunch of his football players right out from under him. Resulted in him getting fired from a big job he had with the agent, Drew Rosenhaus. Went from very high on the hog to no job, no boat, no big house, and no more private jet rides. Interviewed him, liked him, unlikely.

Seven: A guy named Mark Shuman, whose wife Rembert was screwing. Claims he and his old lady had an open marriage and it was no big deal to him. Mort said he was pretty convincing. I'd put him way down on the list, two hundred to one shot.

And finally, suspect number eight: A Russian named Stanislav Dalya-

gin. *Owns a boat that's at least three football fields long. It was moored down at the docks here when Rembert was killed. Motive: Rembert was screwing his girlfriend, who's a six-foot four black Russian basketball player name Anoushka something. Don't think so. Two hundred to one too.*

Shaw shook his head. "Jesus, Charlie, how'd this guy have any time for agenting when he spent half his life boffing chicks?"

"That's a damn good question."

"And also what about Rembert's wife? With all his fucking around, wouldn't that be motive enough for her?"

"Yeah, I hear you. But apparently, she just got to the point where she didn't care what he did. Lived a completely separate life from him even though they lived under the same roof."

"I got ya."

"All right, so like I said before, we gotta find the guy in the black SUV with the bicycle rack."

"But we don't know whether it was a Mercedes, an Audi, or a Beamer? Just something fancy, right?"

"Yeah, well, that's what I need you to find out. There's gotta be some security cam that picked up the shooter's car. Either at or near the Trianon, or where Ott lives on Edgeworth. Take a few guys with you and canvass those areas top to bottom."

Shaw nodded. "Will do."

"So the best thing to find is, obviously, the plate number, but if you can't get that then maybe the make of the bicycle rack."

"I gotcha, so then we can find out who sells 'em in the area."

"Yeah, or if it was ordered direct or on Amazon, then maybe we can find out who bought one in the area."

"I'm on it," Shaw said, "anything else?"

"Nah, that's the key. Find out that info and we got our killer and Ott's shooter," Crawford said, then snapped his fingers. "Oh yeah, find out what kind of car each one of our suspects drives."

"Of course, why didn't I think of that?"

Well, for starters, you ain't Ott.

CRAWFORD CALLED BETTINA WHO WAS MEETING OTT'S MOTHER AND sister at the Fort Lauderdale airport. She said the flight was on time and had just landed and she was waiting for them at baggage claim.

"When you go to Good Sam, find out what the story is with Mort having visitors, will you? They might be just letting family see him at first. Find out when I can see him, please."

"Will do," Bettina said. "I'm hoping I can see him with his mother and sister."

LATER THAT MORNING, DOMINICA CALLED AND SAID SHE HAD HAD A long conversation with the crime scene tech who had investigated Ott's shooting at his house on Edgeworth.

"As best as she can tell, there were at least twelve shots fired. All around Mort, including a few into the side of his house."

"All right. I think this is unnecessary but see if the slugs match up to the ones down in Miami."

"I was going to do that," she said, "but why do you think it's unnecessary?"

"Just 'cause I know they will."

"Understood."

Crawford thought for a second. "Bottom line is the shooter can't shoot for shit. Which again, backs up my theory that he definitely wasn't a pro. By the way, thanks."

"You got it," Dominica said. "You'll let me know when Mort can have visitors, right?"

"I will."

It suddenly occurred to Crawford that he hadn't told Jackie and Ryder Farrell about the shooting. So he dialed the number he had for Jackie Farrell.

"Hello, Charlie," she said. "I was just about to call you."

"I have some bad news," Crawford said. "Mort was shot twice last night," he heard Jackie gasp, "but the good news is he's going to be okay. I went to his room at the hospital this morning and he was conscious."

"Oh, thank God," she said, then he heard her say to Ryder, "Mort was shot last night, but he's okay."

He heard another gasp.

"Looks like the same guy who had Rembert killed and took out the hitter in Miami," Crawford said. "I'll let you know when it's okay to see him."

"But you were there this morning?" Jackie asked.

"Yeah, let's just call it an unauthorized visit."

"How was he?"

"I'd say...groggy."

"Well, keep us informed, please?"

"Definitely," Crawford said. "What were you gonna call me about?"

"Oh yeah," Jackie said. "So Ryder called Rembert's daughter, Muffie. We wanted to speak to her and her husband, who worked for Rembert."

"The Drexels, yeah. How'd that go?"

"She hung up on Ryder."

"I'm not surprised," Crawford said, then described the impromptu visit of Gary, Manny, and silent Chuck.

"No wonder," Jackie said. "Think we'll fare any better with the girl-friend, Weezie Gifford? By the way, what's with all these names? Weezie and Muffie?"

"This is the capital of the cutesy women's names. Men's, too. Let's see, we got a Biff...and a couple of Chips, and, get this, a Pinkie who's a girl and a Pinkie who's a guy."

"You're kidding."

"Nope. A Binkie, too."

"Wow, people I look forward to meeting."

"None are on the short list of suspects."

"Why don't you tell me who is?" Jackie asked.

He laughed. "Jackie, we're glad you came down here, but as far as solving the case goes, you're on your own."

"I get it."

"'Cause, as I'm sure you can appreciate, we'd never hear the end of it from my boss. I can hear it now, 'so, let me get this straight, those girls from Savannah who probably specialize in climbing up trees after stray cats, solved it when you homicide superstars couldn't.' I really don't want to hear those words."

"Professional rivalry, huh?"

"Big time."

"Well, will you just tell me if Weezie Gifford's on your short list?"

"She's on *the* list."

"Meaning pretty far down it."

"That's all I'm going to say."

"All right," Jackie said. "Time to get to work. Let us know when we can see Mort."

"I will. Good luck."

Just as he hung up with Jackie, he heard the unmistakable thudding footsteps of Norm Rutledge walk into his office.

"How's he doing?" Rutledge said, no 'hey', 'hello' or 'morning.' Just a frowning, slightly stooped man in a brown suit that could use a press.

"He's gonna be fine," Crawford said. "I'm gonna go over there in a little while."

Rutledge nodded. "Hey, I thought you planned to keep it quiet that the guy last night was driving a black car—probably an Audi, BMW or a Merc —with a bicycle rack?"

"We were. Why?"

"'Cause it's in the *Post*. Said the suspect was driving a late model black German luxury sedan or SUV with a bicycle rack."

"You're shitting me," Crawford said, shaking his head in disgust. "Who was the source, you know?"

"I don't know. A neighbor who saw it maybe?"

"Well, there goes that."

"What do you mean?"

"I got Shaw looking into what my suspects drive. But if one of 'em had a bicycle rack, they'll definitely get rid of it now."

"Only if they read that article."

"True."

"Guess you gotta burn all the copies of the *Post*."

FORTY-ONE

CRAWFORD'S NEXT CALL WAS TO BETTINA, WHO HE REACHED AT GOOD Sam. It was a long conversation.

She explained that she was with Ott's mother and sister in the visitors' room and that both of them were allowed to visit Mort for twenty minutes. Ott's mother said Mort spoke a few painful words but smiled a lot. Tried to anyway. She said that she spoke to one of his doctors afterwards and the doctor was concerned about several things. Specifically, he did not know exactly what the extent of the damage was to Ott's liver, stomach, or intestines. There also could be damage to his kidney and bladder, he explained. Bettina said that Marie had the foresight to bring along a notebook and pen and took pretty thorough notes on all this, while Bettina herself was using a small recording device.

The doctor went on to say that something called an endoscopy was scheduled for later in the afternoon which might possibly show damage to Ott's esophagus, stomach, or small intestines. He was optimistic that if there was just minor damage then he and his team could repair it on the spot. He told Marie and Kay that various drugs and medicines were administered to treat the pain and prevent infection and that Ott had been given a tetanus shot so bacterial infection would not occur.

He also mentioned that a blood transfusion had taken place the night before due to Ott's enormous loss of blood. He went on to explain all the tubes inserted into Ott's body and their functions. Specifically, the IV was to prevent dehydration and increase blood flow to the major organs. Then something called a nasogastric tube, a long, thin, flexible tube inserted through Ott's nose and down into his stomach, was to remove air, fluid, and blood from his stomach.

At this point, Marie stopped the doctor and asked him if all of this was normal. He replied it was and went on to tell her about yet one more tube called an endotracheal tube, a hollow plastic tube placed in Ott's trachea— at which point Marie stopped him and asked what the trachea was, and he explained that it was his "windpipe" or "airway." He went on to say that basically the purpose of the endotracheal tube was to help him breathe.

Kay then asked if they were going to insert any more tubes in her poor brother.

The doctor laughed and said, "I don't think so. That's enough."

He then told them what he called, "the good news." The good news was that there didn't appear to be the kind of damage to the intestines that might have meant the necessity of wearing a colostomy bag for life.

"Thank God," Marie had said.

And, also, the bullet had not touched his spine which could have resulted in him being either a paraplegic or a quadriplegic.

"Thank God," Marie said again.

The doctor then wrapped it up. "I'm going to give you my write-up which you really don't need to read. In fact, half the words will probably strike you as medical gobbledy-gook, but I'm required to give it to you anyway. I just wrote it up, so it's current and refers to 'postoperative day (POD) 2,' which means today."

He handed her three sheets of paper.

Marie gave it a long look, then stuffed it in her purse. "I'll save it for tonight. It looks like a good way to put me to sleep."

Crawford was glad to hear she had her son's sense-of-humor.

A second later, Bettina put Marie herself on the line.

"Hello, Detective, it's Mort's mother," she said, unnecessarily. "First of all, I want to thank you so much for having Bettina pick us up. And also, for arranging with Sergeant Barnes to take us to the Cleveland airport. That was so nice of you."

"You're very welcome, Mrs. Kowalczyk. Anything for Mort. How is he?"

"Well, I'd say his spirits are good, but he's got a long way to go. He's not really talking but he's writing notes. He said he wants to see you."

"Will they let me? Is that all right with the doctor? I thought it was just family?"

"Well, for one thing, I know Mort regards you as family," Marie said. "And, as far as the doctor...let's just say I had to persuade him."

Crawford laughed. "I bet like your son, you can be very persuasive."

"When I need to be. Anyway, you can go there any time up to six tonight."

"Thank you very much, I'll come right away."

"By the way, Charlie—I'm going to call you Charlie if that's all right—"

"Of course it is."

"That Bettina is a real peach."

"Yeah, she's great. I'm glad she took good care of you and Kay."

"The best," Marie said. "Oh, and by the way, I left a copy of the doctor's medical report at the front desk for you. I don't know, I just thought you might want to read it. I skimmed it...a lot of words I've never seen or heard before...and never will again."

WHEN CRAWFORD WALKED INTO OTT'S HOSPITAL ROOM, THE FIRST thing he noticed was the tubes. One in Ott's nose, one down his throat, plus the IV in his arm. Then he noticed again the large bandage on Ott's left shoulder, that looked like it had recently been changed.

The second thing he noticed was a metal stand, which resembled one of those stands that a musician in an orchestra uses to read music, next to Ott's bed. On it was a yellow pad and a pen.

The third thing he noticed was Ott's eyes. They seemed clear and focused unlike how they had appeared the night before. Those eyes were staring at him now, his head slightly turned to his right.

Crawford smiled at him. "How you doin', old buddy?"

Ott's hand slowly went to the pen on the stand and, with effort, he lifted it and wrote.

I've got a stomachache.

Crawford was relieved. Thank God, same old Ott! His sense of humor was fully intact.

"Any idea when you're gonna get out of here?"

Nope, he wrote.

"Well, I miss you."

Backatcha.

Crawford smiled. "Okay, enough of the small talk. I'm guessing your shooter was left-handed since if he was a righty, it would be pretty hard for him to shoot from the driver's side window. Know what I mean?"

Agree.

"So I got Shaw, who's pinch-hitting for you, running down which of our suspects have black BMW's, Audi's or Merc's and which ones, if any, are lefty's."

Ott gave a slight nod.

"But here's a problem," Crawford said. "Somebody, I'm guessing a neighbor of yours maybe, told a *Post* reporter that the black car had a bike rack on it, so if our shooter reads the article, we're screwed. Meaning he'd take the bike rack off his vehicle."

Another nod from Ott, but then he wrote on the pad: *Check for discoloration.*

Crawford frowned. "Come again?"

Ott wrote: *On the car trunk. Or bumper. Outline of straps from rack maybe.*

"Ah." Crawford nodded. "Good thinking. I'm just not quite sure how me and Shaw are gonna get to see the cars, assuming some of the suspects have black German luxury vehicles."

Ott wrote. *They're pretty common in PB.*

"True."

"Well listen, I was told to keep it short with you. I'll check back in tomorrow...oh, I thought maybe you'd like to get the inside—so to speak—scoop on what's giving you the stomachache. It's the doctor's report he gave to your mother. She left a copy here for me.

"*A 41-year-old Palm Beach Police detective,*" Crawford read, "*presented to our hospital as a trauma activation following a gunshot wound to the abdomen and shoulder. He was taken to the operating room (OR) where abdominal exploration revealed injured segments of the distal small bowel and proximal colon were resected and bowel continuity was restored. Additionally, a smaller sigmoid colon injury near the level of the sacral promontory was identified and primarily repaired. The missile sites were not aggressively debrided, but were irrigated and left to close by secondary intent. Perioperative antibiotics were continued for 12 hours given intra-abdominal contamination. The patient continued his recovery in the surgical intensive care unit (SICU). On postoperative day (POD) 2, he remained hypotensive—*"

Ott lifted a finger and started writing: *Can you translate that crap into English?*

CRAWFORD GOT OFF THE ELEVATOR AT THE GROUND FLOOR AND looked across at the visitors' room.

He saw a tall, well-dressed woman and a shorter, older equally well-dressed woman who hadn't been there when he went up. They were dressed more for a colder climate than Florida. Crawford guessed Cleveland. He walked over to them.

"Excuse me, I'm guessing you're Mrs. Kowalczck and Ms. Ott?"

"Yes," said Marie Kowalczck. "You must be Charlie."

"Yes," Crawford said. "So nice to meet you both. I just wish it was under different circumstances."

"Nice to meet you, too," Marie said. "Mortie didn't say how handsome you were."

"Mom," Kay said, shaking her head.

"I can't help it if I'm still a bit of a flirt. So how's he doing?"

"Mort will always be Mort, thank God," Crawford said. "But I can tell he's in pain. Not bad enough, though, so he couldn't help me on our case."

"Oh, that's good," Marie said.

"Well, we're going to go up and see him now," Kay said. "So nice to meet you and thank you again for all your help in getting us here."

"Yes, thank you," Marie said. "And we need to pay you for our flights."

"Don't worry about it," Crawford said. "It's on the Palm Beach Police Department."

"Are you sure?"

Crawford nodded. "I'm sure. And I'm sure I'll see you ladies again."

"I hope so," Marie said.

———

CRAWFORD DROVE BACK TO THE STATION AND WALKED UP TO ROB Shaw's cubicle.

Shaw wasn't there so Crawford left him a note. *Stop by—CC.*

A half an hour later, Crawford heard footsteps, then Shaw walked in. "Hey," he said.

"Hey. Got anything yet on the suspects' cars?"

Shaw nodded. "All but two of them. Weezie Gifford and Del Lewis. So two of the six

have black German cars. Robert Smallwood and Scott Drexel. Smallwood a Mercedes

and Drexel a Beemer. I don't know if either one's got a bicycle rack, but I'll find out."

"So you paid a visit to DMV?"

Shaw nodded. "Does that mean we rule out...who's left—?" Shaw looked down at a

piece of paper. "Daryl Boone, the other daughter, Sally Hemmes, Mark Shuman and the

Russian, though his car, when he was here, may have been a rental."

"I'm not ruling any of 'em out," Crawford said.

"Yeah, I hear you. But it's a start."

"What about any lefties in the bunch?"

"No to Boone, Sally Hemmes, and Mark Shuman. I'm still working on the rest of 'em."

"How do you plan to see if Smallwood or Drexel have bike racks?"

"Only way I know, go to their offices or homes and see somehow."

"Yeah, you definitely don't want to call and ask 'em. That'll tip 'em off we're

zeroing in on that."

Shaw nodded. "I think we're getting close, Charlie."

Yeah, but if Ott was around, we'd have the guy behind bars by now.

FORTY-TWO

A few minutes after Shaw left Crawford's office, he got a call from Bettina in reception.

"Hey, Charlie," she said. "I've got two women here to see you."

"Check their belts."

"Their belts? What for?"

He was half-kidding, knowing it had to be Jackie and Ryder. "See if one's got a big Q on it."

"They know you, Charlie." She spoke to the two women. "What are your names, please?"

"Jackie and Ryder," Jackie said.

"I'll be right out," Crawford said. "Hey, by the way, Bettina, I tried to find you earlier to thank you for taking care of Mort's mother and sister. Nice job...Marie called you a *peach.*"

"She did? That's nice, but I think a peach is a Georgia thing, not Florida."

On his walk out to the reception area, Crawford fielded a quick call on his cell phone.

It was Shaw with more information about another owner of a black German vehicle.

He clicked off, walked out to the reception area and said hello to the sisters, giving each one a kiss on the cheek.

"So how's it going?" He asked.

"I've never seen a place like this before," Ryder said. "Does everyone here have a Bentley and live in a hundred-million-dollar house."

"Yeah, everyone except me and Mort."

"And me," Bettina piped up.

The three laughed. "Come on back to my office and let's catch up."

They followed him back and he told them about seeing Ott earlier that afternoon. He told them that he thought Ott had a long way to go before he'd be running down killers with his usual blazing speed.

"So it's not like on TV where a cop gets shot, then the next day he's back on the job climbing fences?" Ryder said.

"Nah, I'd say Mort's fence climbing days are over. Come to think of it, I don't recall ever seeing him climb a fence."

"It's not a job prerequisite," said Ryder dryly.

"So we decided after what happened to Mort," Jackie said, "that we want to be on the same team and help you. Just like with Nick Janzek up in Charleston. We started out as competitors, then teamed up."

"But what about the three hundred thou?" Crawford asked.

"Ah, we're not starving," Jackie said. "We'll just take another lunch at Green's."

"The hell we will," Ryder protested. "We'll take a dinner at Le Bilboquet if we help you crack it."

Crawford smiled at her. "It didn't take you long to find out what the most expensive restaurant in Palm Beach is."

"We're fast learners," Ryder said.

"The only thing you can't have there is anything at the Oyster Bar."

"Aw, come on. Why not?'

"'Cause they have a thirty two hundred dollar caviar."

Jackie shook her head. "How in God's name would a Green's guy know about that?"

"Because a friend of mine named Rose told me."

"Is she one of the many billionaires in this town?" Ryder asked.

"Not yet."

"I heard there are something like seventy-two of 'em who live here."

"Sounds about right," Crawford said. "Okay, back to business."

"We were never on it," Ryder joked.

"Right, but since we're on the same team now, have you guys come up with anything yet? Except what the most expensive restaurant is?"

"We had an interesting conversation with Weezie Gifford," Jackie said.

"And?"

"Long shot at best," Jackie said.

"Yeah, that was Mort's take."

"However, she does drive a black Audi," Ryder said.

"But no bike rack," Jackie added.

"How did you know about the bike rack?" Crawford asked, figuring they must have seen the article in the *Post*.

"I'm not sure where we heard about it," Ryder said. "Word seems to get around pretty fast in this town."

"You can say that again," Crawford said.

"It was parked in her driveway," Jackie said. "When we left, we checked out the trunk."

Jackie nodded. "But there were no faded lines or discoloration where the rack might have been."

Crawford smiled. "You thought about that too. I thought only the great Ott could come up with that."

"Come on, Charlie, don't sell us short," Jackie said.

"Yeah, that was pretty routine," Ryder added.

"You said it was interesting? Your conversation with Weezie Gifford," Crawford said.

"What was interesting about it?"

"So we had a pretty long conversation with her. Dishing, as girls will do. You know, couple glasses of wine," Ryder said.

"Yeah, she's quite the chatterbox," Jackie said. "One thing she said was that Rembert, who seemed like he got about what he deserved, was about to fire his son-in-law from his company."

Crawford leaned forward with huge heightened interest. "Really? What for?"

"That's not totally clear," Jackie said. "We asked but she didn't really seem to know. Just something that Rembert mentioned to her."

Ryder chuckled. "You know, pillow talk."

"Gotcha."

"Well, that is very interesting. I wonder why he was gonna do that."

"Can't help you there," Ryder said. "Then she veered off on how Rembert was such a bastard. Wanted not just to dump her but take the ring back. Did you check out that rock, Charlie?"

"Yeah, it's huge even by Palm Beach standards," Crawford said. "Well, thanks for that. Now I've just got to find out why Rembert wanted to can Drex. I mean, guy's a little lame but he *is* his son-in-law. Firing him would make waves in the family. With Muffie, in particular."

"No question," Jackie said. "So who are you gonna ask?"

Crawford tapped his desk. "I'm thinking Rembert's partner, Del Lewis."

"Who I would think would be high on your list. Suspect-wise, I mean."

"He wasn't high on my list. But I just got a call from Ott's fill-in saying he drives a black Mercedes."

FORTY-THREE

CRAWFORD CALLED DEL LEWIS ON HIS CELL AND REACHED HIM AT his office.

"I know what you're going to say," Lewis said. "You found out I have a black Mercedes and now I'm suspect number one."

"No, I just want to ask you some questions."

"Well, go ahead."

"Face-to-face."

"Okay, but you gotta come right over. I have a 4:30 conference call."

"I'll be there in ten minutes."

"See you then."

Crawford walked into the Rembert Sports Management office at Phillips Point at a little past 4:00 p.m.

The receptionist knew he was expected and walked him into Lewis's office.

Lewis looked at his watch. "Twenty minutes until my call. Have a seat."

"That's more than I need."

Crawford looked over Lewis's shoulder at the spectacular 9th story view of the Intracoastal in the foreground, Palm Beach Island beyond, then the endless blue-green ocean.

"This won't take long at all," Crawford started out. "What I've heard is that Jack Rembert was intending to fire his son-in-law from your company."

Lewis nodded and folded his hands. "So I've heard," he said. "Do I know for a fact that he was really going to do it? No, I don't. But that was the story making the rounds. He never said a word to me about it, but I know what the reason for it was."

"That was going to be my next question."

"Well, this is classic the-pot-calling-the-kettle-black. It was because Scott had a number of affairs with women. He was a hell of a lot more discreet about them than Jack, but word definitely got out. Including an accusation that he had used a date-rape drug on a woman at a bar."

Crawford leaned closer to Lewis, his eyes fixed on the agent's. "Where did that go? I mean, was he arrested or what?"

"No, I think what happened was the girl was paid to go away. But Jack knew about it and I'm sure Muffie did too."

Crawford slowly shook his head. "Does seem pretty hypocritical, given all the women Rembert was involved with."

"Ya think? I mean, I couldn't believe it. But Jack and I were all about business, and only business. Our personal lives were off-limits and that's the way we wanted to keep it."

"But Scott Drexel *was* business. I mean, he worked for your company. Rembert never told you directly he was thinking of firing him."

Lewis shook his head. "Nope. Jack was the boss. It was his company. Hell, he could have fired me if he wanted to. But for all I know, it could've just been a rumor—about Scott, I mean—you know as well as I do, Palm Beach is famous for 'em."

Crawford was almost done. "Would you do me favor?" he asked.

"Sure."

"Would you write down Scott's cell number. I thought I had it but can't find it."

In truth, he had the number memorized.

"No problem," Lewis said, taking a pen out of a pen holder. He opened a drawer and took out a pad that said Rembert Sports Management in blue raised letterhead. He wrote out the number.

Del Lewis was left-handed.

FORTY-FOUR

CRAWFORD WENT BACK TO THE OFFICE AND FOUND ROB SHAW. HE told him about Del Lewis being left-handed.

"So does that jump him to the top of the list?"

"I don't know," Crawford said. "It's a stretch to think of him going to Mort's house and shooting him."

"But isn't it a stretch with all our suspects? Unless they got another hitter."

"True. Anyway after I left his office, I went to the garage in the building looking for his car. But no luck. So I just don't know about him. But, in the mean-time, I found out Rembert might have been planning to fire his son-in-law."

"Scott Drexel? Why?"

Crawford nodded and explained. "The source was Weezie Gifford. And Del Lewis seemed to confirm it, though he didn't know for sure."

"How did Weezie Gifford know?"

"Rembert apparently let it slip when he was with her."

"Unbelievable," said Shaw.

"What?"

"I mean, here's a guy who's screwing everything that walked or crawled in Palm Beach and he's gonna fire his son-in-law for doing the same thing... what a dick!"

"I know. So I'm going to have another conversation with Drexel," Crawford said.

"Meanwhile, what should I be doing?" Shaw asked.

"This is a long shot," Crawford said, "but maybe check to see if any of our eight has a carry permit."

"Okay, no harm in trying," Shaw said with a shrug.

"I'll give you some more marching orders in the morning." Crawford reached for his cell phone. "I'm gonna call Drexel now. You might as well call it a day."

Shaw stood up. "Maybe tomorrow's the day we get our man."

"That would be nice," Crawford said, dialing his cell phone as Shaw walked out of his office.

The call went straight to voicemail, and he left a message for Drexel. He was not going to hold his breath about getting a call back that night.

He leaned back in his chair and thought about how strange it was not having Ott around. He missed his wit, his sarcasm, his wisecracks, his insights, his intuition, his brains, his thudding footsteps, his double chin, the few remaining strands of hair on his head, the mole on his left cheek, his uneven sideburns, hell, even his farting. He wondered whether Ott would be the same, or even ninety percent of what he had been before the shooting. He wondered how the incident might affect his psyche, his spirit, his identity. He realized he was terribly worried about the man with whom he'd first been thrown together five years before.

They hadn't hit it off right off the bat. They were polar opposites, after all. Crawford was the six three, handsome, chiseled, former athlete who kept his privileged, Ivy League background as under wraps as he possibly could. But Ott was a detective and found out everything. Ott was the five eight, balding, rotund guy from the bad side of Cleveland, who groused to Norm Rutledge about being assigned to a cubicle and not having an office like Crawford. Hell, he argued—quite convincingly actually—that he had a record every bit as impressive as Crawford's. In fact, his closure rate, it could be argued, was even better. And he'd won every medal in the book in Cleveland.

Crawford, who had signed on with the Palm Beach Police Department two months before Ott, had read the man's resume and was impressed. He was even more impressed when he found out that the resume was not written by Ott, but by Ott's boss up in Cleveland. He had won something called the Medal of Heroism award which was, "awarded to officers who demonstrate extraordinary bravery or act in an exemplary and extraordinary manner while at substantial risk of personal harm" when he was twenty-nine. Two years later he won the Medal of Honor Award, the, "highest commendation presented to a Cleveland Division of Police officer for acts of personal bravery performed beyond the call of duty and involving an incontestable risk of life." Four years later he was the winner of the Samuel H. Miller Police Officer of the Year Award, "which honored outstanding police service significantly above and beyond the call of duty."

What Crawford wondered was, with all that heroism and bravery and risk-taking, why Ott had never caught a bullet before. Just lucky, he concluded.

Sure, Crawford had won a few things and was a Gold Shield up in New York but it almost all paled in comparison with super-cop Ott.

Man, he missed the guy.

Shaw was fine, he'd do in a pinch, but no man but Ott was Ott.

FORTY-FIVE

CRAWFORD HAD NOT HEARD FROM SCOTT DREXEL BY TEN O'CLOCK the next morning. Knowing he often worked remotely, he decided to go straight to his house and question him about whether he had actually been fired by Jack Rembert. Certainly, a solid motive to kill his father-in-law, realizing that he was being tossed off the gravy train. Then there was his purported use of the date-rape drug. On his way there, he got a call from Ott's mother, Marie. She said she had a suggestion from Mort who had asked her to pass it along to him. It was, like Ott, simple but smart in its brevity. He thanked her as he drove into Scott Drexel's driveway.

He got out of the Crown Vic, walked up to the porch, and rang the doorbell. Muffie Drexel opened the door a few minutes later.

"Thank God! I was afraid it might be those three crazy men again," she said.

"Hi, Mrs. Drexel. I don't think you have to worry about them coming around again."

"I hope not," she said. "Did you want to see Scott? Because if so, he's not here."

"Is he at his office?"

"I assume so."

"Well, actually I have a question or two for you, ma'am."

"Okay, you want to come in?"

"If you don't mind. It won't take long."

He followed her into the living room, and they sat down.

"Ms. Drexel," he paused, wondering how to frame the question, "I have heard…" he took a deep breath, "what I'd call an unsubstantiated report that your father was either thinking about firing, or maybe actually had fired Scott, at the time of his death."

There was no shock on her face. And no words came out of her mouth.

Instead came a deep frown, then she scrunched her eyes and a tear rolled down her cheek. Next came a flood of tears. Crawford almost wanted to put his hand on her shoulder and say that whatever it was that had suddenly gotten her so upset would be all right. Then she put her hands up to her face and started sobbing.

"Please leave," she said in between sobs.

He put up a hand but had to ask his last question. He never got a chance to ask it because she suddenly blurted. "My dad was just trying to protect me after Scott date-raped some girl in a bar. He tried to talk me into divorcing him and I was going to…but didn't because…I found out I was pregnant."

Then, he did put his hand on her shoulder. "I'm sorry, Ms. Drexel, I'm very, very sorry."

Slowly, she nodded. There was nothing more to ask or say. Nothing he could do for her. He turned and walked toward the front door. As he got to the front door, he saw a garage door clicker and remembered the message Ott had relayed via Marie. He picked up the brown remote and walked out the front door.

Standing on the driveway, he clicked the remote and heard the door whirring to the up position. He walked into the open three-car garage and saw what he was looking for almost right away. It was sitting on a wooden work bench.

It was black and had a number of plastic straps and round metal tubes and on one side in white letters it said, THULE 910XT Two Bike Carrier.

Thank you, Mort.

FORTY-SIX

CRAWFORD DROVE UP TO THE PHILLIPS POINT OFFICE BUILDING AND took the elevator to the offices of Rembert Sports Management. He smiled at the receptionist and said he was there to see Scott this time. She said that he had gone out a half hour before. He asked her where and she said she didn't know. He asked when she expected him back and she replied she didn't know, and offered, "his hours are kind of unpredictable." He asked if Del Lewis was there and just then Del Lewis walked out into the reception area.

"I thought that was you," Lewis said, "come on back."

Crawford followed him to his office.

"Thanks, but I'm going to make this brief," Crawford said, remaining standing, "I'm looking for Scott."

"He was here but left a little while ago."

"So I understand. Do you have any idea where he went?"

"I just know I heard his cell phone ring and he left right after that," Lewis said. "Hang on a second—" he hit an intercom button. "Sherri, do you know who that was who called Scott?"

"Ah yes, it was Ms. Delgado."

"Thanks, that's what I figured," Lewis said, then to Crawford. "Okay, you didn't hear this from me, but I'm gonna guess that wherever Valentina Delgado is staying, is where Scott is."

"Valentina Delgado the tennis player?"

"Yup. Scott's her agent." Lewis added with a scoff, "And also a *special* friend."

Crawford nodded. "I see. So you think she's here staying at a hotel maybe."

"That would be my guess," Lewis said. "She just played at a tournament down in Miami. Won it, in fact."

"So, if I'm understanding it, Scott probably went there for some reason other than business."

Lewis smiled. "You catch on quick, Charlie."

"Okay, well, if he comes back here, please don't mention I was looking for him."

"Okay, but why?" Lewis said, then shook his head and held up a hand. "I don't need to know. That's your business."

"Thank you," Crawford said. "Well, all I need to figure out now is what hotel Ms. Delgado is staying in."

"Good luck with that."

Crawford turned and walked out of Lewis's office.

He walked into the reception area. "Sherri, I would appreciate it if you wouldn't tell Scott I was looking for him."

"Okay," she said, but Crawford figured it was fifty-fifty she might.

He got in the elevator, took out his cell phone and called the station.

"Hello, Charlie," Bettina answered.

"Hi, Bettina. Your next assignment is to call around to all the hotels in Palm Beach and see if the tennis player, Valentina Delgado, is staying in one. Oh, get Shaw on it too. You can divvy up the calls."

"On it," she said and was gone.

———

He decided that since he was in West Palm that he'd take a run up Flagler Drive to The Ben hotel. It was only five minutes away and he knew it was a place where celebrities sometimes stayed if they didn't stay at a hotel in Palm Beach. The thought crossed his mind that maybe she'd be using an alias, but figured she was hardly a big name like Serena or Venus Williams and chances are she would use her own name. The woman at the desk said Delgado wasn't registered there.

Ten minutes later, he walked into the station.

"Perfect timing," Bettina said. "Your tennis player is staying at the Brazilian Court."

"Thanks," Crawford said, giving Bettina a fist bump. "Good work."

As he was about to do an about-face and go back to his car, he spotted Dominica on the other side of the lobby. He flagged her down and walked over to her.

"You doing anything?" he asked her.

"Nothing that can't wait."

"I need you."

She smiled. "It's good to be needed."

"Come on." Together, they walked out the front door and over to Crawford's double-parked Crown Vic.

On the short drive to the Brazilian Court, he caught her up. He told her where he expected his suspect was and that he had probably gone there to "visit" his client who had just won a Miami tennis tournament.

She snapped her fingers.

"Got an idea," she said. "Quick detour to the liquor store we just passed."

She pointed at a wine and liquor store on County.

"What?"

"Just trust me."

He U-turned, pulled up in front of it, and she hopped out. "I'll be quick," she said.

He just shrugged. Not a clue what she was up to, but yes, he trusted her.

A few minutes later she came out with a bottle in a brown bag.

"Are you going to clue me in?" he asked.

She took the bottle out of the bag. It was Dom Perignon 2013 Brut champagne. She gave him a quick explanation as they made the short drive to the Brazilian Court.

He parked and they walked into the hotel and up to the main desk.

He showed his badge to the man there, who had a gold name plate on his left breast pocket that said *Peter*.

"Did a man come in earlier and go up to Valentina Delgado's room?" Crawford asked.

The man got a little twitchy and his eyes strayed away from Crawford's. "Sir, we're discouraged from discussing anything about our guests here at the Brazilian Court."

"You may be, but this is official police business, *Peter*, and I need to know. Did a man come here a little earlier and go up to Ms. Delgado's room?" he repeated.

Peter didn't answer for a few moments, then lowered his voice. "Yes, sir."

Crawford described Scott Drexel and Peter just nodded nervously.

Crawford looked over at Dominica, who had the bottle of champagne in her hand.

"What are we waiting for?" she said.

Crawford turned back to Peter. "Okay, here's what we need you to do," he said. "You're going to call Ms. Delgado's room and say a big fan of hers dropped off an expensive bottle of Dom Perignon champagne to celebrate her big victory in the Miami Open."

Peter looked at him warily. "O-kay, but I-I-I don't know if Ms. Delgado is going to like being interrupted,"

"Of course she will," said Dominica and held up the bottle. "For this, you bet she will."

The girl could sell most anything.

"So now, what's her room number?" Crawford asked.

Reluctantly, Peter gave it to him.

"Okay, so give her a call, please, and tell her the porter's gonna drop it off."

Peter eyes started blinking and one hand seemed to shake. "I could get in troub—"

"Just say we put a gun to your head," Dominica said,

Peter looked frightened.

"Kidding," she said with her million dollar smile.

"So what are you gonna say?" Crawford asked.

"Um, okay...hi, Ms. Delgado, this is Peter at the front desk...a big fan dropped off a bottle of Dom..."

"Perignon."

"Dom Perignon champagne for you for winning the Miami..."

"Open," said Crawford. "Okay, say it again."

He did and this time he got it right.

"Okay, call her."

Peter exhaled deeply and put his finger on the house phone.

"Come on, it's easy," Crawford said. "And sound excited, not scared."

Peter dialed. Then a few moments later. "Oh hi, Ms. Delgado, this is Peter at the front desk. Um, a big fan dropped off a bottle of, um, Dom Perignon champagne for your victory at the Miami Open. I'm going to send it up if that's all right...yes ma'am, right away."

Crawford shot him a thumbs-up and started to walk away with Dominica at his side, then he turned back. "Oh, and Peter, don't call her and warn her 'cause if you do, you're in really big trouble. Think jail."

Peter nodded nervously, a sweat bead or two on his forehead.

"We clear?"

He nodded again.

They walked to the elevator, and he pressed the button for the top floor.

They got off the elevator and found the room where Valentina Delgado was staying.

Crawford knocked on the door and a few moments later the door opened a crack. Valentina Delgado's deeply tanned face peered out.

Crawford pushed the door open, and Valentina stumbled backward. She was wearing nothing but an 800-count Egyptian percale sheet around her. Across the large suite was a man in bed with a deep frown creasing his unlined, boyish face.

Dominica burst into the room holding the bottle. "Hey, nice going down in Miami," she said. "Hell of a victory."

"Scott Drexel," Crawford said, raising his voice. "You're under arrest for the murder of your father-in-law Jack Rembert and Gretchen Bull."

"You're out of your goddamn mind, Crawford," Drexel said. "I'm gonna nail your ass for this."

"I don't think so."

One eye on Drexel, Crawford went to a closet, reached in, and took out a white bathrobe with BC spelled out in bright blue letters on the breast pocket. "Put this on," he told Drexel, "then go change in the bathroom."

Dominica walked into the bathroom to make sure there was no means of escape and nodded at Crawford.

He tossed the bathrobe to Drexel, then turned to the ashen-faced tennis player who seemed to be momentarily incapable of speaking.

"Well, are you going to give me that?" Valentina asked Dominica, pointing at the bottle.

"Oh sorry," Dominica said, shaking her head, "this was just a prop. I gotta take it back. See, a two-hundred-ninety-six dollar bottle of Dom Perignon is just not in the budget."

FORTY-SEVEN

CRAWFORD WAS IN OTT'S ROOM AT GOOD SAMARITAN HOSPITAL.

"It was 'cause of your idea to check suspect's garages that got this thing solved."

Ott wrote something on the stand next to his bed. *Happy to help. LOVE the champagne gambit*—he punctuated it with three bold exclamation points after "gambit."

"Yeah, well, team effort," Crawford said.

Ott leaned forward and wrote out, *So how'd you figure it all out, genius?*

"So glad you finally recognize my brilliance," Crawford said, patting Ott—lightly—on his non-IV'd hand. "Well, first of all, when I heard Drexel was accused of drugging a woman, I made the obvious connection. Same thing happened to Jack Rembert. He got roofied."

Ott smiled and nodded.

"The other thing was," Crawford said, "I don't know if you remember, but when we were driving down to Miami the first time, I called Drexel about going to question him and let it slip we were on our way to Miami."

Ott nodded and started writing. *Aha, so he figured he better take out Gretchen right away.*

"Yup, dead women tell no tales."

Ott gave a faint nod and wrote. *About who hired 'em.*

"Exactly," Crawford said. "So when you getting out of this dump?"

Ott thought for a second, then wrote slowly. *They got more to do on this old, beat-up body. A week maybe.*

"Shit, you mean to say I got another week with Shaw?"

He's not so bad, Ott wrote.

"Yeah, well, just hope Palm Beach remains murder-free 'til you're back."

Crawford debated for a few moments as he stared down at Ott, whose face was wan and ghost-like. Suddenly, he welled up with emotion that he'd almost never felt before.

"You know, Mort, I'm going to say something I've never said to a man before and I guarantee you I'll never say again...I love you, man."

A smile flashed across Ott's face for a split second before it went back to being wan and ghost-like. He wrote, *I'll just pretend I never heard that.* But, with effort, he flashed that smile again.

"All right, enough of the mushiness," Crawford said and smiled.

CRAWFORD DIALED JACKIE FARRELL'S NUMBER. HE TOLD HER THE killer was in jail, and he'd give the sisters all the details when they had dinner at Le Bilboquet that night at 7:00 p.m.

"Charlie, we don't want to break the bank," Jackie said. "Ryder and I actually have pretty simple tastes in food. We really don't need to go to the most expensive restaurant in Palm Beach."

Crawford had done some research on the subject with his epicurean friend, Rose Clarke.

"Turns out to be the *second* most expensive restaurant in Palm Beach," Crawford said. "But it's on my boss...though he doesn't know it yet."

Jackie laughed. "Oh well, in that case," she said. "Hey, also, this friend told me that when in Palm Beach we should check out a place called Swifty's."

"Yeah, I hear it's quite the scene," Crawford said, "so let's do this, drinks at Swifty's at seven, then dinner at La whatever-the-hell-it's-called at eight? Sound good?"

"Okay, but we're buying at Swifty's."

"No way in hell, my boss insists."

FORTY-EIGHT

CRAWFORD OFFERED TO PICK UP JACKIE AND RYDER, BUT THEY SAID they'd meet him at Swifty's in the Colony Hotel because they first wanted to drop by and see an old friend. He got there and a few minutes later the sisters pulled up to the valet in Ryder's Jeep. Crawford opened the door for Jackie and she got out.

"Looks like a pretty snazzy place," Jackie said, gazing up at the shocking pink exterior of the Colony Hotel.

"Piggy pink, that's my color," Ryder added, giving it a thumbs up.

"Supposedly," Crawford said, under the canopy outside, "they used to pack big name singers in this place."

"Like who?"

"Jazz singers mainly."

"Enough talk. I'm a thirsty girl," Ryder said, tugging at Crawford's sleeve. "Come on, let's go."

They went inside the hotel, walked through it, and out the back area to Swifty's, where tables were set up on all sides of a large pool.

Since it was off season and the place wasn't packed, they sat right down at a table next to the pool.

Ryder looked around at the young and pampered. "Is this one of your regular haunts, Charlie?"

He shook his head. "I don't have any in Palm Beach."

"Why not?"

"For one thing, I don't eat or drink with people I might have to arrest one day and, for another, I can't afford any place except Green's," Crawford said. "And, by the way, even Green's is getting pretty expensive. My sardines are a buck more than when I started going there."

"Oh no," Ryder said. "A whole buck!"

Jackie laughed. "Where are you originally from, Charlie?"

"Connecticut."

"No wonder," Ryder said. "A New Englander."

"Yeah, so?"

"New Englanders are notoriously cheap."

"I prefer, thrifty."

"So do you have regular haunts in West Palm?" Jackie asked.

"Not really."

"Why not?"

"'Cause I'm kind of a home body," he said. "Give me a good series on Netflix or Hulu any night."

"Yeah, I'm with you," Jackie said. "Ryder's the night owl in our family."

Ryder smiled. "Used to be. Until Nick Janzek came along. Another homebody."

They ordered drinks.

Ryder looked around at the tables near them. "I've never seen more Derek Lams and Peter Soms," she said to her sister.

Crawford had no clue what she was talking about.

"Rent the Runway," Jackie explained to him and Ryder nodded.

"What's that?" Crawford asked.

"This place where you can rent dresses for fifty bucks, instead of buying 'em for five hundred."

"Who knew?" He proceeded to update them on all the details about the capture of Scott Drexel and the clues that led to it, including the big one the sisters got from Muffie: that Jack Rembert was about to fire his son-in-law for drugging a woman with a date-rape drug.

"Both of 'em," Ryder said, "were bad news."

"Have you ever heard the expression," Crawford said, "like father-in-law, like son-in-law?"

"No, but it works," Jackie said.

"What a bunch of pigs," Ryder said. "I mean, how do men like that get away with it?"

"Well," said Crawford. "Turns out they don't."

"Yeah, but so many do."

As Crawford glanced over Jackie's shoulder, he suddenly saw a man stand, whip off his shirt, drop his pink pants down to his boxers and jump in the pool. A woman followed, taking off her top and skirt, and wine glass in hand, jumped in.

"What the hell?" Ryder said, as a male waiter ran up to the edge of the pool.

"Hey!" the waiter shouted. "You can't do that!"

The man dog-paddled to the side of the pool and extended a hand to the waiter who was bending down to pull him out. The man grabbed the waiter's out-stretched hand and pulled him into the pool.

Jackie shook her head in disbelief and laughed. "Is this normal?"

The maître d' and several other staff members ran to the side of the pool and barked commands at the barely-clad swimmers.

"I like this place," Ryder said, with a shrug. "Reminds me of when I was in college. Kids cuttin' up and goin' wild."

"Drunken kids," Crawford said.

"At 7 o'clock?"

Crawford chuckled. "People get early starts around here."

The waiter in the pool had an arm around the man in the boxers and swam him down to the shallow end where two staff members hauled him out. The girl in bra and panties pulled herself up onto the pool coping and stood, dripping. Her friend at the table started clapping for her performance. A young man, who might have been her date, had his mouth agape, incredulous at what he had just witnessed.

A few minutes later things were back to normal, except the swimmers and their friends had either left on their own volition or, more likely, had been asked to leave.

Jackie shook her head and smiled. "Palm Beach kinda seems like a place where just about anything goes."

Crawford didn't disagree with her.

LE BILBOQUET WAS LOCATED ON WORTH AVENUE, JUST AROUND THE corner from Swifty's. It was down a narrow entrance way which opened up in the back. Crawford had requested an outside table and a hostess led then back where they sat down at their table.

"Pretty crowded for the off-season," Crawford said, looking around at the surrounding tables, only a few of which were empty. "I remember back to when this town dried up in the summer."

"A little older crowd here," Jackie observed.

The waitress came to their table with menus, and they ordered drinks.

"I don't dare look at the menu," Jackie said.

"Hey, it's on my boss, so get whatever you want," Crawford said. "It's a small price to pay for providing the clue that led to Scott Drexel."

Jackie shrugged. "It was a team effort," she said. "It started with what Weezie Gifford told us, then Mort came up with the idea to check suspects garages for the car bike rack," she turned to Crawford, "then you and Dominica nailed him with the champagne gambit."

"That was Dominica. I just tagged along."

Ryder put her wine glass down. "Hey, how's Mort doing anyway?"

"Better. But he's probably got another week in the hospital. I tell you, all those tubes and drips and IV bags don't look like fun."

"Yeah, but consider the alternative," Ryder said getting up. "I gotta hit the ladies room."

Ryder walked across the courtyard and spotted two couples at a table. One of the women looked vaguely familiar. Then it hit her when the woman looked up as she approached their table.

"Oh my God," Ryder said. "Flora? Flora Hendricks?"

"Oh, hi," the woman said with a smile. "Alexandra Farrell, right?"

"Yes, but now it's Ryder. My first name, that is."

The woman nodded and smiled. "And my *last* name is now Peabody."

Flora introduced the others at the table, including her husband, Frank. Ryder zeroed in on the gigantic diamond ring on Flora's finger. Then she took in her clothes. Rent-a-Runway didn't rent clothes nearly as expensive as hers.

"So are you still in banking?" Ryder asked.

Flora laughed. "I'm in nothing."

"Except spending my money," Frank said.

"How 'bout you, advertising right?" Flora asked.

"Believe it or not, I'm actually a private detective," Ryder said.

That produced a major frown on Flora's face. "What?" she said, incredulously.

Ryder just nodded.

"And I always thought you were going to be the star of our class," said Flora.

Ryder nodded very slowly. "Well," she said, "nice seeing you again." And she beelined into the powder room.

A few minutes later she walked out and went past Flora's table with nary a glance at her.

"Who was that?" Jackie asked when Ryder got back to the table.

"An old classmate...who was not too impressed with our profession," Ryder said, then under her breath. "Screw her."

Crawford laughed. "You tell 'em."

Ryder picked up the menu as their waitress returned to the table.

"Are you folks ready to order?" she asked.

Ryder didn't hesitate. "Yes, I'm going to have the Caviar Ossetia Imperiale for four hundred and ninety dollars, then...let's see, the pickled rhubarb for twenty-nine dollars, then bouillabaisse royale for fifty-four dollars and then wash it all down with a nice bottle of Caymus Cabernet, 2018 for two hundred and fifty dollars."

Crawford's face blanched.

Jackie patted his hand. "Don't worry, she's kidding."

Ryder smiled up at the waitress. "I'll just have a hamburger, please."

The waitress smiled back at her. "Sorry, no hamburgers. But we do have a wonderful tartare de boeuf."

Ryder tapped her fingers on the table. "Um, how 'bout a wonderful...*le hot dog avec moutarde?*"

A HALF HOUR LATER, CRAWFORD PUT HIS FORK DOWN ON HIS PLATE. "I noticed something when I was making the reservation for this place."

"What was that?" Jackie asked.

"You know how they have those stars for everything? From one to five."

Jackie and Ryder both nodded.

"Well, you'd expect for how much everything costs here, this place would be 5-stars, right?"

Jackie nodded.

"At least," said Ryder.

"Would you believe, only 3.5 stars, and guess who it's tied with? Who else has only 3.5 stars?"

"Um, I don't know...Burger King?" Ryder said.

"Would you believe the Palm Beach Police Department?"

"You're kidding?"

"Nope, look it up. But the only kind of food we ever have there are Ring-Dings and Hostess Twinkies."

EPILOGUE

THE DAY AFTER THEIR DINNER AT LE BILBOQUET, CRAWFORD said good-bye to Jackie and Ryder before they drove off into the sunset.

"Let's keep in touch," Crawford said as they got into Ryder's Jeep. "We're only six hours apart."

Ryder corrected him. "Five, with me at the wheel."

Three days after that, Ott's mother and sister flew back to Cleveland having been reassured by Ott's doctor that Mort would be as good as new in no time. Ott's mother even extracted a promise from her son that he'd come home for Christmas. No longer—if ever—a big fan of cold weather or shoveling snow, Ott agreed but was very careful not to specify which Christmas and which year.

PALM BEACH PSYCHO
Charlie Crawford Palm Beach Mysteries
Book 16

Someone is killing corrupt billionaire fat cats in Palm Beach...and the whole town is cheering him on!

In the sun-drenched opulence of Palm Beach, a sniper's bullets are targeting the corrupt elite, sending shockwaves through the community. Detective Charlie Crawford, alongside his partner Mort Ott, navigates the glittering parties and shadowy back alleys of the rich and infamous, racing against time to stop a vigilante with a chilling agenda.

The killer is a phantom in plain sight, taunting the police and the public alike. The victims are chosen through a disturbing social media poll that's gone viral, not only shocking the locals, but exposing their morbid fascination...and their complicity.

With the city on edge, Crawford and Ott must outsmart a foe who is always one step ahead, and whose precision is unmatched. Where justice and revenge blur, they must stop the killer before the body count reaches the double digits.

Featuring an unforgettable cast of characters, *Palm Beach Psycho* is a masterful exploration of the darkness that lies beneath Palm Beach's shiny exterior. Turner's sharp prose and relentless pacing ensure that readers are hooked from the first page to the last.

**Get your copy today at
tenhutmedia.com**

PALM BEACH PSYCHO
Charlie Crawford Palm Beach Mysteries
Book 16

Someone is killing corrupt billionaire fat cats in Palm Beach...and the whole town is cheering him on!

In the sun-drenched opulence of Palm Beach, a sniper's bullets are targeting the corrupt elite, sending shockwaves through the community. Detective Charlie Crawford, alongside his partner Mort Ott, navigates the glittering parties and shadowy back alleys of the rich and infamous, racing against time to stop a vigilante with a chilling agenda.

The killer is a phantom in plain sight, taunting the police and the public alike. The victims are chosen through a disturbing social media poll that's gone viral, not only shocking the locals, but exposing their morbid fascination...and their complicity.

With the city on edge, Crawford and Ott must outsmart a foe who is always one step ahead, and whose precision is unmatched. Where justice and revenge blur, they must stop the killer before the body count reaches the double digits.

Featuring an unforgettable cast of characters, *Palm Beach Psycho* is a masterful exploration of the darkness that lies beneath Palm Beach's shiny exterior. Turner's sharp prose and relentless pacing ensure that readers are hooked from the first page to the last.

**Get your copy today at
tenhutmedia.com**

ABOUT THE AUTHOR

A native New Englander, Tom Turner dropped out of college and ran a Vermont bar. Limping back a few years later to get his sheepskin, he went on to become an advertising copywriter, first in Boston, then New York. After 10 years of post-Mad Men life, he made both a career and geography change and ended up in Palm Beach, renovating houses and collecting raw materials for his novels. After stints in Charleston, then Skidaway Island, outside of Savannah, Tom recently moved to Delray Beach, where he's busy writing about passion and murder among his neighbors.

Learn more about Tom's books at:
www.amazon.com/stores/Tom-Turner

f facebook.com/tomturner.books

a amazon.com/Tom-Turner/e/B00W4ASVJG

BB bookbub.com/authors/tom-turner